Reaching the Summit

Reaching the Summit

Catherine MacDonald

CREATIVE ARTS BOOK COMPANY
Berkeley ♦ California 2000

Copyright © 2000 by Catherine MacDonald

No part of this book may be reproduced in any manner
without the written permission of the publisher,
except in brief quotations used in articles or reviews.

For information contact:
Creative Arts Book Company
833 Bancroft Way
Berkeley, California 94710
(800) 848-7789

Reaching the Summit is published by Donald S. Ellis and
is distributed by Creative Arts Book Company.

The characters, incidents, and situations
in this book are imaginary and have no relation
to any person or actual happening.

ISBN 088739-227x
Library of Congress Catalog Number 98-89656

Printed in the United States of America

The City
part 1

Chapter 1

It was an early spring evening, one of those evenings where flowers fill the air with their heavy aroma and birds are courting each other with their mating songs, when Debbie first had a gut feeling that something was not right in her marriage. Her mind was not on the task at hand. "Damn," she muttered as she burnt her hand on the lasagna she was pulling out of the oven. She placed the pan on the granite countertop, closed the oven door, and went to the sink to stick her hand under the water. A woman with all my culinary skills should remember to use potholders, she thought.

"Are you okay, Mom?" Jenny yelled from the family room, where the TV was blaring.

"Yes," Debbie yelled back. "I just burnt myself."

"You do too many things at once, Mom. Slow down."

Debbie laughed. Her twelve-year-old daughter was the family's miniphilosopher. Jenny was always spouting wisdom. "I'm going to be late for my meeting, and I want to be sure you and your dad have a healthy meal."

Jenny walked into the kitchen and leaned against the countertop of the fabulous state-of-the-art kitchen they had put in several years ago. "Let me help, Mom. I'm not helpless."

Debbie turned toward her and took off her apron. "Okay, you win," she said with a grin. "You can toss the spinach salad in the refrigerator and set the table. I've got to freshen up; I'm going to be late."

"Go, Mom. I can handle it." Jenny stood with her hands on her hips and a look of authority in her eyes.

Debbie gave her thin, long-legged, bespectacled daughter a hug, hung up her apron, and went upstairs to finish getting ready. She was chairing another committee meeting, and she didn't want to be late.

As she ran up the stairs, her footsteps were muffled by the thick white carpeting. The master suite glowed with the pink tinge of sunset, the light entering softly through the floor-to-ceiling windows that overlooked Golden Gate Park. As she appraised herself in the mirror, the nagging thought about Sam, her husband, didn't seem to disappear. There was something wrong; he had never worked this hard before. Something wasn't right.

"It's just a big project, like he said," a voice from inside told her, trying to quench her fears. She straightened her outfit—an elegant white silk blouse with matching pants—and ran a brush through her shoulder-length blond hair. She touched up her minimal makeup, used the bathroom, and gathered up her purse. She didn't have time to eat, but she could afford to miss a few meals.

"I'm home," she heard Sam yell as he came in the back door.

"Hi," she answered as she rushed downstairs to greet him. As she gave him a kiss, she noticed that his blue eyes were heavy-lidded with tiredness, the lines around his mouth deeper when he tried to smile.

He loosened his gray silk tie. "You look good, Debbie." He put his briefcase down on the well-scrubbed pine kitchen table.

"Work again, Sam?" It seemed that even when he was home, which was not often, he was working, and lately he spent Saturdays at the architectural firm he worked for.

"This project has to be done by Monday. The clients are in a big hurry." A long sigh escaped his lips.

They were interrupted by Jenny, who came bounding in like a puppy. "Hi, Daddy!"

Sam turned around, and a huge smile spread across his face. "How's my girl? Are you ready for our night alone? What do you have planned?"

She gave him a big hug and stood back. "After dinner I need some help with my math, then how about we play Nintendo?"

"Sounds like a plan." Sam liked Nintendo as much, or more, than Jenny. Sometimes Debbie felt envious watching the father/daughter exchange that took place between them. Her own father had died when she was thirteen. She shuddered as she remembered that night.

Sam walked into the entry hall, almost tripping over the UPS boxes that littered the floor. "More shopping, Debbie?" he asked sarcastically.

"Just a few things I ordered out of the catalog," she quickly answered as she went to the hall closet and pulled out a black trench coat.

Sam crossed his arms and looked sternly at her. "When are you going to stop shopping, Debbie? When is enough enough?"

She put on her coat and avoided the question. She didn't want to get into that old argument again. "I've got to be going. Dinner's ready. I'll be home later." She gave them each a kiss, ignoring Sam's displeased look. She picked up her purse and went out to the garage and got into her white BMW with the license plate frame that read: "I'd rather be shopping at Nordstrom."

Driving home later that night, along the busy streets of San Francisco, she mentally went over the evening. The meeting had gone well; they had gotten quite a bit accomplished for the silent auction that was coming up. She was the chairperson, and she loved the control and power the position offered. Besides shopping, eating, and spending money, Debbie was good at organizing and motivating people.

She pulled into the driveway and skillfully drove the car into the tight garage. Tomorrow was another day, and there were more shops to conquer.

Debbie awoke to the sun streaming through the bedroom windows. She glanced over at Sam's place and saw it was vacant. He must have left early for the office again, she thought as she lazily stretched in bed and looked at the blue sky through the windows. It was going to be another beautiful San Francisco day.

She reluctantly pulled herself out from between the satin sheets and padded over to the calendar on her antique white writing desk to refresh her memory of the day's activities. Let's see, she thought. Lucy, the housekeeper, is due at nine, then I have a luncheon and a shopping date with Jan. The new spring fashions have arrived at Nordstrom. And it's not my day to drive the car pool!

Debbie went downstairs and saw Jenny off to school. "I'll see you after school," she yelled, watching with love as Jenny sauntered down the walkway. She then put herself in motion for the day; she had a fairly rigid routine in the mornings. When her personal trainer wasn't coming, she usually did ten minutes of an ab workout, followed by stretching, and then she got on the stair machine and climbed the non-existent hills to the sounds of *Good Morning America* droning in the background. After completing her exercise ritual, she showered and had a light breakfast while reading the paper. She was religious about her routine since she wasn't blessed with a fast metabolism like Sam and Jenny. She had to be extremely careful about every bit she put into her mouth; it had a habit of finding her hips. And going out to lunch and dinner often didn't help. She was still carrying around extra pounds from Jenny, partly because she lacked self-discipline around desserts.

"Good morning, Mrs. Burke," Lucy said as she eased her plump body through the doorway. "How is everyone today?"

"Everyone's great, and I'm glad to see you. I've got a dinner party tomorrow night, and Jenny's having friends over this evening, and as you can see, the house is a mess." Lucy glanced around the kitchen and saw the remains of last night's dinner stacked in the sink and Jenny's cereal bowl and juice glass, which had been carelessly left on the kitchen counter.

"Not to worry. It'll be shining by this afternoon." She set down her large vinyl purse, straightened her button-down house dress, and fluffed up her short, curly gray hair. "Shall I start upstairs?"

"Please, and don't forget to change Jenny's sheets."

"I won't. Sorry about last Friday. I just forgot."

"Don't worry about it," Debbie reassured her. Lucy was a blessing. She had worked for them for the last three years, arriving early every Monday, Wednesday, and Friday. She did most of the laundry and all the cleaning. With her busy schedule, Debbie felt she was a necessity, although Sam had been asking if they could cut back to once or even twice a week. She convinced him she desperately needed Lucy.

Debbie finished her coffee and newspaper and checked her nails, then and went into her office and started returning some phone calls that were long overdue. Sitting on so many committees was almost like having a full-time job, she had discovered. She had once asked Sam, jokingly of course, if she could have a personal assistant. "That's way over the line," he had angrily replied. "You spend too much as it is on your shopping, trainer, and your housekeeper." She had never brought the subject up again, but a girl could dream.

Debbie loved her office, which she had designed several years ago. It was small and off the kitchen, but she had transformed it into a cozy fortress. The room had a large oak desk that held the telephone, fax, and computer. Bookcases lined the walls, filled to the brim with all the books of her childhood and her many collections. There was a yellow-and-white chintz-covered couch under the window, and flowering plants were everywhere. On the floral wallpaper-covered walls, she had hung all the awards she had collected from her years of volunteering. Jenny also loved her mom's office, and she often came in during the afternoons while Debbie was busy on the phone and curled up on the couch with her homework or a good book.

Debbie glanced at her watch and, noting the time, realized she'd better get going if she was to meet Jan at Cafe Della Stelle on time. Yelling to Lucy that she was leaving, she grabbed her purse and left.

Jan was already seated in the homey restaurant when Debbie strolled in. Jan waved her over to the table.

"Hi, Debbie! What took you so long?"

"Sorry I'm late, but I couldn't find a parking space, and this place doesn't offer valet," she said as she sat down at the table.

"Tell me about it, but this is the new place to be. I had to make the reservation a week ago."

Debbie sank back into her seat and took in the surroundings. The café was small, maybe twenty tables, the walls were painted a butter yellow, and bottles of wine and vinegar cluttered the counter space by the kitchen. There were large plants everywhere, in corners and hanging by rope from the vaulted ceiling. Debbie deeply inhaled the smells of Italian cooking that were seeping from the kitchen. She picked up the menu. Yum, she thought while scanning its contents. She was definitely going to have to break a sweat on her walk this afternoon to work off all the fat and calories that lurked in the delicious food.

"What are you going to have?" she asked Jan after a few minutes of studying the menu.

Jan put her menu down and ran a perfectly sculptured red nail through her thick blond mane. "Teresa didn't show today, so I'd better be good and have the fresh salmon and the house salad, sans dressing."

"Why didn't she show?" Teresa was the personal trainer they both used. She was a body builder herself and tough as nails. She pushed and pushed them until every muscle in their bodies screamed. Every muscle in Teresa's tight, thin, tanned body glistened with sweat as she tortured them.

"She said she was sick."

"Think so?"

"Yes, I do. She's such a health freak, she doesn't drink anything stronger than mineral water, and this is the first time I can ever remember her calling in sick."

The waiter came and took their orders. Debbie decided on the portabella mushroom sandwich with the pasta salad. They both ordered white wine.

After the waiter left, they got down to the business aspect of their lunch, discussing the damage they would do to their husbands' credit cards. Jan loved to shock her husband with her monthly statements. David was a doctor and spent many hours at the hospital in the company of a certain nurse, or so the gossip indicated. If it bothered Jan, she didn't show it; she just spent more and more money.

Debbie and Jan had been friends since high school. Jan was a former cheerleader who attempted college, dropped out, then went to work in an insurance office. She met David one day when he was a struggling intern shopping around for car insurance for his ancient Austin Heely. He fell hard and deep for the blond, blue-eyed girl, who seemed to have legs that stretched forever, and courted her like a star-struck young lover.

They married, and Jan fell into the role of being an up-and-coming doctor's wife. She produced two children, hired a nanny, and spent the rest of her time spending the money David worked so hard for. Every time they had a fight, she would call up Debbie and drag her out shopping.

"What are we looking for today?" Debbie asked.

Jan took a sip of her wine and sighed. "We have a function to go to next week at the hospital, and I was hoping to find a beautiful and sexy suit. What about you?"

Debbie exhaled. She had been shopping so much lately that she must have at least seven new outfits hanging in her already bulging closets that she hadn't even worn yet. But shopping did seem to fill the hole that was getting deeper in her life. She and Sam were drifting further and further apart; something was wrong, she just couldn't put her finger on it. Jenny was spending more time with her friends and glued to the phone, and even Debbie's aunt was rarely home when she called to chat. Aunt Jane seemed to be busier in her retirement than she'd been when she was director of the children's library.

"I could use some new workout wear," Debbie replied. True, even though the only ones who saw her in them were Teresa and Lucy.

"That's all? What about something fun?"

"I'll look," Debbie said to get her off the subject. All of a sudden she didn't feel like shopping.

They finished their lunch and walked down to Union Square amongst the throngs of shoppers. Jan led the way. After much searching, Jan finally succeeded in finding the perfect suit and didn't seem to flinch at the price tag—an amount that would feed a family of four for months. Debbie did manage to pick up some new workout wear, a silk nightgown, and a few items for Jenny, but her heart was not in it.

As they stood in the brilliant sun outside Nordstrom, she turned to Jan. "I've got to get Jenny and take her to ballet. I'll call you next week."

"Take care. I'm going to go and do some more damage." And Jan gave her a hug, turned, and headed down the street in search of more conquests.

Debbie looked at her watch. She was going to be late.

Sam spent most of Saturday at the office getting an important project finished. He arrived home late, tired, but luckily for Debbie, he did remember to pick up the wine she had ordered. Jenny was spending the night at a friend's, so they had a few hours to relax before their guests arrived. Debbie walked into the family room and found Sam curled up on the couch watching The Golf Channel. She took off her apron and crawled up next to him.

"Not now, Debbie. I'm tired."

The rejection hit her like a slap and she pulled away. Their lovemaking was almost nonexistent. She pulled her arms around her body as if to protect herself from his refusal. Something's wrong, she thought. Sam's always had such a high sex drive.

He turned and looked at her, almost in disgust. She tried to make light of the situation. "Maybe you'll feel like it later," she suggested. "Can I get you a soda?"

He turned his eyes back to The Golf Channel. She could tell he was under a great deal of stress by the fine lines that were etched around his green eyes. Funny, she thought, they weren't there a few months ago.

"That would be great, Debbie. I just need to relax before our company comes. I hope you don't mind."

"No, no problem." She got up and went into the kitchen, where she poured him a glass of diet soda and added a few ice cubes.

"Here you go," she said as she handed the crystal goblet to Sam. "I need to attend to some things in the kitchen." He took the glass from her and didn't even look up from the TV.

Frustrated, she went back into the kitchen, where she began pulling down shiny copper pots from the brass pot rack that hung over her cooktop, then she pulled out the ingredients needed to make pasta carbonara. Cooking always soothed her soul. She had already prepared the salad, baked fresh bread, and had made a delicious tropical cheesecake. (Sam's favorite, she was hoping.)

What's going on with Sam? she wondered as she began cooking the bacon the recipe called for. As she grated the Parmesan cheese, she decided she would have to bend Aunt Jane's ear if she could catch her home.

The dinner party went off without a hitch, the meal was a huge success, and everyone stayed late, sipping brandy and telling funny stories. As laughter filled the dining room, she noticed that Sam seemed to relax and fall into the role he had played so well in the past: the charming and gracious host.

The next day the three of them went over to Point Reyes for a hike and a picnic. It was a chilly but beautiful early spring day, and Debbie watched with pleasure as Sam and Jenny bantered back and forth. As they enjoyed the lunch Debbie had prepared earlier that morning, Debbie put away her self-doubts and joined her family in the moment. Nothing was wrong. Sam must just be working too hard. The three of them were together. They stopped and had an early dinner at a small Italian restaurant in North Beach on the way home later that evening. Over the flickering of the candles, the soft music, and the magic of the wine, Debbie convinced herself once more that she had an overactive imagination.

"Hello," answered the familiar voice on the other end of the phone.

"Aunt Jane! Where have you been? I've been trying to reach you for days. I wish you would get an answering machine like everyone else in the nineties."

Debbie's aunt laughed. "Over my dead body," she chuckled. "What's new, dear?"

Suddenly Debbie didn't want to burden her aunt with her mundane problems. "I just called to see how you were and ask if you'd like to come for dinner.

"I'm fine, dear. Busy as usual. I just got back from a weekend gambling trip to Reno. I even won fifty dollars."

Debbie smiled. Since Aunt Jane had retired two years ago at the young age of seventy, she was always on the go.

"I'm not too busy this week," she continued. "But next week a group of us are going to Las Vegas. I hope my luck holds out." She paused. "How are Jenny and Sam?"

Debbie decided to dive right in. "Jenny's fine. She's busy with school and ballet, but Sam seems preoccupied. I don't know if it's something at work, or if there's something else on his mind. He just doesn't seem here."

The line was silent on the other end.

"Aunt Jane?"

"I'm here, dear. I don't know what to say. I was never married. I think you need to ask advice from someone with a little more experience than me."

Debbie thought out loud. "Well, maybe it's just this project he's been working on. Anyway, can you come for dinner Wednesday night?"

"Love to. Can I bring anything?"

"No, just your charming self. I don't know what I'm going to make yet. What sounds good to you?"

Debbie could feel her aunt's grin through the phone. Aunt Jane had trouble microwaving popcorn.

"Anything's fine with me. You know me; my idea of a gourmet meal is Lean Cuisine."

"Aunt Jane, that stuff is like eating cardboard! You need real food."

"I'm still alive at seventy-two; there must be something in there that's working. What time would you like me Wednesday?"

"Come around six. We can have a nice visit. I know Jenny would love to bore you with her latest escapades."

"Okay, see you Wednesday. And Debbie . . . "

"Yes?"

"You take care of yourself."

"I will. Bye." Debbie hung up the phone and got up from her chair and stretched. She heard Lucy downstairs vacuuming. Looking at her calendar, she saw she was free until a doctor's appointment at one. She decided to get some paperwork done.

The thought of Aunt Jane on a gambler's special, charging up to the slots in Reno, put a smile on her face. She loved her aunt, who had stepped in when Debbie's parents had been killed in a fiery one-car crash on Highway 50. They had left her with Aunt Jane that early spring afternoon and headed up the hill, preoccupied with each other. Her parents had been madly in love; Debbie had always felt like an outsider around them.

Debbie sighed as she picked up a framed wedding photo of her parents. She shook her head. She'd never forget that night as long as she lived. Two young officers had come to Aunt Jane's door with news of the accident. She heard the hushed voices from the guest room where she was sleeping and heard Aunt Jane crying, the door softly closing. Debbie drifted back to sleep, never realizing the horror that awaited her in the morning. It seemed her father had gone off the road by Kyburtz. Witnesses said they saw the two of them sitting close to each other, and they thought they saw her father lean over to kiss her mother. At that instant, a deer ran across the highway. Debbie's dad swerved to avoid hitting it and ended up going down the embankment. Neither of her folks had been wearing their seatbelts. They were thrown clear from the car.

She took the silver-framed photo of her parents and curled up on the chintz couch. As she stared at the happy couple, she tried to remember that period in her life. Memories were fragmented; it was as if she had blocked it all out to protect herself. She sighed as she did remember a neighbor coming to stay with her while Aunt Jane went to the morgue to make the identification, and she remembered going to her house in San Jose to pick out clothes to bury them in. She never understood why; the caskets were closed. Aunt Jane insisted Debbie's mother wear her favorite hat and pumps and kept the pearls for Debbie, which she gave to her when she married Sam. To this day, she'd never worn them.

She barely remembered the funeral. Both coffins had been heavily draped with beautiful white roses—her mother's favorite flower—and many people had attended the heart-wrenching service. Everyone went back to the house in San Jose, where Aunt Jane had held a reception.

Debbie got up off the couch and put the picture back. She picked up another picture of the three of them and gazed fondly at the family holding hands. Debbie's father, Arthur, was twenty years older than her mother, Claire, a soft-spoken, beautiful woman who had been fascinated by Jackie Kennedy. Claire had imitated Jackie's look; the only thing different about the two of them was that Claire had blond hair and only one child holding her white-gloved hand.

Arthur, an engineer, was tall and thin with sandy blond hair. To Debbie, he had always seemed larger than life with his booming voice and energy. He indulged both his girls' every whim. They lived in a three-bedroom, two-bath ranch house with beautiful gardens, within walking distance of Debbie's elementary school.

Debbie put the picture down and thought back to her childhood. Even though she had lived in the shadow of her parents' ongoing love affair, she did have a wonderful childhood. She remembered a great deal of hugs and laughter and vacations spent at Lake Tahoe and Santa Cruz. How she used to love the roller coaster! Dad loved to go with her, holding up his hands as the car went down the track, screaming like all the other kids. Mom would never go; she didn't want to ruin her Jackie-like hair.

They often went to the city to attend plays, concerts, and to visit Aunt Jane, Arthur's sister and only living relative. They would all go out for a meal in one of the many restaurants San Francisco offered. Arthur and Claire would leave Debbie in the tender care of Aunt Jane once or twice a year while they took their torrid love affair on holiday. Aunt Jane always managed to take time off from her duties at the library, and the two of them would explore the city together. There was so much to do and see in San Francisco that Debbie never got bored. She loved to go down to the wharf, watch the ships come in, and fantasize about what exotic ports they had come from. Her father had promised her a trip one day, a trip she had never been able to take.

Debbie picked up another picture of herself and her mother taken when she was around eight, about the same time the hippies had overtaken the beautiful city in the psychedelic 60s. A little girl stared back at her wearing a starched white-and-pink ruffled dress with shiny black Mary Janes on her feet. Claire had disliked the smelly, dirty people who wore flowers in their hair and their music. Looking back now, Debbie thought the hippies must have thought her family was just as strange: the older distinguished gentleman, his Jackie clone, who had her white-gloved hand wrapped through his arm, and the doll-like child by his side.

After her parents' deaths, Camelot was gone. She remembered going with Aunt Jane to meet a real estate agent to sell the house. She was able to take her own things and a few of her parents' items into her aunt's large apartment, which was located in the Marina district of the city, near the water.

Debbie changed schools and slowly made new friends and a new life for herself. She missed her parents terribly at first, but then she figured they were up in heaven continuing their love affair. She imagined they would take time out from each other periodically and smile down at their only child, then go back to spending eternity with each other.

Debbie put the picture down and stared at another taken of a young Aunt Jane. Her loving face beamed back at Debbie, and Debbie thought she must have been a challenge for her aunt. Aunt Jane had never married; she claimed she had lost the love of her life when her beau was killed in a plane crash in the early sixties. Then, in her fifties, she became the guardian of a thirteen-year-old hormonal girl. Claire's family came from the East Coast. They disowned her when she ran away with Arthur at eighteen. To this day, Debbie had never met or exchanged even so much as a Christmas card with them. It was as if they had erased Claire from their lives.

Aunt Jane became the only family Debbie had, and the two of them clung to each other and braved the adolescent hormones together. Aunt Jane was a wonderful surrogate mother who devoted all her time to Debbie.

Debbie glanced at a current picture of her, one that she had taken over Thanksgiving. Aunt Jane was still a tall, handsome woman. Her steel-gray hair was cut short and permed, and her green eyes twinkled with life and excitement. She still looked like the librarian she had been for forty years with her glasses around her neck attached by a thin gold chain and sensible shoes on her feet.

Aunt Jane had gotten Debbie an after-school job at the library; it wasn't far from the high school she had attended. High school was all right for her, but she always felt sad when she watched the other families gather for school activities. But Aunt Jane would be there, and she would pick up on Debbie's sorrow and indulge her every whim. Debbie pushed the pain and loneliness deeper and deeper into her subconscious.

The money from her parents' estate was put into a trust, which Aunt Jane administered. Arthur had done well in the stock market, and Debbie was allowed full access to the money when she turned twenty-one.

She managed to get herself accepted to UCLA, where she majored in communications. She received good grades, made many friends, dated a great deal, and always had a beautiful tan. She was the quintessential California golden girl: long blond hair, blue eyes, a great body, and a dark tan, which she spent many hours running to achieve.

After completing college, and gaining access to her trust fund, she moved back to San Francisco, bought an elegant townhouse by

Aunt Jane, and went to work in the public relations department of a major company. She enjoyed the lifestyle and indulged her every desire by dining, traveling, and shopping. It was rare for her to go through a day without purchasing something. Quickly her apartment and closets overflowed with beautiful things. It was as if she tried to fill an ache in her soul–only the hole kept getting deeper and deeper.

But she did enjoy her job, and she was good at it. She attended many power lunches and cocktail parties, wearing her smart designer suits and dresses showing off her tight body. It was at a cocktail party that she met Sam Burke, tall and cool, a perfect ad for a Brooks Brothers suit. They were introduced by her boss; Sam was an architect who was doing a project for Debbie's firm. He was several years older than Debbie and the most handsome man she had ever seen. Tall, with sandy brown hair that was rather long and ice blue eyes–she immediately fell head over heels in love.

Sam was an alumni of Stanford, and he asked her to go to the big game the next weekend. She hid her dislike for football, said yes, and planned the perfect outfit in her head. Stanford beat Cal that year, and Sam won her heart. They dated for a year, and were married in his parents' backyard in Oakland. Neither one of them was terribly religious. Debbie had lost her faith when God took her parents, and Sam was a self-proclaimed agnostic.

Debbie's eyes glanced over to a picture of the two of them on their exotic honeymoon to Acapulco, where they stayed in a tiny bungalow complete with its own private pool and pink Jeep to drive around. The couple in the picture smiled back at her. They had been so in love! She sighed as she remembered those two weeks and the hours they spent secluded in their love, exploring each other's dreams and bodies. Where had that couple gone?

After the magical two weeks, they jetted back to San Francisco and to their busy careers and new life. Debbie threw herself into the role of being the perfect wife while continuing on with her career. After all, it was the early 80s and the women's movement had a strong hold in society. She took cooking classes, read many decorating books, and even hired the most prestigious decorator in the city to help her transform the beautiful Victorian-style home they had purchased in Pacific Heights with a hefty down paybent from Debbie's trust fund.

Sam came from a modest background; his father, Don, was an insurance salesman, and his mother, Muffy, was an elementary school teacher. They had always lived well above their means and had been able to send their only son to Stanford on a partial scholarship. Sam had an older sister, Sally, who lived up in Oregon somewhere. She had shunned her folks' constant quest for materialism and fell hard for the philosophy of the 60s. She still practiced the lifestyle to this day, living on a self-sufficient farm where they grew much of their own food. Her husband, Keith, was a carpenter who made furniture. Their two children, Sunshine and Destiny, were grown now, living their own lives farther up north.

Debbie loved her home; it was her pride and joy, and their beautiful kitchen was the center of their existence. Debbie loved to cook and entertain friends. She had gutted and moved walls in the late 80s, ripping out the ugly brown linoleum, gold appliances, and old oak cabinets that had been put in by the previous owners. Debbie had created a kitchen with a taste of France, where they had gone on their one-year anniversary. She had fallen in love with the French countryside, food, lifestyle, and people.

She became pregnant on that trip, blaming the wine. She threw herself into motherhood and created a beautiful nursery for their child. She gave birth the following spring to a beautiful baby girl. Her life was now complete. She quit work and spent her time trying to be the perfect wife and mother. The three of them were inseparable. She hired a nanny, Mary, who took care of Jenny when Debbie and Sam went on their many trips and attended the many social obligations that filled her calendar. Aunt Jane was always in the background in case she was needed, and Sam's parents saw Jenny occasionally. They were hard people to get close to, and Jenny preferred the warmth and laughter of Mary and Aunt Jane.

So, once again, Aunt Jane filled a major role in Debbie's life. She was Jenny's only link to the older generation. She loved Jenny completely and was a terrific grandmother. At the time, Debbie threw herself into the role of being the perfect San Francisco matron. She found herself sitting on many committees, entertaining lavishly, and attending many openings and parties. When she honestly thought about it now, outside of producing Jenny, she had not done anything else of substance.

Looking back now, Debbie could see that she and Sam had started drifting apart when Jenny was around nine. On the outside they still had the most enviable marriage, but they no longer shared pillow talk. She became more and more enthralled with being Mrs. Sam Burke, and Sam seemed to be working more and more at the office. His travel schedule picked up, and he was gone several times a month. She had too much going on with her own "work" to accompany him, even though Aunt Jane offered to stay with Jenny. (They had let Mary go when Jenny was around ten.)

Debbie's life consisted of shopping, lunching, networking, and socializing. The three of them did some traveling together; their last family vacation was over Christmas, when they went to Aspen to ski. Jenny was a good skier; she spent quite a bit of time skiing with Sam. Debbie watched their two lithe bodies traverse the slopes from her perch behind the picture window of the ski lodge, where she sat nursing a twisted ankle. She had skied the first day and fell and spent the rest of the vacation hobbling from store to store and reading juicy novels by the roaring fire.

Chapter 2

Debbie heard Jenny shout from the foyer, "Mom, hurry up, we'll be late."

Debbie looked at her watch; she's right, she concluded. "I'm coming. Let me just brush my teeth." She went into the bathroom and glanced at her appearance. Not too bad for a woman of thirty-eight, she told herself. The navy blue crepe suit she was wearing hugged her in all the right places. The new muscles she had worked so hard for were starting to show, and her hair dresser had done a good job with her new cut and color. It was a blessing having blond hair; the gray didn't stand out as much as it did on her friends with dark hair. She slid her feet into her new navy blue pumps and stood back from the mirror to get the entire picture. Looking good, she told the image in the mirror. Hopefully, Sam will take notice.

"Mom!" she heard again.

"Coming. Get in the car," she yelled back and picked up her matching purse from the antique writing desk. Tonight was Jenny's ballet recital, and she had been rehearsing for weeks. This was her first recital on pointe, and Sam had promised he'd meet them there. Recently he had traded his Volvo for a flashy red convertible Porsche and had started wearing a small diamond earring in his left ear. Maybe it was a midlife crisis. He had been working longer hours and was traveling more. She had resorted to going through his things to find receipts, credit card bills, anything that would shed some light on the situation. Nothing.

The ballet recital was beautiful. Jenny danced in three numbers. Her tall lithe body stood out among all the other girls on stage. Sam arrived just as she began her last number.

"Sorry, I was hung up in a meeting," he said as he slipped into the seat next to her.

Debbie held her tongue.

After the performance, they stood in the lobby waiting for Jenny. The silence was piercing between them. Aunt Jane stood possessively next to Debbie with a worried look on her face.

"Daddy, Daddy!" Debbie heard from behind. "Did you like the recital? I'm so glad you made it. I was worried you wouldn't be here." The three of them turned around, and there stood Jenny, her cheeks flushed with excitement and exercise.

"You were wonderful," Sam exclaimed as he gave her a big hug.

"You danced like a princess, Jenny," added Debbie, watching Sam play the role of the proud father.

Aunt Jane gave Jenny a big hug. "You were wonderful, dear, the best dancer of the group."

"Did you like my solo? I worked on it for weeks."

"It was wonderful," responded Sam, beaming with pride.

"Yes, absolutely breathtaking," Debbie added.

"Let's go and have some dessert to celebrate," suggested Aunt Jane.

"Great," said Jenny. "I'm starved. I'll be right back; I want to say goodbye to my teacher." And the three of them watched her slip off in her pirate costume.

Sam turned to Debbie. "I've still got some work to do, Debbie. Would you mind if I bowed out? I'll make it up to her this weekend."

"Sam, this is her night. Can't it wait until tomorrow?"

He sighed. "No, the project's due tomorrow. I'm going back to the office. Don't wait up; I'll be home late. I'll go and explain it to Jenny." And he gave her a peck on the cheek and left. Debbie looked over at Aunt Jane and saw that her worried look had deepened.

The three of them joined several other families, and they all headed for a favorite ice cream parlor. They got a large table and spent an hour laughing and talking. Several of the other girls were there without fathers. Divorce was pretty prevalent in their age group. Debbie told herself that Sam was really working.

Later that evening, as she sat on Jenny's bed letting her recount her night's success, Jenny asked why her father hadn't come to the celebration. Debbie asked her what he had told her.

"He said he had a big project to get in to his boss by tomorrow, but Mom, I think he's lying. I could see it in his eyes."

Debbie gave her a kiss. "Not to worry, Jenny. You just have an overactive imagination. Now, get a good night's sleep, my little ballerina."

"Mom," she said as Debbie was leaving the room, "everything's all right with you and Daddy, isn't it?"

Debbie felt her heart sink. "Why of course, honey. Why would you think otherwise?"

Jenny turned her back to Debbie. She could tell the child was hurting. Damn him.

"Good night, darling. See you in the morning," she said and softly closed the door. She padded into her own room, closed the door, and sat down at the foot of the oak four-poster bed. She looked out at the fog slowly covering the city like a thick, fluffy blanket, sighed, and flopped back on the thick white comforter, exhaling deeply. What was going on here? Why was Sam working so much? Granted, they enjoyed a high lifestyle, but Sam was a wonderful provider, and they still had some of her trust fund. Lately, he did seem to be preoccupied about something. When she did ask him why he was working so much, he always had some lame excuse about a project that was due.

Debbie lay on the bed thinking for quite a while. She finally glanced over at the clock on her cluttered nightstand. It was 12:10, and he wasn't home yet! There had to be something going on. Even the president of the United States didn't work this hard.

She decided to get to the bottom of the problem. As she got ready for bed and performed her beauty routine, she decided to take the Scarlett approach: she'd worry about it tomorrow. She slipped into a deep sleep.

Teresa was at the door bright and early the next morning. "You're looking tired, Mrs. B," she chirped as she set up her equipment. "Let's get some blood pumping through those veins, and you'll feel better."

Debbie smiled at Teresa's attempt to humor her, pulled her hair back in a clip, and grudgingly let Teresa put her through a series of exercises designed to strengthen her quads, hip flexors, hamstrings, and stomach muscles. Debbie moaned and groaned at the end of the strenuous exercise session.

"Next time we'll work on the upper body, Mrs. B. I've got to run; I have another client in a few." And Teresa gathered up her torture items and let her tight, lithe body out the back door.

Debbie just sat on the floor massaging her muscles and trying to stretch. She decided she did feel better. She must have sat on the floor thinking for quite a while, about what she really didn't remember, but a litany of thoughts crossed her mind. She finally got up, poured herself a glass of orange juice, and glanced at the paper Sam had brought in early that morning. Funny, she thought, I didn't hear him come in, and he was up before the sun. He had mumbled something to her about his project almost being done, and then he would be home more. Debbie suddenly realized there would be more projects after this one. A sickening feeling grew strong at the bottom of her stomach.

She decided to call Jan and see if she knew anything or had seen something she was trying to protect her from. Years ago a group of women had sat around one gal's kitchen table drinking red wine—whose, she really didn't remember—and they vowed to each other that if they ever saw or heard about one of their husbands with another woman—or guy, this was San Francisco—they would tell the wife, gently. They collectively decided that if they were the "victim," they would need to be proactive, know what they were up against. Sadly, several of the women around the table that night long ago had already split from their husbands. Unfortunately, the pact hadn't helped them. One of the husbands had kept a mistress in another city. Another one had no mistress; he just came home one day, told Sara he didn't want to be married anymore, said he wanted to be free, packed his bags, and left everything—his job, the house, her, and the kids. It took Sara a long time to find him; he was holed up in a remote cabin in the mountains, fishing.

The really sad part of all this divorce was how it affected the children. She shuddered as chills ran through her body. The thought of Jenny shuffling between two parents' houses, her precious things packed in her overnight bag, was too much to handle.

Hey, you're way ahead of yourself, Debbie chided herself. Maybe Sam really is working all these long hours. Maybe the Porsche and the earring are just a midlife crisis.

Slowly, she dialed Jan's number and got her machine. She left a message for Jan to call her back as soon as she could, took a shower, and decided to go shopping. Saks was having a sale, and shopping always made Debbie feel much better.

She took her time with her appearance and glanced at her calendar. She had a meeting at one, so she still had a few hours to do some damage.

And she did. She found several dresses and matching pumps that she had to have. She treated herself to a bagel and coffee at the coffee bar before she headed over to her meeting.

"Debbie? It's Jan. What's up? Sorry I didn't return your call earlier, but I was having the most wonderful facial and massage. I feel marvelous."

Debbie looked over at Jenny, who was at the table struggling over a math problem. "I'm going to take this in the other room, so I won't disturb you," she said to Jenny as she covered the mouthpiece.

"Don't go far, Mom. I may need your help again."

"Okay, sweetheart."

Debbie took the cordless phone into her office and curled up on the chintz couch. "Jan, you remember that pact we made years ago while sitting around that gal's kitchen table drinking red wine?"

"At Patty's?"

"That's her name. I forgot."

"Yes, what about it? It's too bad we couldn't help Sara and Beth."

"Yes, but now I'm asking you. Have you seen Sam with anyone or heard he's been seeing anyone? Even if it's a so-called rumor, I want to know."

Debbie heard Jan struggle on the other end. Finally, she answered, "No, not really. I haven't heard anything. Why would you ask?"

But her tone wasn't convincing. She knew something. Some friend, Debbie thought. She won't even tell me the truth. She's trying to protect me. "Are you sure, Jan? You haven't heard anything?"

"No, Debbie. That's silly. Why would I hear anything?" Jan quickly changed the subject to an upcoming luncheon they were going to.

"Thanks anyway, Jan. I've got to run." She quickly hung up the phone.

As luck would have it, Sam called a few minutes later informing her that he had to work late again. "The project had a few problems. Don't wait up for me, and give Jenny a kiss."

"Mom, could you help me with this problem?" she heard Jenny yell as she hung up the phone. "I don't get this. Math is stupid." Suddenly Debbie felt tired, and she was tired of playing single mom.

She went into the kitchen and gazed at her child as she feverishly worked on her homework. She suddenly felt all the motherly love she had in her cells at that moment swell. Damn Sam! What was he doing to them?

"Let me see, honey." She took the chair next to Jenny, and they spent the next hour finishing up her homework. Jenny was an A student and pushed herself in all her subjects.

"When's Daddy coming home?" she asked as she closed up the books and put away her materials.

"He has to work late again."

Jenny put her pencil down and stared at Debbie. "Mom, in case you haven't noticed, he's always working late. Why?"

Debbie looked at her daughter and felt the tears rush to her eyes. She quickly stood up and pretended to do something on the kitchen counter so Jenny wouldn't see the tears she was trying so hard to hold back. "I don't know, Jenny. He says he has a lot of work to do." She quickly changed the subject. "Why don't we go out to dinner tonight? What about that restaurant you love?"

"The Jade Palace?"

"Sure." Debbie was in the mood for Chinese food.

Jenny's eyes lit up. She loved to eat, and lucky for her she had a high metabolism and spent quite a bit of time on the dance floor. "Can I have a Coke tonight?"

Debbie felt her spirits rise to meet Jenny's. She was very careful in allowing her daughter to drink soda because she was still wearing braces, but tonight would be a special treat. "Sure. Let's get ready; I'm starved." Suddenly, Debbie remembered she hadn't eaten much all day.

She slept deeply that night; she didn't even hear Sam come in. She awoke the next morning to see him ready for the new day and stuffing a few papers in his briefcase. She quickly closed her eyes so he wouldn't see she was awake. He didn't even turn around to see if she was, and he snuck out of the room like a thief in the night.

It was a brilliant spring day. The sunshine warmed her spirits as she prepared Jenny's breakfast, saw her off to school, and performed her exercise routine. Lucy was upstairs scrubbing bathrooms, and Debbie had a luncheon at noon to attend. She softly padded over to her walk-in closet and chose an ivory linen pantsuit: a single-breasted long jacket with a V-neck collar that was paired with elegant flowing pants. The price tag still hung from the sleeve. Debbie put on the suit and admired herself in the floor-length mirror. She added gold loop earrings, a sparkling diamond pendent, and a small gold bracelet to complement the outfit. She brushed her shoulder-length blond hair and dabbed her favorite perfume, Jessica McClintock, on her wrists.

"You look wonderful, Mrs. Burke," Lucy said as Debbie descended the stairs. Lucy was cleaning the living room, or moving the dust. Debbie and Sam hadn't entertained lately.

"Thank you, Lucy. Have a good day and please don't forget to dust the shutters."

"I won't."

Since it was such a glorious day in "the City by the Bay," she decided to open the BMW's sunroof and feel the sun's warmth on her body. She quickly sped up and down the hills of the city; she was running late, as usual.

As she drove through the heavy traffic, with the sounds of The Eagles playing, she looked ahead and saw a red Porsche that resembled Sam's. There were two people riding in it, the top was down, and the passenger's long brown hair flowed in the air as the driver took off when the light changed. There were many red Porsches in the city, she told herself; it was probably someone else's, but just in case, she decided to follow it anyway. She sped up, managed to edge herself in behind the red Porsche several cars back, and followed for several blocks. Whoever was driving did resemble Sam, and the woman, whoever she was, looked to be laughing at something he had said. A sick feeling overcame her, followed by a nagging voice that said there was someone else—and there she was.

As Debbie continued to follow them, her hands began to shake. It took all her strength to hold on straight to the steering wheel. That used to be me! screamed a voice inside of her head. Who the hell was she?

She finally managed to get one car behind them, praying he

wouldn't notice. And he didn't, he was too caught up in her, and yes, it was him. Debbie saw the light catch the diamond in his left ear.

She continued to follow them for several more blocks. Maybe it's just business, she tried to rationalize with herself. Maybe she's just a client. Debbie watched as the other woman swung her hair and flirted with Sam. No, she decided, it looked like something more.

She followed them down to Pier 39 and into the parking garage. They still hadn't noticed the blond-haired woman with large sunglasses on who was driving the car Sam had leased for her last year. Sam and the other woman parked, and Debbie quickly parked in the next row over. She slid down in her seat and watched in horror as Sam walked around the car and opened the door for the other woman. Out she stepped, a tall, long-legged brown-haired woman wearing a long striped dress with a mock turtleneck. She had on a belt that cinched her tiny waist—probably only twenty inches—which had obviously never seen childbirth, and the slits in her dress showed off spectacular legs. She swung her hair around, and Debbie could see that it flowed down to the middle of her back. I had hair that length when I first met Sam, she remembered, and a waist like that too.

She watched in disbelief as the two of them walked away, hand in hand. The other woman was as tall as Sam with her heels on, and she held on to him as if for support. Debbie just sat there in her car, numb, and felt her entire self-created world fall apart that brilliant spring day in April.

Follow them, urged a voice from within. Find out where they are going. She decided to heed the command—just to make sure that it was really Sam, and not her mind playing tricks on her—and quickly got out of the car and walked toward Pier 39. She could see them way up in front: two tall, beautiful people ambling slowly toward their destination.

She quickly caught up to them—the woman seemed to have trouble walking without his help in her high heels—and saw them stop at a street vendor, watching in awe as Sam bought her a single red rose. The woman smiled widely, took off her sunglasses, and gave Sam a big kiss on the lips. She was gorgeous, the man was Sam, and this was not a client.

Debbie made her way through the throngs of people ambling along the pier, trailing behind them just enough so they couldn't see her. The couple entered a small seafood restaurant, and Debbie watched from outside as they were led to a small table near the window. Couldn't you be a little more discreet? she thought as she hid behind a large fern. What happens if someone we know sees you?

She quickly ducked into a shop and pretended to be interested in its souvenir merchandise. As she examined the seashells and other items for sale, she came to the realization that this other woman was the reason he hadn't touched her in months. After a few minutes, she went out and took a post where she could keep an eye on them without their knowledge.

Debbiestood outside that restaurant for what seemed like eternity, waiting for them to emerge. Finally, they ambled out into the dazzling sunshine, arms wrapped around each other, and headed in the direction of the parking garage. She followed them, feeling like a private eye and worried they'd see her, but they were too wrapped up in each other to notice anything. She painfully remembered that that was the way she and Sam used to walk together, years ago.

She stayed several hundred feet behind them and watched as they got into the car. Sam held the door open for her and kissed her deeply before he shut the door. Debbie quickly got into her car and managed to follow them at a safe distance. Either her sleuthing was that good, or they were so entangled in each other they didn't notice her following several cars back.

Traffic was heavy, but Sam's red Porsche was not too difficult to keep her eyes on. She followed them to a quaint hotel on Geary Street and watched in disbelief as Sam and the woman got out, and a valet took their car and parked it. The couple strolled into the elegant little hotel as she sat double-parked on the other side of the street. She couldn't hold back the tears any longer, and as she opened the floodgates, huge tears and a gut-wrenching sob were released from her body.

How long she sat in her car and sobbed, she didn't know. There was a tap at her window. "Hey, lady," the man said gently as she pressed the window button down. "You need to move your car." Debbie just looked at him and continued to sob.

"Hey, you okay?"

Debbie looked at him again and tried desperately to stop crying.

She managed to smile weakly. "I'm fine. I'll be going now. Sorry." She quickly put the car in drive and began what seemed like the longest trip of her life toward her home.

She flung herself on the family-room couch when she entered the silent house. She felt depression grip her body and soul, and she just stared at the ceiling as if waiting for divine inspiration. What was she going to do? How would she face her friends? What would happen to them? And Jenny, how was she going to handle this? She had always been "Daddy's little girl"—or had been until the "other woman" took over both their roles.

She glanced at the clock and saw it was almost time for her to pick Jenny up from school and get her to ballet. She was going to have to pull herself together for both their sakes.

And she did. She reluctantly got off the couch, touched up what was left of her makeup, which had streaked down her face from the river of tears, grabbed her keys, and headed out to the car and the afternoon of obligations that awaited her.

Later that afternoon, while Jenny was chewing on the end of her pencil over some math problem and Debbie was fixing dinner, the phone rang.

"Debbie?"

She instantly recognized the voice as her new-found enemy. I'm sure he's thinking up some other excuse as to why he has to work late again, she thought.

"I'm sorry, I have to work late again. Something came up suddenly today, and I wasn't able to finish the project. I've got to finish it tonight."

Debbie felt the vomit rise to the roof of her mouth as she tried to swallow his lie. How dare he lie to me again, she thought. But looking at their sweet, innocent daughter diligently doing her homework, she concluded that now wasn't the time or place, even though she felt like ripping every hair out of his head.

"All right, Sam. When do you think you will be home? We need to talk."

"Is everything okay?" the guilty inquired.

"Fine, there's just an issue with Jenny." Two can play this game, she decided.

Debbie heard a sigh. "I'll try to be home by nine. Give her a kiss for me." And he hung up.

She looked at the kitchen clock. That gave her several hours to plan her attack.

The phone rang again. "Hey, where were you today? We missed you at the luncheon. Did you get hung up at Nordstrom?" Jan jokingly asked.

"Something unexpectedly came up. I can't talk. Can I call you tomorrow?"

"Sure. Is everything all right?"

"Fine. I'll talk to you tomorrow." As Debbie hung up the phone, she decided she was going to have to find the strength from somewhere down deep to confront Sam.

Later, after dinner, while Jenny chatted with a friend about some upcoming dance, Debbie lay sprawled across her bed lamenting her predicament and planning her attack.

She heard Sam sneak in late. She looked at the clock; it was midnight. She watched through one eye as he slowly took off the clothes she was sure had already been discarded in a flaming love moment and crawled in quietly on his side of the bed. A few minutes later, she heard him snoring. I'll confront him in the morning, she decided and she spent the rest of the night tossing and turning.

She got up very early the next morning, even before the sun cast its light through the thick fog that covered the city like a glove. She padded down to the kitchen, put the coffee on, and sat at the table, rehearsing the words she would say to Sam. There was no need to cry anymore. She had cried enough tears yesterday to fill a lake. Everything finally made sense. The other woman was the reason he wasn't home and he didn't touch her. How long had this affair been going on?

She finally heard the shower on upstairs. Sam must be up. She took her coffee and went upstairs.

Chapter 3

"WHAT'S HER NAME, SAM?" she asked as he stepped out of the shower. He picked up a fluffy white towel and began to dry off his lean, firm body.

"Come again?" he responded, sleep still deep in his words.

Debbie sat down at the vanity and placed her coffee cup on the counter. "I saw you with her yesterday, Sam, having lunch on Pier 39. Don't deny it. Who is she?"

He turned around slowly, as if he were a child caught with his hands in the forbidden cookie jar. He sighed and hung up his towel. He turned to face Debbie. "Her name is Donna, Donna Richards."

Debbie asked very quietly, "Are you in love with her?"

Sam looked her deeply in the eyes. "Yes, Debbie, I am. And I'm sorry. I never meant for this to happen, and I never meant to hurt you."

Debbie felt her soul shatter into a thousand pieces. Tears choked her words. Slowly she said, "I am deeply hurt, if you're interested. Now what do we do?"

"I honestly don't know, Debbie. All I do know is that I love her, and she loves me. She makes me feel alive, sexy, and she's a wonderful listener."

"Ouch, that hurt, Sam. And I take it I don't?" Debbie wiped the tears from her eyes with her bathrobe sleeve.

Sam looked sad. "You used to, Debbie, but lately, well, I don't know. I really don't want to get into it right now."

"You don't want to get into it right now?" she yelled in disbelief. "You bastard!"

"Calm down, Debbie, you'll wake Jenny."

Debbie toned down her voice for Jenny, not for him. She didn't want to deal with Jenny right now; she needed to gather herself and make some sense of this mess. "You're telling me that you're in love with another woman, and I'm supposed to be calm," she whispered angrily.

"I'm telling you that now is not the time to talk about it. I'm late for work."

"When is it a good time, Sam?" she replied, the sarcasm dripping from her voice.

He went over to his closet and pulled out a gray suit. He looked at her for a moment. "How about tonight, after dinner? We'll sit down and figure out what to do."

Stunned, Debbie walked over to the bed, sat down, and watched her husband dress. "What do you want to do, Sam?" She couldn't believe she was having this conversation. Never in her wildest dreams did she think she would be talking to her husband about his girlfriend. That happened to other people, not her. "Do you want a divorce?" she asked meekly.

Sam looked at her with tears in his eyes. "Yes, Debbie, I'm sorry, but I think I do." And he left the room. A few minutes later she heard the garage door open and close. She threw herself back on the bed, and huge, heart-wrenching sobs escaped her fragile soul.

The rest of the day passed in a haze. Somehow, she managed to get Jenny off to school, suffer through Teresa's grueling exercises, and get to the grocery store. The phone rang a few times, but she let the machine do its job. She drove the girls to ballet, and luckily Jenny was too busy chatting with her friends to notice her somber mood.

Sam did make it home for dinner. She fixed broiled salmon, baby red potatoes, and a fresh salad and served ice cream for dessert. Jenny chatted animatedly about her day with Sam, and how he managed to eat unnerved Debbie.

"Mom, are you okay?" Jenny asked as she cleared the table. "You hardly ate anything."

"I'm fine, Jenny. I just have this pounding headache," she answered as she glared over at Sam, who wouldn't catch her eyes, and focused on the remainder of his ice cream. "Leave the dishes tonight; I'll do them later. Why don't you go and do your homework. I'll be up later."

"Great." She bounded from the kitchen with a spring in her step. How young and innocent she is, Debbie thought as she watched her leave the room. What is this going to do to her?

Debbie cleared the remainder of the dishes and stacked them on the counter. "What do we do now, Sam?"

"I don't know," he muttered. "I guess this is where I pack up and leave."

"That's it? You don't want to discuss this? This is what you really want, to destroy our family?" Debbie walked over to the table, sat down, and studied him.

Sam wouldn't make eye contact, and Debbie could tell this discussion was difficult for him. "I didn't mean for this to happen, Debbie. I didn't go out purposely and look for her; it just happened. All I do know is that I love her. She makes me feel alive, and I found that I have to be with her. I know this sounds trite. I don't want to hurt you, but I am miserable living here."

Tears filled Debbie's eyes.

He reached for her hand, and she quickly pulled it away. "Debbie, you're a wonderful mother and a great person, and we had wonderful times together; it's just that we're not growing in the same direction."

"And you and Donna are?" This was unbelievable!

"I think so," Sam said gently. "Donna is a beautiful, fun, intelligent woman who is interested in many of the same things I am interested in."

"And I'm not?" She couldn't believe what she was hearing. "How old is she, Sam? Eighteen?"

"For the record, she's almost twenty-six."

"Almost jail bait, Sam."

"Debbie, I don't want to hurt you. I'm actually glad you saw us. I'm tired of living a lie and having to sneak around all the time. It's taking its toll on me, and it's not fair to anyone, least of all Jenny."

Debbie shook her head in disgust. "You didn't look concerned about Jenny the other day, when you were parading around town with your young thing."

"Debbie," he said gently, "I'm going to sleep in the guest room tonight, then tomorrow I'm going to pack some things and find a place. We'll each get lawyers. I want you to know that I'll take care of Jenny."

Debbie felt herself detach from the scene that was playing. It was as if she was outside her body, watching this poor, pathetic woman who was trying so hard to be brave at this moment. It was like watching a bad movie, a movie where you knew the ending was going to be horrible.

"Debbie, are you all right?"

She stood and stared at Sam. "Sure, Sam, I'm fine, never better. My husband of fourteen years has just informed me that he's in love with another woman and he wants a divorce. But don't worry about me. Rush off to your little hussy." Debbie felt like screaming, ripping the diamond earring off his ear, and scratching up his handsome face.

"I'm sorry, Debbie." And he left the kitchen.

He did have the good sense to pack after Jenny left for school the next morning. Jenny was surprised to see him still home, and he informed her he would pick her up after school. He had the gall to ask Debbie to be with him when he told Jenny what was happening.

"You're the one who is breaking up the family, not me. Do it yourself," she angrily spat as she watched him pack him clothes. He sighed and turned away, guilt plastered all over his face. Suffer, you bastard, she thought bitterly.

Later that afternoon, Debbie was trying to read a book to keep her mind off reality when she heard the door slam.

"Mom, where are you? Why is Daddy leaving?" Jenny came into the family room, tears streaming down her innocent young face. She threw herself on Debbie's lap. "I don't understand, Mom."

Debbie wrapped her arms around her and held her as she cried. "I'm sorry, Jenny. This has nothing to do with you. He's not leaving you, he's leaving me. He still loves you." Jenny's tear-stained face looked up at Debbie. "Sometimes people just fall out of love."

"Why did Daddy fall out of love with you?" She sat up and studied her mother.

"I honestly don't know, but I do know that we'll get through this ordeal together, Jenny."

"Oh, Mom, I'm so sorry. Maybe if I'd been a better kid, Daddy wouldn't have left."

Debbie shook her head and held Jenny's young body tight in her arms. Damn you, Sam, she thought. Now Jenny joins the ranks of millions of other children who have split-up families.

Debbie canceled her appointments for the next several days and decided she wouldn't leave the house until she gained control over her emotions and figured out what to do. Most of Sam's personal belongings were gone; she realized he wasn't coming back. And he didn't rent his own place. She overheard him talking to Jenny on the phone and giving her Donna's number. He repeated that he was there for Jenny if she needed him.

But who was there for her? She, who had been there for everybody and had done everything, was without anybody. What did she do to deserve this? Was she too good a wife? Should she have had a dazzling career? Should she have not tried so hard to cook nutritious meals and keep a beautiful house? What is going to happen to me? she thought. What do I do now?

Great waves of grief rolled over her body again, and she gave in to the self-pity. After several hours of crying, she fell into a deep, dreamless sleep. When she awoke the following morning and glanced over at Sam's side of the bed, hoping it all had been a bad nightmare, she saw it was empty. Reality set in. This had really happened. He had left her.

She pulled her weary body out of bed, went to wake Jenny for school, and put a call in to Lucy, telling her not to come. Lucy seemed confused on the phone, but Debbie told her it was a paid holiday and to go and have some fun. She just didn't want to deal with anyone.

"Mom, I don't feel good." Jenny dragged herself into the kitchen and sat down at the kitchen table, where Debbie was sipping a cup of coffee. "Can I stay home from school today? Please?"

Debbie looked up from her coffee and smiled. "I don't want you to miss any school. We have to go on, and you need your education. Besides, it's Friday; you'll have the whole weekend to relax."

"I just don't think I can face anyone today, Mom. Do you understand?"

"Of course, sweetheart." Debbie thought for a moment. "What

do you think about escaping the city for the weekend?" she asked as she got up and went over to the cupboard and pulled down bowls for cereal.

"Just you and me?" Jenny sounded like a small child and not the preteen who lived in the house.

"Yes, just the two of us. We could go to Carmel, stay at a nice hotel, go to the aquarium, and do some shopping. What do you think?" Debbie began to warm up to her idea and began to feel better. She needed to get out of this repressive city.

"I don't know. Kim is having her slumber party tonight, remember?"

"You're right. Do you really want to go?"

Jenny played with her cereal. "Not really. Everyone will be laughing and giggling, and I don't feel like doing that; so yes, I think it would be good to get away for the weekend. Do you think I could skip school and ballet?"

"You can skip ballet, but you need to go to school. How about when I pick you up from school, we head on down to Carmel."

"I can't skip school?"

"No, young lady. You need to go to school. Finish eating and run up and put some things in your suitcase."

Debbie did Lucy's chores that day. It felt good to keep busy. Scrubbing the kitchen floor seemed to calm her. She heard the phone ring several times, but she just let the machine in the den take the messages. She decided she would have some kind of a plan by Monday, then she would deal with Sam and everyone else. She did place a call to Aunt Jane, who wasn't home. Maybe she went up to Reno on a gambling junket, she decided.

She then called her favorite resort in Carmel, the Normandy, and luckily they did have a room available for them. Debbie was beginning to feel better. She took her checkbook out of the drawer and looked at the balance. She would need to transfer some funds on Monday from her trust. Luckily, she had money. She couldn't imagine going through this without money.

She picked Jenny up that afternoon, and they sped down the coast to Carmel. It was warm, and she opened the sun roof and let the sun's golden rays lighten their spirits. Jenny chose the radio station, and they let the music carry the conversation the duration of the trip, each of them alone with her own private thoughts.

They pulled up to the inn just as the sun was lowering across the Pacific. They were shown to their room, quickly unpacked, and headed down to the ocean before darkness descended. Jenny played in the waves, and Debbie sat on the sand allowing the ocean to soothe her aching soul. Later that evening, they had dinner at Clint Eastwood's Hog's Breath Inn and turned in early.

The weekend proved to be good for them. They were away from home, where Sam had been, and they went to the aquarium, explored the wharf, and wandered through the many shops. Jenny purchased a few things, but Debbie, for once, did not have the slightest desire to buy anything.

As they headed home late Sunday afternoon, Debbie still didn't know what to do about the situation, but she did feel better. The tears had finally stopped, and her head felt clear.

"What do we do now, Mom?" Jenny asked as they pulled into the driveway.

"I don't know, but I'll figure something out."

"I miss Dad, Mom. I'm sorry."

"Oh, Jenny, don't be. This is not about you. You did nothing to cause this. This is between Daddy and me."

"Mom, does Dad have someone else?"

"Why do you ask?"

"When Amber's parents split up, it was because her father had a girlfriend. Does Daddy have a girlfriend?"

Debbie sighed. It was time to tell Jenny the whole truth. Obviously Sam had not. "Yes, he does. Her name is Donna, and your father says he's madly in love with her."

Jenny just shook her head, got out of the car, and slammed the door.

Monday morning dawned cool and foggy, and Debbie still had not come to a decision about what to do. The weekend had given her some distance from the situation, though. She sent Jenny off to school, gave Lucy her instructions, and called Aunt Jane, who luckily was home, and arranged to meet her for lunch. She exercised, returned some phone calls, and dug around for the divorce lawyer's name a friend had given her long ago. She had tucked it away after some close friends had gone through a nasty divorce, just in case.

She dressed with care, choosing a black knit pantsuit and a diamond pendent, brushed her hair until it shone, and left the house shortly before noon. The fog was breaking and a cool wind was blowing off the bay.

Aunt Jane was waiting for her at the restaurant, sitting at a small table in the corner. She was sipping a glass of white wine and pondering the menu as Debbie came up. She took off her glasses and exclaimed, "Hi, Debbie. How wonderful to see you! Did you have a good weekend? I thought I saw Sam at the opera this weekend. Couldn't have been him, because you weren't with him," she rambled on.

Debbie gave her a hug, sat down, and took her hand in hers. "I'm sure it was Sam you saw, Aunt Jane. Jenny and I went to Carmel for the weekend."

She looked confused.

Debbie continued. "Sam left me. He's in love with another woman. I believe her name is Donna. Anyways, she makes him feel alive and sexy, so he says."

Poor Aunt Jane, she really looked confused. "Oh, Debbie. I'm so sorry. I don't know what to say. You sure?"

Debbie smiled. "Yes, Aunt Jane, I'm sure, and I need your help." Debbie proceeded to tell her about the entire horrible affair, the reason why he left, and Jenny's reaction. Aunt Jane just sat there, regal, taking it all in. She didn't interrupt Debbie once. When the waiter came over to take their orders, Aunt Jane ordered Debbie a glass of wine and then asked him to come back later. Debbie finished the story.

Aunt Jane sat back in her seat. "I'm so sorry, Debbie," she finally said after she had processed Debbie's story. "I always thought Sam was such a nice young man. What's gotten into him? Do you think it's a phase?"

Debbie shook her head. "He says he loves her, and I did follow them last week. They look very happy together."

"What does she look like?"

"She's young—twenty-five to be exact—tall, and she has long brown hair that falls to the middle of her back. I couldn't really see her face, but knowing Sam, she's gorgeous. Aunt Jane," she stammered, "I don't know what to do."

"Does he want a divorce?" Aunt Jane drained her wine glass.

"Yes."

"Do you think it's any use fighting for him?"

"I did at first, but no, not now. He's called several times and left the name of his lawyer, and he's pretty much moved out. He took most of his things, even his golf clubs." Sam hadn't played golf in years. Maybe Donna does, Debbie thought wryly.

Aunt Jane suddenly looked old. Debbie felt terrible; she didn't want to worry her again. Lord knows her aunt had her share of troubles with Debbie when she was younger.

The waiter came back again, and Debbie and Aunt Jane both ordered a chicken Caesar salad.

"Well," Aunt Jane said suddenly. "You're just going to have to pull yourself together and get tough. Find a lawyer and make sure you get what you deserve out of this marriage. How's Jenny taking it?"

Debbie told her about Jenny's reaction but then emphasized how the trip away had been good for both of them. Because, when you came right down to it, he was really leaving the two of them.

The waiter brought the salads, and they both dug in. Aunt Jane ordered another glass of wine. Debbie was suddenly hungry and realized she had skipped breakfast. In fact, she hadn't eaten much over the last few days. Somehow food seemed revolting. Food was a celebration of life, and she had been in no mood for celebrating anything lately.

Aunt Jane put down her fork and looked directly at Debbie. "You know what you should do?"

"What, Aunt Jane?" Debbie's interest was piqued. Aunt Jane usually never offered suggestions. She had told Debbie once she didn't want to interfere in her life.

"Jenny and you should get out of town. Spend the summer somewhere else. Get away from Sam and the situation and give yourself some time to reflect on the problem so you don't make a rash decision."

Debbie chewed on a piece of romaine lettuce and digested Aunt Jane's words. That didn't sound like such a bad idea.

"Hmmm, and where do you propose I go for the summer?"

"Why not go to Lake Tahoe and rent a cabin? You still have your trust money, I presume. Sam hasn't gotten a hold of that also?"

Debbie thought it over for a moment. She and Jenny loved Lake Tahoe. She could find a cabin, and even a job if she had to. She hadn't looked at her trust statements, but she was sure she had lots of money. When Sam and Debbie had first married, she had put Sam's name on the accounts. She suddenly hoped all the money was still there.

"That's not a bad idea, Aunt Jane. In fact, it's a wonderful idea. I could find a place, and I should still have lots of money left. It would only be for the summer."

Aunt Jane smiled. "Let's go up this weekend and look, shall we? And we can stay at the Crystal Bay Club. My treat."

Debbie smiled. The Crystal Bay Club was located on the Nevada side of the lake. Aunt Jane loved her gambling.

Debbie felt much better as she drove home. Now she had a direction, a purpose, even if it was only for the moment. She wasn't sure how Jenny would like the idea of spending the summer away. School was out in five weeks, and she would have to finalize all this quickly if she wanted it to happened.

She wondered what her parents would think if they were here. Would they be disappointed in her? She had been around Jenny's age when they died, a long time ago.

The news of Sam's affair and departure spread like the Oakland fire through her friends' phone lines. Debbie found herself the object of pity. If she heard "Oh, you poor thing" one more time she felt she would vomit. Something snapped in her, and she decided from that point on she was not going to play the victim. She decided to rise like a phoenix from the ruins of her past existence.

Jenny was initially upset with the idea of spending the summer away from her friends. Debbie let her rant and rave about how she wouldn't have anyone to hang out with and how there'd be nothing to do. After it was out of her system, Debbie gently asked her to try and think of this as an adventure. She told her that when she was a young girl, Lake Tahoe had been a great place to meet boys. Jenny could go to the beach every day, and Debbie was sure she'd meet other kids who were spending the summer there. That seemed to pique her interest, and later Debbie heard her on the phone telling some friends about all the cool guys she was going to meet over the summer.

Sam had called Jenny twice during the week, but he never did find the time to come and see her. He told her he had a big project due, and he needed to get it in on time. Debbie imagined Donna took a great deal of his creative energy. Sam and Jenny made a date for the following weekend, but Debbie could tell Jenny was disappointed. She too had been displaced by the other woman.

Aunt Jane, Jenny, and Debbie left for Lake Tahoe that Friday. It was early spring up there. Patches of dirty snow still lingered on the sides of the roads, and the temperature was cool. But the sky was a brilliant blue and the air fresh and invigorating.

They arrived at the Crystal Bay Club, and Jenny and Debbie took a walk after they had settled in. It had been a four-hour trip, and they needed to stretch their legs. Aunt Jane hurried to the slots, and Jenny and Debbie went in search of a real-estate office.

They visited several and were given lists of available cabins. One realtor explained that the rentals were quickly filling up for the summer, and that if they found a cabin they liked, they should put a deposit on it as soon as possible.

Armed with a list of furnished cabins, they began their search with Mrs. Dennis, a middle-aged, heavyset woman who offered to show them some properties that day. Many of the cabins they visited were too primitive for their San Franciso blood, and several were too big for just the two of them. Debbie began to feel discouraged. Maybe she should rent a condo. Mrs. Dennis informed her that there were several available, but Debbie had her heart set on a cabin. She specifically wanted a log cabin with a fireplace and heavy on the mountain charm to help her through her grief.

And as if the Tahoe angels were guiding her, one of the last cabins on her list fit the description. They pulled up to a log cabin with a huge stone chimney and green shutters. As they got out, Mrs. Dennis explained that the owner had died over the winter, and the children, who all lived back East, were arguing among themselves whether to sell or keep it. Yesterday they had decided to rent it until they could come to an agreement. The cabin had sat vacant since the owner had used it last summer, and as Mrs. Dennis opened the flimsy lock, a small gray mouse scurried across the floor.

"Yuck!" shrieked Jenny. "I don't want to stay here."

They all entered the cabin, and Debbie was immediately struck by its charm. There was a large stone fireplace that took up most of one wall. An old tattered couch, a trunk that doubled as a coffee table, and several pine chairs filled up the living room. Off to the right, Debbie could see the kitchen, with its knotty pine cupboards, a large kitchen table, and enough counter space to hold all her treasures. There was a stairway that led to the upstairs, where she presumed the bedrooms were.

"It has potential," Debbie said, ignoring Jenny's moans.

"I know it's dirty, but with a little love, some plants, pillows, throws, and books it could be transformed," Mrs. Dennis suggested. "Why don't you think about all the cabins you've seen, discuss them, and call me at the beginning of the week?"

Chapter 4

"You've been spending money like the federal government," her lawyer scolded as he examined the records Debbie's banker had faxed over. "What did you expect?"

Debbie sat back in the soft leather chair. Never had she imagined this! Mr. Blair, her lawyer, had informed her that they had been living well beyond their means; the trust was depleted.

"But Sam made a good living, and I had the money from the trust. I don't understand."

Mr. Blair ran a hand through his short, curly, salt-and-pepper colored hair. Very patiently, almost as if he were speaking to a small child, he tried again. "Your expenses ran more than the two incomes combined." He looked at a legal pad with some figures scratched on it and continued. "You have a hefty mortgage on the house in Pacific Heights, a lease on a BMW 740il, the lease on the Porsche, a maid, a personal trainer, Jenny's private school, ballet lessons, Sam's gym, your credit card bills, and your travel and dining out. Sam had to dip into the trust principle more and more each year to cover the expenses, and it looks like he also made a few poor investments. There have also been some substantial cash withdrawals. The only real asset you have is the house."

"Which Sam wants to sell," Debbie added bitterly. Her house was her showcase, her pride and joy, and now it would be gone.

"You should have been asking questions," Mr. Blair continued.

Debbie sighed. "I guess so. I never thought about it. Sam never said anything, so I just assumed everything was all right. How much cash do we have?"

Mr. Blair shuffled some papers and finally came across the information he needed. "According to Sam's attorney, he's living paycheck to paycheck. There's around five thousand left in your trust fund account. You shouldn't have let Sam have access to that money."

"Who would have thought," she answered bitterly. "We did take vows to love, honor, trust, and obey. Obviously, Sam didn't take those words very seriously. Why would he do this to us?" she asked, deeply confused.

"Who knows? I've seen this too many times. Money and people are strange bedfellows. I suggest you make some decisions here as to your lifestyle, how you want to proceed, and get back to me."

Debbie stood up and smoothed her linen skirt. "Thank you for your time, Mr. Blair. I'll be in touch."

Debbie felt like she had been beaten over the head with an aluminum bat. The tears rushed to her eyes, and she ducked into the nearest ladies' room and took up residence in a stall. "How are we going to live? What am I going to do?" she sobbed as she sat down on the cold, hard toilet seat. "I'm so afraid. This is so unfair! I didn't do anything to deserve this. How dare Sam ruin my life!"

There was a message on the machine from Sam when she arrived home. As she hit the play button, the voice that she had loved for years barked, "I want to sell the house now. I've found a realtor I like. I'm willing to pay a thousand a month for Jenny's support, but you're not going to bleed another dime out of me. Try it and I will quit my job. Make sure you get an attorney!"

Just as Mr. Blair predicted, this was going to be ugly.

Walking into the den, she sat down and made a few calls. She canceled her trainer and her nail appointment for the next day, left a message for Lucy to call her, and phoned the realtor at the lake. "I'll take the log cabin for the summer. The deposit will be in the mail tomorrow."

She made herself a cup of lemon herbal tea, took it over to her favorite chintz couch, and pondered her predicament. She was in deep shit. Her cash flow situation was not good. She had several thousand dollars in a checking account that she used to pay the household bills and ten thousand dollars in a mutual fund that was just hers, waiting for a rainy day. Well, it was raining!

Suddenly her life was turned upside down. Not only did she find herself out of a marriage, but she was going to be without a home soon, and to top it off, she was almost broke. Now what?

Everything in her life had always been handed to her, and she never really had to work for anything she needed or wanted because Sam, Aunt Jane, or the trust fund had made sure it was there for the taking. Now Sam had found someone else, the trust fund was almost gone, and she certainly was not going to trouble Aunt Jane. It was time to grow up and start taking care of herself and Jenny. Going to Lake Tahoe and living in that rustic cabin would be a good start. She was going to have to find some kind of a job for the summer, she decided. Anything. They would make it. She was determined!

After picking Jenny up from school and dropping her off at ballet, she dropped in on Aunt Jane, who was surprised but happy to see her. She explained what she had discovered at the lawyer's, and Aunt Jane looked as shocked as Debbie had. They discussed Debbie's new twist in the road of life.

"I still think it's a wonderful idea for you and Jenny to go to Tahoe for the summer. Perhaps the clean fresh air and tall majestic pines will mend your broken spirits. You know, dear, I do have some money if you need it."

"Thank you, but no," Debbie replied gently. "I'm going to do this on my own."

And having said those words aloud, it was as if a new sense of purpose resonated from her being. She had direction now, a reason for getting up in the morning. She wasn't really sure what her new purpose was, but definitely something different than being the self-absorbed shopping little twit she had been before.

Debbie found herself back in Mr. Blair's office at the end of the week signing papers, which included the listing on their one-point-two-million-dollar home. Sam was extremely eager to dump it, but Mr. Blair held firm at the price he thought the market would support. Mr. Blair handed her the Sam's first child-support check, and there were papers to sign to get the wheels moving for the divorce. Under California state law she was entitled to half of the years they were married in alimony. Sam didn't want to pay her alimony; he wanted to give her most of the proceeds from the sale of the house.

"You're entitled to more," Mr. Blair urged.

"I just want what's mine." Thanking him, she left the office to deposit Sam's check in her dwindling bank account. She paid the stack of bills, took several outfits back to Nordstrom that still had tags on, and sent Lucy a severance check. Mr. Blair had informed her that Sam was refusing to pay the lease on her car, so she decided to turn it in and get something cheaper. The last thing she wanted to do was deal with car salesmen, but she had been thinking that she'd need another car for the mountains anyway.

That weekend she turned in the BMW and went down to a used car dealer and purchased a white 1991 Ford Bronco with four-wheel drive, just in case she decided to stay longer in Tahoe. The cost of the Bronco closed out her mutual fund, but at least she wouldn't have a car payment.

The For Sale sign was up in the yard on Saturday. Sam picked up Jenny for the weekend, and Debbie spent the time alone, grateful for the solitude and the chance to think and air out her thoughts. She puttered around her beautiful home, rearranging her favorite items, lost in her own thoughts. She packed the things she wanted to take to the lake and boxed some things she wanted to store. Sam had presented Mr. Blair with a list of things he wanted. She played around with the thought of throwing his precious stereo and collection of old albums out on the front lawn and having a massive bonfire. Maybe she'd invite the neighbors over for a marshmallow roast.

But she didn't. She did succeed in burning them in a wonderful daydream, though, complete with Sam running up the steps trying to save his beloved items with Donna close behind. Debbie just stood to the side laughing, and when Donna wasn't looking, Debbie pushed her into the fire. The fire engulfed her, and she sank in her own evilness like the Wicked Witch of the West.

"I'm home, Mom," Jenny yelled when she came through the back door late Sunday afternoon.

"How was it?" Debbie asked as she met Jenny in the kitchen.

"We went to Grandma's house. It was all right. She was there; she's nice, I guess."

"Tell me about it, please." Debbie took a seat at the kitchen table and listened attentively.

"Well, Grandma and Grandpa didn't really know what to make of the whole situation. They tried to be pleasant. Daddy seems happy. She orders him around a lot, and he follows her like a puppy dog."

"What's she like?" Debbie was dying of curiosity.

Jenny paused, went to the refrigerator, opened it, and retrieved a small bottle of Sunny Delight. She flipped off the top and took a long, thirsty gulp. "Mom, I'm not going to lie to you and say she's ugly and horrible because she's not. She's pretty, tall and thin, and she has long brown hair, big brown eyes, and she wears glasses. She seems real smart. I overheard her telling Grandma that she graduated from Brown."

"Did your father tell you how they met?"

"Yeah, he said something about how she works for a regional lender, whatever that is, and they met while he was giving a presentation. He did say he never meant for any of this to happen. He told me to tell you he's really sorry."

Debbie shook her head. "He doesn't act that way, throwing us out of our home."

"I have a feeling it's her idea and not his."

"Why do you say that?"

Jenny finished the rest of her drink. "Oh, I heard them talking. Donna was telling Dad that you acted like you were super wealthy and you threw your money around to try and impress people."

Debbie's eyes grew big. "She's never even met me; how dare she!"

"Calm down, Mom. If you ask me, she seems very impressed with herself."

"Do you think they want to get married?"

"I think she does, Mom, but I'm not sure about Dad. To be honest, he seems a little overwhelmed by the whole situation."

"How did Muffy and Don like her?"

"She kissed up royally to them. I could tell Grandpa was impressed when she told him who her father is; she said he's some kind of big developer in Sacramento. Grandma was polite."

I bet, thought Debbie. I'm sure Muffy is having a hard time with the impending divorce. She won't know what to say to her bridge and golf buddies. Debbie gave Jenny a big hug. "I'm glad you're home. I missed you terribly."

Jenny smiled and gave her a kiss. "I'm glad too, Mom. If I have to look at the two of them all over each other again, I think I'll puke. Mom, I've been thinking."

"What, sweetheart?"

"I think it'll be good to get away for the summer. I'm sorry I put up such a fuss."

Debbie gave her another big hug. "I love you, Jenny."

Jan came over to see Debbie a few days before they were scheduled to leave. "Hi, Jan," Debbie said as she answered the door.

Jan entered. "I would have come over sooner, Debbie, but you know how busy it gets at the end of the school year."

Debbie ushered her into the kitchen, and they sat down at the table. "Can I get you something to drink? I don't have much, but I can offer you some iced tea.

"No, Debbie, I can't stay long. What I came to say won't take too much of your time, but my conscience has been bothering me."

Debbie looked her friend directly in the eyes. "What's this about?"

Jan studied her nails. "I haven't been honest with you, Debbie, and I'm sorry."

"Honest about what?"

"I knew Sam was having an affair with Donna; in fact, I've run into them on several occasions. In a twisted way, I guess I was almost glad."

"Glad? Why? I thought you were my friend?"

"I am, Debbie; it's just that you always had everything going for you—the perfect marriage, house, and child—and I know my husband's been cheating on me for a long time. I was just glad that I wasn't the only one."

Debbie just shook her head in disbelief. "So you lied to me when I asked you, when I came to you for help."

Jan picked at a hangnail on her perfectly manicured nails. "I guess so. I am sorry. I never meant for this to hurt you. I hope we can be friends."

"I don't think so, Jan. This hurts deeply. You know the way out."

"But Debbie, I'm sorry."

"With friends like you, Jan, I can't imagine how my enemies feel about me." Debbie got up and left the kitchen.

✦ ✦ ✦

Debbie awoke early several mornings later and looked out the bay window. The horizon was just beginning to explode with color, emerging from the dark, cool night into the promise of a bright new day. Muted shades of purple and pink were dotted by streaks of golden sunlight that struggled to become dominant. The city was free from fog, and a light breeze ruffled the tops of the trees in the park across the street.

Getting out of bed, she stood before the spectacular event, stretching; she inhaled and exhaled the promise of a new beginning. They were leaving tomorrow for the lake, and she was ready. Not only had she lost her husband, but her best friend had betrayed her. She noticed some of her other friends were avoiding her; it almost seemed that they were afraid they could catch the divorce bug by being with her.

The house still hadn't sold, but they had quite a few lookers. Debbie disliked the intrusion into their lives, the opening of drawers and closets, the poking into nooks and crannies, and the constant list of questions: What type of heat do you have? Where's the circuit breaker? What are the power bills like? What kind of insulation do you have? What day is garbage pickup? And on and on went the litany of questions these noisy intruders asked. Of course Sam, the reason for all this misery, wasn't here to deal with it. She wondered how many of the potential buyers had been told of her situation. She thought she saw several pitying looks. Maybe it was her imagination, though. But as of tomorrow, she told herself, she wouldn't have to deal with this any longer.

Debbie had reserved a U-Haul trailer, and they packed it full of the things they'd need for the summer. Aunt Jane was going to follow them up in her car with more of the things they couldn't cram into the trailer. Debbie still hadn't decided what to do about Jenny's school in the fall when they returned, but she did know that the hefty private tuition was going to be a luxury of the past. She hadn't dropped that bomb on Jenny yet; Jenny had been in the same school since the first grade.

She had to hand it to Jenny. She seemed to be handling this entire situation like an adult. She told Debbie that she was going to have an adventure this summer. She was sure she was going to meet a boy, and she had begun to beg Debbie for a puppy. They had never had a dog before; it had always seemed to be too much of a hassle, not to mention the mess, but now it seemed like a good idea.

Jenny had seen Sam several other times, but never overnight again. She made an excuse to Sam each time he asked if she wanted to spend the night at Donna's. He really didn't seem too sad to see her go for the summer. According to Jenny, Sam and Donna had several trips planned.

Muffy and Don came over the day before they left to say good-bye to Jenny. They said few words to Debbie and made polite small talk with Jenny. As they were leaving, Don pressed some money into Jenny's hand and told her to call if she needed anything. Jenny promised to write to them when they were settled, and they told her they might make it up in August for a week. Sam had promised to visit also with Donna.

As they drove across the Bay Bridge, they both turned around and took a look at the city they loved so much. Debbie adjusted the mirror and waved to Aunt Jane, who was following right behind them, anticipating the slots she would visit later that evening.

As Jenny fiddled with the radio dial, Debbie's mind went back to the day several weeks ago when Sam and Donna came over to divide up their things. Debbie had just stood there, appalled by the gall of Donna, who walked around Debbie's house like she owned it. She pointed out things to Sam she wanted, and Sam just followed her around, okaying her choices. Debbie had raised objections, but Sam told her that they could do this in a civilized manner, or drag this into court. At that point, Debbie was so tired and beaten up by the situation that she withdrew.

She just stood back and watched Donna lead Sam around, commenting on Debbie's taste and arrangements. He produced a list of things he felt he deserved. Debbie felt total detachment and disgust by that time. It was as if he had beaten every bit of hope out of her.

"Just take what you want and leave," she snapped back. "Get out before Jenny comes home and has to witness this."

As she watched them tag his items, she observed Donna. This is who he has left me for, she mused. Donna was just like Jenny's description, only plainer than Debbie had imagined, no real sparkle or beauty, she just had the flame of youth going for her. I guess I thought the woman would be a complete knockout. She must be something in bed, she decided as she watched them leave. And I wonder if those breasts are real?

"Hey, Mom! Can we stop in Sacramento for something to drink? I'm thirsty."

Debbie glanced at her watch. "I don't see why not. I'm sure we're all in need of a bathroom break." They were driving through Davis. "We'll be there in twenty minutes. Look for a place."

Several hours later their car pulled off Highway 80 into Truckee, and they took Highway 267 over to the lake. They both rolled down the windows and inhaled the sweet, fresh mountain air. Spring was just beginning in the mountains and the green hills were dotted with clumps of purple and white wildflowers. Debbie felt her mood lighten as she turned off the air conditioning and drank in their surroundings. Maybe this is what my broken spirit needs, she concluded as she drove along the uncrowded road, savoring the beauty and serenity of the mountains.

They pulled up to the realtor's office shortly before closing. Luckily, the realtor was still there, and she gave Debbie the key and had her sign some papers. "Enjoy the cabin and your summer," she said breezily as she locked up her office and headed off into the dazzling sunlight.

"Well, this is it, Jenny," she said as they both got back in the car. "Ready?"

"Let's go, Mom. I'm tired, and I'd like to unpack and maybe walk down to the beach."

Debbie leaned out of the car and spoke to Aunt Jane, who had parked right next to them. "Aunt Jane, you ready?"

Aunt Jane grinned. "I'll say. Let's get there, unpack, freshen up, and then go over to the Crystal Bay Club."

Jenny and Debbie shared a smile. The slots were calling.

They pulled up to the log cabin a short time later. Debbie peered at the cabin through her window and thought about the hours and hours of work it was going to take to get the cabin in shape. And no Lucy! It's funny, she thought as she got out of the car, I used to love cleaning and taking care of my own home, then for some strange reason, I decided I had to have a maid like all my other friends. She chuckled as she thought about the first few times she'd had Lucy over. She had gone around the house cleaning and straightening up before Lucy arrived. Debbie didn't want her to think they were slobs. But gradually she had gotten used to the luxury of having more and more time to shop, lunch, and volunteer.

Well, I'm not going to be shopping much anymore, she concluded. She was in no financial situation to blow her money on things that were not a necessity.

They all tromped up the walkway, and Debbie opened the front door and they all peered in. It was just as she remembered: quaint, cozy, and very dirty.

"Yuck, Mom. Why couldn't you have had someone come and clean?"

"Because, darling Jenny, we can't afford that lifestyle any longer."

"It'll be good for you," said Aunt Jane. "Hard work builds a healthy appetite and develops muscles." She winked at Debbie.

"Sure will. There's no more personal trainer for me, and ballet lessons for you are on hold. We'll need to get our exercise the old-fashioned way."

Jenny rolled her eyes in disgust and went up the rickety stairs to the bedrooms.

"We need your help down here, young lady!" Debbie yelled after her.

"I'll be right down, Mom. Just let me check out my new room."

After a quick dinner later that night in the coffee shop at the casino, they went out into the gambling area and watched as Aunt Jane attacked the slots. Jenny and Debbie stood off to the side and watched her squeal with delight as every once in a while a machine repaid her efforts with a handful of quarters. Debbie had a feeling they would see quite a bit of Aunt Jane over the summer.

The cabin was located several miles from the California/Nevada border. On the Nevada side of the imaginary line sat several small casinos. Aunt Jane had already made noises about going over the Mount Rose highway into Reno, which had larger casinos. Debbie knew one day they were going to have to indulge her. Aunt Jane went to Reno often on the gambling junkets, but there were several other clubs the buses didn't run to that she wanted to try.

"I'm ten dollars ahead," she said with a wide grin after what seemed to be an eternity. "Let's go back. I can come back tomorrow and see if I can double my win."

Jenny and Debbie laughed and followed her out into the cool, starry night.

"Look at all the stars, Mom!" Jenny shrieked. "There are millions of them. I've never seen so many."

Aunt Jane and Debbie stopped alongside of her, and they all gazed up. The sky was littered with a multitude of twinkling stars. Debbie took a deep breath and felt the invigorating mountain air fill her with a sense of peace.

The next day she awoke to sunlight streaming through the dirty windows in her bedroom. She glanced over at the side of the bed where Aunt Jane had slept and saw it was vacant. When she smelled coffee, a smile spread across her face, and she lazily stretched. Aunt Jane used to get up early when Debbie was a kid, sip her coffee, and read the paper. When Debbie finally emerged, wiping the sleep from her eyes, Aunt Jane would fix whatever breakfast she wanted.

Thank goodness some things don't change, she chuckled as she got out of bed and followed the coffee aroma.

"Good morning, Debbie. How'd you sleep? Would you like some coffee?"

"Love some," she answered as she sat down at the kitchen table. "I haven't slept this good in a long time. How come you're up so early?"

Aunt Jane got up and went to the cupboard and took down a bright blue mug. She poured Debbie a cup of coffee and handed it to her. "It's a beautiful morning, and we have a great deal to do, so when the birds woke me with their lovely songs, I decided to get up. Besides, I don't sleep as much as I used to. I find the older I get, the less sleep I need."

"Not me–I think I need more." Debbie took a sip of the coffee Aunt Jane had placed before her. Scanning the kitchen, she could see that Aunt Jane had already been busy. The counters were clean and sparkling, and she had placed the dishes in the open cupboards, arranged the spices, and scrubbed the stove. Debbie's utensils and pans were draining in the sink. Jenny was going to have to get used to washing dishes by hand.

"Looks great, Aunt Jane, but you should have waited for me."

"Nonsense. It's my pleasure." Aunt Jane looked pleased with herself. "Now, how would you like your eggs?"

"Scrambled, please."

"Coming right up."

By the time Jenny emerged a few hours later, Aunt Jane and Debbie had cleaned the living room, washed the windows, shaken the rugs, dusted the furniture, cleaned the bathroom, and run several loads of laundry.

"Hey, thanks for all your help, sleepyhead!" Debbie gave Jenny a hug.

"I'm sorry, Mom. I zonked out last night. I was so tired."

"Let's get you some breakfast, and then we'll tackle your room," said Aunt Jane.

"Where do you get your energy?" Debbie asked as she followed her aunt into the kitchen. She was exhausted, and they still had the upstairs to do.

Aunt Jane just smiled.

Later that morning, tired from their hard work, they sat on the front porch sipping herbal sun tea Aunt Jane had made earlier and composing a grocery list. Debbie read from the list. "Bread, milk, eggs, fruit, lettuce, tomatoes, rice, chicken, ice cream, paper towels, toilet paper . . . anything else?"

"Coke?" suggested Jenny.

"You know how I feel about that, Jenny. It's not good for your teeth."

"Ah, come on, Mom. Just this once."

Debbie looked at her daughter sitting on the ledge, dangling her long legs, and her heart went out to her. *Damn you, Sam,* she thought as she wrote down Coke. "I suppose just this once."

"Cool, and could we get some chips? I seem to be hungrier up here. Cool Ranch, please."

Debbie wrote down chips, took a sip of her tea, and sank back in one of the wicker rockers they had found in the back room. They had dragged them out, cleaned them up, and placed some pillows on them to add some comfort and color. *It will be wonderful to spend the warm summer evenings in these, gently rocking away our worries,* she concluded. She observed Aunt Jane enjoying hers with eyes closed and a satisfied grin on her face.

Some time later, Aunt Jane looked at her watch and started making the motions of getting up. "It's going to take me a while to get home. I think I'd better get on the road."

"Do you have to go so soon?" Debbie pleaded.

"Yeah, Aunt Jane, please stay longer. We could go to the Crystal Bay Club again tonight?" Jenny argued.

Aunt Jane smiled. "That certainly is tempting, but I have a few things to attend to tomorrow, and you both need some time to get used to your new home. I'll be up in a few weeks—that is, if you want me."

"Of course," they both yelled in unison.

Jenny and Debbie followed Aunt Jane into the cabin and watched her gather up the few things she had brought. Debbie gave her a big hug.

"Thanks so much again, Aunt Jane. I appreciate all your help and support."

My pleasure, dear. Now you just focus on taking care of yourself and Jenny. And Debbie?"

"Yes?"

"Carry a lighter load. Try to have some fun."

"Thanks. I'll definitely try."

Aunt Jane turned to Jenny, who was leaning against the bathroom door. "And you, young lady, help your mom and have a wonderful time."

"I will, Aunt Jane. I'll miss you."

"And I'll miss you both. Keep those slot machines warm for me. I'll be back," she said with a twinkle in her eye.

Jenny and Debbie stood hand in hand and watched Aunt Jane back out of the narrow dirt driveway. They waved until she was out of sight and then turned silently and looked at each other. I sure hope I know what I'm doing, Debbie thought as she gazed back at her daughter's innocent eyes.

The Mountains *part 2*

Chapter 5

SLEEP DIDN'T COME GENTLY THAT NIGHT. Debbie tossed and turned, worrying about her financial situation. In the past, she had let Sam worry about money; she had just worried about spending it. But that life was over now, and she was the one in charge of the economics. And she was scared to death!

Turning on her bedside light, she got up, put her pink chenille bathrobe on, and gathered up her checkbook and lists. The balance stared her straight in the face: $1,500. And the list of monthly fixed expenses took a big chunk out of that. She was definitely going to have to go job hunting in the morning. After doing the math, it looked as if she needed to bring in around eight hundred dollars a month to get by comfortably—provided Sam kept sending the monthly check. Once the house in the city sold, her cash flow problems would ease, but she couldn't count on that yet. Her once-secure future was gone. They had spent all their money and they didn't have any money put away for Jenny's college. How pathetic! Why didn't Sam talk to me about our finances? she thought. How could he do this to Jenny? Who would have thought she would be in this situation now? If even a few months ago a psychic would have predicted this turn in her life, she would have laughed in her face and demanded her money back.

❖ ❖ ❖

Today's the day I find a job, Debbie thought as she lay in bed early the next morning staring at the knotty pine ceiling. Glancing through the cotton curtains, she saw blue skies. A good day to run into the town of Kings Beach to get a paper, she decided as she got up. Debbie left a note Jenny, who was still fast asleep, locked the front door, and stood on the porch stretching. Her muscles felt stiff in the cool, early morning air.

It's now or never, she told herself. Let's go. And she took off down the hill. Her legs talked back for the first half mile, and she struggled to breathe in the thin mountain air. After a while her body began to wake up, and she started to feel alive. Hey, this feels wonderful, she decided. Why did I give this up?

She made it to town and ran along the main street, looking in the windows of the stores and restaurants that faced the road as she slowly plodded along. She jogged by gift stops, bathing suit stores, expresso stands, and a book store. Several places had "Help Wanted" notices, but none interested her until she came upon Zak's Saloon and Grille. "Help Wanted: Waitress," the sign read.

I think I'd like working here, she decided as she tromped around the property. The restaurant was located on the beach. There was a large wooden deck that faced the water. Picnic tables sported bright blue umbrellas to protect customers from the intense Tahoe sun. Peering in the windows, Debbie saw the place was decorated with many hanging plants and pictures of the lake taken at various times in the year. Large wooden booths made the restaurant seem cozy and homey. The sign on the door stated that the restaurant opened at eleven for lunch.

She ran home to tell Jenny her discovery.

"It looks like you have a gap in your employment record," the young manager stated as he carefully reviewed her completed application. "What have you been doing for the last twelve years?"

Debbie stared at the young man, who barely looked old enough to shave, her potential boss, the key to her new job, and turned on all her womanly charm. "I've been at home, raising a daughter, tending a large home, taking care of a husband, and volunteering."

"And what finds you here at Lake Tahoe looking for work as a waitress at your stage of life?"

Debbie smiled sweetly, but secretly she wanted to strangle his scrawny neck and rip the earring that jutted out from his eyebrow. "It's personal, if you don't mind. I don't think my reason for being here has any relevance on my ability to perform the job. As you can see from my prior work experiences, I did quite a bit of waitressing in college."

The manager looked at her application again. One would have thought she was applying for the job of CEO of a large corporation instead of a waitress in a thirty-year-old restaurant. "Okay, you're hired. Be here at ten tomorrow. And I don't tolerate late people."

"Thank you," Debbie said as she got up. "You won't regret it. I'll work very hard, and I'll be on time."

"Sure, whatever, lady. I just don't want you calling in because your kid's sick."

"I won't, Bruce," she replied, focusing on his name which was prominently displayed on his name tag along with the word "Manager."

Bruce strolled over to the bar, flipped on the small TV to a music video station, poured himself a drink, and began to get the bar ready for the upcoming lunch crowd.

As Debbie walked into the dazzling sun, elation swept her being. I'm employed! And it feels good! As she began the walk home, she started to reassess her financial situation. If I could make enough money in tips, she thought, I could put away a chunk of Sam's monthly check for Jenny's college and maybe save some for my retirement. The future suddenly looked brighter, and savoring the feeling, she walked over to an expresso stand and treated herself to a large nonfat latte.

"I got the job, Jenny," she yelled as she came in the front door.

"Cool, when do you start?" Jenny asked as she came out of the kitchen, drying her hands on her cutoffs.

"Tomorrow at ten. What are you doing?"

"I made us tuna-fish sandwiches for lunch. I don't know about you, but I'm starved."

Debbie hugged Jenny, and she could have sworn Jenny had taken another growth spurt. She was now almost as tall as Debbie, who stood five-seven. "What did I ever do to deserve a kid as great as you? How about doing something fun after we eat?"

"Sure, Mom."

Debbie followed Jenny into the small kitchen and took a place at the table Jenny had lovingly set with placemats and their nice dishes. Jenny had placed a cobalt-blue pitcher filled with beautiful wildflowers in the middle of the table.

"It looks beautiful," Debbie exclaimed as she took a sip of her iced tea.

"Thanks, Mom. I just figured we needed to treat ourselves well and keep our sense of family, even though Daddy's not here."

I have some kid, she thought as she took a bite of the tuna sandwich. "Delicious," she said and then she proceeded to tell Jenny about her new job and her young boss. "Are you going to be all right while I work?"

"Mom, we've been through this before. I'm almost thirteen. I'll be fine. Besides, I'd like to look for a babysitting job. I could really use the money. Then I won't have to ask you for money for things I want."

"You don't have to work yet, Jenny. You have your entire adult life to work. You should have some fun. Perhaps we can find a camp or something."

"No, that's for babies. No, Mom, I've thought it through. I want to do something useful, and I want to help you out."

Damn you, Sam, Debbie thought bitterly. You've taken away your daughter's childhood, and all because you had an itch in your groin. She took Jenny's hand. "Thanks, Jenny. We'll get through this."

"Of course we will, Mom. We can't play victim. Now, what would you like to do?"

After much discussion, they agreed to go to Sand Harbor for the afternoon. It was the cheapest of all their suggestions, and Debbie was still having difficulty adjusting to the new way of living, while Jenny actually seemed to enjoy finding cheaper ways to have fun and purchase groceries. In fact, Debbie had to admit as she watched her daughter clear the table and wash the dishes by hand, Jenny seemed to be maturing in the process. Not once had she heard Jenny complain about the situation being unfair or about how she missed her old life. Jenny had become a symbol of strength and determination to Debbie. It was her own weak character that needed work.

Still early in the season, the beach was uncrowded. Debbie and Jenny had no trouble finding a spot close to the water. They laid their towels out, slathered their virgin white bodies with sunscreen, and flopped down on the sandy beach. Jenny turned on the small portable radio to a station they could both tolerate. The sounds of the waves soon lulled Debbie into an altered state, and the warm sun began to penetrate her body. She vaguely heard Jenny get up after a while and head into the water.

"Hey, Mom, you're getting awfully red. You might want to put a shirt on."

Groggily, Debbie lifted her head and looked at her arms. It was hard to tell how red she was in the direct sun. Jenny stood over her with another girl around her age.

"Mom, this is Kate. She's spending the summer up here with her family. Do you think she could come over some time?"

Debbie smiled at Kate. "Sure, that would be fine. It's nice to meet you, Kate. You girls have fun; I'm going to flip and burn the other side."

And she did. Even though she had applied sunblock, she still went home with a red glow all over. But she didn't care. It had felt marvelous to soak up the warm rays of the sun.

"My name is Anne, and I'll be working the lunch shift with you." Debbie looked up and saw a tall, willowy woman whose hair hung down her back in a thick blond braid. The lines around her liquid blue eyes revealed that she was around Debbie's age. Excellent health radiated from her being.

"Nice to meet you. I'm Debbie. Have you been working here long?"

Anne gathered up the salt and pepper shakers and put them on a tray. "I've been here several years now. The money's good in the summer and the ski season, but the rest of the year can be slow."

"Do you like it here?"

"Yeah, it's fine for now. I'm kinda in a holding pattern for now while I figure out what to do with the rest of my life."

Debbie followed her around the restaurant with a tray filled with condiments. As they prepared all the booths for the lunch rush, she listened as Anne continued talking.

"It's nice to see another woman my age here. You said your name's Debbie, right?"

"Yes, Debbie Burke. Anne?"

"Correct, Anne Montgomery. So, what brings you to the lake? No wait. Let me see if I can guess. Divorce, and you had to get away."

Debbie smiled. "You're right. How'd you know? Am I that obvious?"

"No, not really. You just have that look about yourself. Many women end up here in our situation. Why are you still wearing your ring?"

Debbie looked down at her left hand. The one-carat diamond Sam had placed on her finger with love sparkled. "Funny, I forgot I had it on. It's been there for so many years. But, I guess it's time to take it off." Debbie slid the ring off her finger and stuck it in the pocket of her khaki shorts.

At that moment, Bruce strolled into the dining room. "I see you two have met. The other waitress called in sick, so it's just you two today. Can you handle it?"

"Of course," replied Anne.

"Good. Let me know if you need help." He went to his position behind the bar.

Debbie followed Anne back to the kitchen, where they completed the rest of their side work. "What's he like to work for? He kind of gave me a hard time yesterday when he hired me."

"Bruce? His bark's worse than his bite. He's young, maybe twenty-four, and he takes this manager business seriously. After work I'll buy you a beer and you'll get to know him better. He's cool."

"Good. He had me worried yesterday."

The restaurant was extremely busy, and Debbie felt she had never worked so hard. When she finally got a break, it was around three. She quickly called Jenny, who was waiting for Kate to come over. "I'll be home in a bit," she told her daughter. Stiff and sore, she limped over to the faucet, poured herself a tall glass of water, and sat on a stool to rest her throbbing, weary legs. It had been a long time since she had waited tables, and her legs and arms were out of practice.

"Feet hurt?" Anne asked as she came around the corner carrying a tray loaded with dirty dishes.

"Yes, they're killing me. I forgot how hard this work is."

Anne smiled and punched her time card. "Come on. I'll buy you that beer before I have to go and get my kid."

Debbie got up and followed her to the large oak bar and eased her aching body into a seat. Anne dumped all her tips out on the counter. She counted out several dollars and ordered two Coors from Bruce.

"On the house today," he said as he placed the ice-cold bottles down. "Thanks for helping Debbie learn the ropes. It got kinda crazy today. And Debbie, good job."

"Thanks." Debbie took a big swig of the icy beer. It tasted delicious as it quenched her thirst. "How old's your kid?" she asked Anne.

"Chloe's eight and a wonderful little girl. Do you have any kids?"

"Yes. I have a daughter, Jenny, who's almost thirteen."

Anne's eyes got large. "Does she babysit? School's out on Friday, and I haven't found a sitter yet. I'm desperate."

"Funny you should ask. She's thinking about finding a babysitting job. She hasn't had a great deal of experience, just our old neighbors, but I have to say she's quite responsible."

Anne took a long, thirsty drink. "Terrific. I wouldn't need her until Saturday. My days off are usually Monday and Tuesday. What days did Bruce give you? It would be fun if we had the same schedule. I could take you hiking. You do like to hike, don't you?"

"I used to love to, but I haven't done much hiking living in the city. I'll talk to Bruce. How about if you and Chloe come over tomorrow and meet Jenny. I'd ask you over today, but she met a friend, and the kid's spending the night."

"No problem. Chloe went to a friend's today after school, so I have a long run planned for this afternoon."

"How long have you been running?" Debbie asked, her interest piqued. No wonder Anne had quite the body, she thought. Working all day in the restaurant, running, and mothering an eight-year-old certainly paid off.

Anne finished the rest of her beer and gathered up her things. "I started running in college, but it wasn't until I moved up here that I really began to get serious about it. Running has helped me get over Chris, Chloe's dad, and has given me the time and space to sort out all my head problems. I guess you could say running's been like a good therapist, only cheaper. Do you run?"

"I ran yesterday for the first time in years and enjoyed it immensely, but I found it's hard to breathe up here."

Anne put her sunglasses on and fumbled for her keys in the bottom of her large, tan backpack. "You get used to it; it takes a while, but you'll be in better shape by training up here. We'll have to go running soon. See you tomorrow."

"Thanks for the beer." Debbie watched as Anne breezed out of the restaurant and got into her Jeep Wrangler. The car fit her personality exactly. Debbie imagined Anne driving to all kinds of remote places, putting on her hiking or running shoes, and hitting the trails. She gathered up her things and stiffly headed for the door. Her body ached, and her spirit needed a long hot soak in the bath.

"Mom, they're here," Debbie heard Jenny shout from the living room. Jenny had seemed excited when Debbie told her of the potential babysitting job. She urged Debbie to have Anne and Chloe for dinner so she could get to know Chloe. She had already made plans for the money she would earn if she got the job.

Debbie took off her apron and paused to look at the beautiful table she had so carefully set with her blue-and-white bone china. It felt good to be cooking for company again, and she had spent considerable time preparing chicken cacciatore, a fresh green salad, homemade bread, and even a chocolate cake for dessert. Wonderful smells now filled the cabin.

Jenny let Anne and Chloe in. Chloe was a tiny version of Anne and stood shyly behind her mother. Jenny immediately took charge and asked Chloe if she wanted to see her room and her doll collection. Chloe's face broke out in a wide smile and she took Jenny's outstretched hand and raced off to her room with her.

"It's a match!" Debbie's eyes followed the girls up the stairs.

"Thank goodness," Anne sighed. She handed Debbie a bouquet of roses. "Chloe was extremely nervous about coming. She's an awfully shy child; she reminds me of Chris."

Debbie inhaled the roses pungent smell and felt her nostrils clear. "Thanks for the flowers. They're beautiful. Jenny's the opposite. She was born talking and has never had a problem making friends. Would you like a glass of wine?"

"That sounds wonderful."

Debbie took the yellow flowers and arranged them in an elegant crystal vase and gently placed them in the middle of the kitchen table. They seemed to catch the dwindling sunlight and cast their beauty and fragrance throughout the room.

Anne followed Debbie into the kitchen. "Those look great," she said as she observed Debbie's handiwork. I just love having fresh flowers in my home."

"I do too. When I was living in San Franciso there was always an abundance of fresh flowers in season. They seem to be a little harder to come by up here."

Debbie and Anne took their wine into the living room. Evenings were still cool, so Debbie lit the logs she had laid carefully earlier in the stone fireplace and joined Anne on the couch. Sounds of laughter could be heard from upstairs. Debbie sank back in the fluffy cushions of the well-worn couch and took a sip of her crisp white wine. Anne seemed to be soaking in the aura of the cabin.

"Great place. How'd you find it?"

Debbie preceded to tell her about the trip with Aunt Jane and the multitude of cabins they had looked at that weekend. Anne asked some questions about Debbie's former life, and Debbie gave her all the juicy details.

"How awful!" Anne exclaimed after hearing Debbie's saga. "And after all those years of martial bliss!"

"Obviously, to Sam it wasn't marital bliss. In the beginning I felt horrible and embarrassed, but now I don't know how I feel. I used to hate Sam, hate her, hate what he did to Jenny and me, but now, maybe it's because I'm up here and away from the situation, but it doesn't sting as much. Maybe I'm numb."

Anne smiled sympathetically. "I understand where you're coming from. When I left Chris and our lifestyle in Laguna Beach and fled here, it really helped that I had put some distance between myself and him. It helped me heal, focus on Chloe, and start developing my own self. When I caught Chris fooling around with that woman, I don't know, but I guess I just snapped."

"How long were you married?"

"Oh, we were never married. We lived together for about ten years. We had decided early on that we didn't need a piece of paper to have a loving, committed relationship." She laughed wryly. "I guess Chris never wanted to be that committed."

"Does Chris ever see Chloe?"

Anne sighed. "Maybe once a year. Sometimes he comes up and takes Chloe out for the day. He's never been a very good father. What about Sam? Is he a good father?"

Memories of the three of them together laughing, talking, and being a family flooded Debbie's mind. She tried to hold back the tears, but they were too strong. Between sobs, Debbie answered, "Sam really was a good father. He loved Jenny, made time for her, came to all her school functions and dance performances, and even took his turn getting up with her when she was a baby."

"You used the word was. I take it he's not acting like this anymore." Anne pulled a tissue from her pocket and handed it to Debbie.

"No. Since Donna, he doesn't seem to have any room in his life for Jenny. He's abdicated his role as a father. Now the only contact she has with him is when I have her call him once a week. The phone lines only seem to work one way," Debbie added bitterly.

Then she changed the subject quickly. "What did you do before you worked at Zak's?"

Anne looked longingly at the fire crackling in the hearth. "In my former life, I was a stewardess for Pan Am. I met Chris on a flight from New York to London. After the airline folded, I did some substitute teaching, then my relationship with Chris took off, and I found myself moving in with him and performing all the wifely duties. We did have some great times, and I was free to travel with him. Then one day I discovered I was pregnant. It was an accident; I really don't know what happened, but she was there. Chris urged me to have an abortion. He said he wasn't ready to become a parent. But I was, and I convinced him to have the baby with me. The first few years of Chloe's life were fine, but then I sensed Chris was beginning to drift. He was gone on more trips, and when he was home, he was preoccupied with work. One day Chloe and I came home a day early from a visit to my sister's, and I caught him in bed with Nicole. I threw them out, but, of course, I had to let him back in—after all, it was his house. Chloe and I went to live with my sister, and then I decided I wanted to get away from everything, so we came north to Lake Tahoe. And I haven't regretted it once."

"Does Chris send you any child support?"

"Yes, that's one thing he's good about. The first of every month I receive a check. I just wish he'd make some room in his life for her. She asks questions about him, and it's getting harder and harder to answer them."

"And Nicole?"

Anne thought for a moment. "I really don't know what ever happened to her. I surmise there's been a succession of Nicoles throughout the years. I have met a few of them when he's come up to see Chloe."

"How sad!" was all Debbie could answer.

"It used to be, but now it just is. Chloe and I do fine on our own. We don't need a man to define us."

"Do you date?"

"Sometimes," Anne answered. "I had a relationship with a dentist for about a year, but he wanted to get married, and I'm not into that right now. Chloe's my first priority, and I don't want to put her needs behind a man's right now."

Debbie got up to refill their glasses and check on the chicken simmering in the oven. "I can see where you're coming from. I don't think I want to get involved with anyone either."

Anne followed her into the kitchen. "I can tell you that the further the incident is behind you, the less intense the pain seems."

"I look forward to that feeling. Hey, girls!" Debbie yelled up the stairs. "It looks like dinner's ready!"

The rest of the evening passed pleasantly, with no more references to the past. They focused their attention on the present, the extraordinary summer weather, the outdoor opportunities, and the good times to be enjoyed. Anne and Jenny figured out a babysitting schedule. It was decided Jenny would walk or ride a bike over to Anne's. Debbie had left Jenny's bike in the city, but Anne graciously offered to lend Jenny hers until Debbie could get Jenny's up there. Perhaps Aunt Jane could bring it up in a few weeks when she came?

As Anne and Chloe were leaving, Anne asked if Debbie wanted to go hiking their next day off together.

"Go for it, Mom. I'll watch Chloe. It'll be good for you," Jenny championed.

Debbie laughed. "Okay, if you promise not to kill me."

"I'll take it easy on your soft city body," Anne chuckled in return.

Chapter 6

Debbie drove over to get Anne and drop off Jenny the morning of the hike. According to Anne, it was a four-hour round trip, so they promised the girls they'd go to the beach in the afternoon. Debbie's body was already stiff from the week of grueling physical work, and the chill that lingered in the early morning air sunk into her bones. She stood outside Anne's house stretching and breathing deeply, trying to warm herself up as Anne bounded out of the house with enormous energy.

"Don't you feel great?" she asked. "It's a glorious day for a hike. Let's go tackle that mountain."

Debbie looked at her in amazement. Had she had an entire pot of coffee? She climbed in beside Anne in the Jeep, buckled herself in, and tried to gather her wits. Anne turned the radio to a rock station and tore down the road, the wind whipping their hair around their faces.

She glanced over at Debbie. "You ready? This is a great hike."

"I guess so. How do you have so much energy so early in the morning? Aren't you exhausted from working?"

"Nope. I feel wonderful. I've found the better shape I'm in, the easier everything else is for me. You'll get used to the waitressing, and you'll get in shape too. I promise."

Debbie sank back in the seat and glanced around at the gorgeous scenery. Funny, she thought, I used to think I was in shape because

I had a trainer over twice a week and walked quite a bit. That might have been fine for living at sea level, but trying to do everything I used to do and more at sixty-three hundred feet above sea level was a killer. Debbie found herself out of breath a great deal of the time, and she could barely keep her eyes open until nine in the evenings; in fact, many evenings Jenny lovingly removed her glasses, picked up the book that lay on her chest, kissed her, and turned off the lights. The roles were now reversed.

But she was determined to get in real shape, mountain-woman shape, even if it killed her. It had become a goal that Debbie had decided to pursue. She was planning to participate in a fun run in the fall to prove to herself that she could be strong and was able to overcome all obstacles in her path, so she had begun jogging after work. She found it easy to jog down her street—it was the uphill part that she struggled on. She had promised herself that by the end of July, which was approaching quickly, she was going to be able to run up the hill without stopping.

Debbie was determined to do things on her own now and not rely on another person. In her former life, hired help had done most of the chores, and Sam had earned the money. All she had done was sit back, have her nails done, and enjoy the fruits of others' labors. She looked down at her once-elegant hands as she thought about all the hours she had sat in the salon. The artificial nails had long since been removed. Keeping her nails short was a priority now with all the things she did with her hands. She turned her hands over as the Jeep sped along. To be honest, she decided, she really didn't miss them. Her hands looked like they had a purpose in life, and she felt much freer now that she didn't have to worry about breaking a nail.

Slowly her life was beginning to change, and she was beginning to feel a sense of purpose, even if it was just waiting tables. She found she enjoyed her job, and she tried very hard to give her customers good service. Her tips were excellent, and she had opened a savings account and was beginning to save a good bit of money. Her plan was to be able to survive on Sam's support check and her small paycheck so that she could save all her tips.

So far, so good. There was no shopping to speak of at the lake. In fact, she found even groceries a challenge. Luckily for her the catalogs had not found her yet. She chuckled at her former love affair with the UPS man. Unopened boxes of stuff she had ordered used to litter her entry hall.

Anne pulled off the side of the road. "We're here, Debbie. Let's go. The mountain's waiting."

Debbie got out and stretched again. Here I go, she thought as she followed Anne. The trail started out flat, and Debbie was able to keep up with Anne, chatting about all sorts of topics. A little while later, the trail started to climb. Anne seemed to gain speed and leap up the mountain, while Debbie struggled with the ascent and the lack of oxygen. "I'll wait for you at the top. Take your time," Anne yelled. Debbie paused in the wake of her dust, gasping for air.

She had no choice but to take her time—this was one tough hike. "I thought this was supposed to be an easy hike," she muttered to a chipmunk that stood off to the side of the path, watching her huff and puff. She dug her feet into the dusty ground and slowly, step by step, trudged up the path that crisscrossed the massive granite mountain. After what seemed like an eternity, she saw the top and saw Anne sitting on a large boulder waiting patiently.

"Hey, you're doing great! It's all flat from here on out," Anne yelled down at her.

"I need to rest!" Debbie yelled back.

"Sure, come on up, sit awhile, have some water and a bite to eat."

Debbie plopped down by Anne. She took a long drink from her water bottle and opened the granola bar Anne handed her. Never had water tasted so delicious or food so satisfying. They sat atop the rock in silence drinking in the breathtaking beauty of the high Sierras. Several other groups of hikers made their way past them, shouting greetings. "You ready, Debbie?" Anne asked as she got up. Debbie could tell she was anxious to go, so she stiffly stood up and gathered her small daypack.

The rest of the hike was easy, just as Anne had said, and after an hour, they found themselves at the edge of a small, crystal-clear mountain lake. Anne opened her backpack and produced juice, muffins, string cheese, and apples. Debbie's mouth drooled.

They sat, enjoying the nourishment, cleaned up their mess, and headed back down the trail so they'd be home in time to take the girls to the beach as planned. Debbie found it was much easier going down, and she was able to keep up with Anne. They talked about all kinds of things. Anne described growing up in Southern California, her parents, who still lived there, her sister, and her college years in San Diego. She told Debbie about how, when she was fresh out of college and dreaming of travel, she had applied at Pan Am, was hired, went for training, and spent the next ten years flying the exotic routes to Paris, London, and Frankfurt. "Sometimes I still miss the excitement, but I need to be here for Chloe," she added.

Finally, through the trees, Debbie saw the outline of the red Jeep. Elation swelled up through her being. She had done it!

"Great job, Debbie." Anne hopped into the Jeep. "Next time I'll take you farther."

As Debbie crawled into the Jeep, she felt her muscles scream back. She laughed. "We'll see!"

As she took a drink of her orange juice, Debbie realized that this was going to be the first Fourth of July without Sam in fourteen years. The Fourth had always been a special holiday for them. While it marked the official beginning of summer, it also marked the time of year Sam usually took off three to four weeks and they vacationed. Many years they went to Santa Cruz, rented a beach bungalow, watched the fireworks from the pier, took Jenny to the Boardwalk, and just enjoyed time together. But that time was over, and now Donna was in her place. She felt hot tears rush to her eyes. She wiped them quickly and went to the kitchen to prepare a potato salad for the picnic they were having with Anne, Chloe, and some other people from work that evening. Jenny was spending the day with a friend, and suddenly Debbie felt sorry for herself because she had to work. She used to pity people who had to work on a day dedicated to family, fun, and food.

Jenny had seemed excited, and she had already changed her bathing suit three times. She had been invited to go water-skiing with Kate and her family. Debbie felt envious of her daughter, who seemed to be enjoying herself immensely. Jenny had already managed to meet several boys at the beach, and the phone was beginning to ring like it had at home. The only one who wasn't calling was Sam, but Jenny was too caught up in her life to notice.

But Debbie did notice. It bothered her. The newness of her current situation had worn off, and the uncertain future stretched out in front of her. What was she going to do with the rest of her life? Would their house ever sell so she could get some cash? And would their divorce ever be final?

Yes, she was at the point where she knew the divorce was going to occur. In the beginning, she had truly believed that she would get Sam back, that he would tire of his midlife crisis and his young thing and would come rushing back to them. Then she believed that this was all a bad dream. But she never woke up in her home in San Francisco with Sam snoring softly next to her, no matter how hard she pinched herself.

But as the situation was put further and further behind her, and as the reality sunk deeper and deeper, she knew her fairy tale wouldn't end in either of those ways. It was time to face the music and learn to live her life without him.

Her lawyer called often. Sam was continuing to play hardball with her. He had cut back his hours at the firm, and her lawyer thought he was trying his hardest to hide income from her. If he completely quit paying child support, she was screwed. She needed that house to sell.

"Hey, Mom!" Jenny yelled. "Kate's brother's out in front. I'll see you around six. Don't work too hard." Debbie heard the front door slam.

"Have a wonderful time," she yelled back as she walked over to the living-room window and observed her daughter climbing into the back seat of a Ford Explorer. Kate sat in front with her brother, a tall, thin boy with a big grin on his face, and they drove away laughing.

The Fourth had fallen on a Friday that year, so the restaurant was busier than normal when Debbie arrived. She quickly put on her apron, did her side work, and went out to greet her first customers, a family of five.

This is what I used to have, Debbie thought as she placed the food in front of them and watched with envy the familial exchange between the members. The parents looked to be in their late thirties or early forties, and they had two girls, around ten and eleven, and a darling little tow-headed boy she imagined to be around four. The girls were eagerly anticipating the fireworks and asked Debbie if she had any suggestions of where to go for the day. She suggested the beach at Sand Harbor or the Ponderosa Ranch for an afternoon of horseback riding and a visit to an old western town.

The father thanked her and told her they were from Michigan, on their way to his niece's wedding in Concord, California. It was their first trip west, and they were enjoying the sights. Debbie told him to make sure and allow enough time to really see her city, San Francisco. She told them they would love the cable cars, Fisherman's Wharf, Golden Gate Park, and China Town. She gave them the names of several hotels and restaurants.

The family thanked her profusely, and when they finally left, she noticed a large tip on their crumb-covered table. A smile spread across her face.

That night the fireworks illuminated the night sky with their dazzling display of color. Debbie, Jenny, Anne, Chloe, and the others all sat huddled together on the sandy beach with warm blankets wrapped around them to keep them cozy and with full tummies from the picnic dinner, marveling at the spectacular sight as a local radio station played patriotic music. Jenny sat next to Debbie, huddled under the blanket, dressed in a warm sweatshirt and jeans. Her face was burnt from her afternoon on the boat, and she seemed to be enjoying herself. Jenny leaned into Debbie, and Debbie wrapped her arm around her. "This is way cool, Mom. It's been one of the best Fourths I've ever had. Too bad Dad isn't here."

Too bad, Debbie thought.

A week after the holiday, Debbie came to the realization that if she was ever going to get serious about her running, she was going to have to start pushing herself because there was no one else here to do that for her. She had been taking short two-or-three mile jogs every other day, but she didn't think that was going to get her where she wanted to be in a year's time.

She mapped out a route that stretched five miles from the front steps of the cabin and back. The run would take her down along the beach, across the highway, then up into the hills and back home. Hill training would give her the strength she so desperately needed. She decided to run in the early mornings, before the stresses and the heat of the day built up. She purchased a training diary at the local running store Anne had recommended, along with her first pair of official running shoes.

"Eighty-five dollars!" she had exclaimed in horror at the price for the pair of Asics. But Anne swore by those shoes. The old Debbie would even not have batted an eyelid at the price, but now every cent was precious. The sales clerk, a runner himself, stressed how important good shoes were to training and how they would save in medical costs in the long run. Reluctantly, Debbie had counted out her tip money and planned several meatless meals in her mind to help make up the dent in her wallet.

Bright and early the next morning, after two cups of strong, black coffee, she stood on the porch stretching her hamstrings, quads, and Achilles tendons. She took several deep breaths of the crisp air, tucked her hair into a baseball cap, and started plodding down the street. Her body resisted the early morning assault on her muscles, and her lungs began to scream for oxygen, but her mind took up the mantra from a favorite children's story: I think I can, I think I can . . .

And for the next forty-five minutes she played that saying over and over in her head despite the strong backlash from her feet and legs. Suddenly, she was overcome by a stitch in her side and was forced to walk.

"Shit, will I ever get strong? It's always something." She was forced to walk for a while, but finally the stitch seemed to subside, and she slowly picked up her pace. The last hill stared her in the face, the hill that led to her house, to the shower, and to the couch. She resisted the strong urge to walk—it was tempting—and changed the mantra to: I know I can, I know I can.

Relief flooded her legs and lungs when she saw the cabin through the trees. She attempted to sprint in, opened the front door, and plopped her weary body down on the couch. Elation filled her mind. She had done it! She ran the five miles, and she still could breathe.

She lay on the couch for some time, and when she looked at the clock, she saw it was time to get ready for work. She eased herself off the couch, gently woke Jenny up, and hopped in the shower. As she scrubbed her fatigued body, she remembered all the years Jenny had been an early riser, often before six. But ever since puberty had taken hold of her body, she was sleeping in later and later, and Debbie literally had to pull her from her warm cocoon many mornings.

She limped into work that day, but she had a smile on her face. Completing the five miles was a first for her, and she was elated.

Chapter 7

One of the perks of working at Zak's, besides the free lunch, was the opportunity to observe the kaleidoscope of people who dined in the restaurant. One perfect, crystal-clear summer's day, Debbie had the good fortune of having a wealthy couple sit in her station. The wife was bejeweled, well-dressed, and sported huge diamond earrings and a diamond Rolex. She spoke loud enough for Debbie to overhear as she was attending to the table next to theirs. The woman hung on her husband's arm as they waited impatiently for Debbie to come and take their order.

"Finally," the woman said as Debbie approached their table. "I'd like a daiquiri, without the salt." She brushed a stray strand of jet black hair away from her heavily made-up face. The rest of her hair didn't move in the breeze that came off the lake.

Debbie tried very hard to squelch the laughter that bubbled from deep inside her. "Salt's on margaritas. What flavor of daiquiri would you like?"

"What flavors do you have?" She seemed somewhat embarrassed as she checked her long, red, elegant artificial nails. Debbie decided the woman must do nothing with her hands, and she looked down at her own hard-working hands.

Debbie recited the list of flavors, and the woman wrinkled up her nose at the suggestions. Finally, she decided on strawberry. As

Debbie left their table with the cocktail order, she actually chuckled. Was I ever that self-involved?

She served the drinks and asked if they were ready to order.

"I believe we'd like to enjoy our drinks. Could you check back with us in a few?" The woman took a small sip of her drink, careful not to smear her expertly applied lipstick.

"Sure, I'll be back later," Debbie replied as she went to check on other customers.

That particular couple stayed for several hours on that beautiful summer's day, drinking a number of cocktails and finally ordering chicken Caesar salads. When they finally staggered off, Debbie noticed that the husband, who had never even uttered a word, had left a twenty. I wonder if they won big at the clubs or if the money was out of pity, she thought as she scooped it up and put it in her pocket.

But twenty dollars was twenty dollars, and Sam had been a week late with his check. When it finally arrived, there had been a note attached saying he was sorry for the delay, but he and Donna had been vacationing in the San Juan Islands. How wonderful for him, Debbie thought bitterly. While I work my nails to the quick because of the itch in his groin, he's sailing up north. He also said he was coming up to see Jenny sometime around the middle of August because he had something important to tell her. Debbie hoped she wouldn't have to see him, and she wondered if he would have the gall to bring Donna.

"Mom, Aunt Jane called from Truckee. She said she should be here within the hour." Jenny sat on the couch watching the small color TV. Debbie put the bags of groceries on the kitchen counter. She had planned a special dinner for Aunt Jane and was looking forward to her visit. Aunt Jane was planning on spending several days, and luckily for Debbie, Bruce had given her the time off. Jenny had come up with a list of activities, but Debbie knew the first item of business for Aunt Jane would be a visit to the Crystal Bay Club and its toys.

She quickly put away the groceries and decided to take a shower. As the warm water pounded her back, she felt the stress of the day wash off her body. Toweling off, she observed her body in the mirror. All the physical work she was doing was beginning to pay off.

Her legs looked shapely, her waist firmer, and her arms had small muscles that peeked their heads. As she combed out her hair, she noticed several hairs that looked too white to be blond. "I'll just pull these little suckers out," she told the lightly tanned woman in the mirror. "And next time I'm in the grocery store, I'll pick up some Loving Care."

"Mom, she's here!" Debbie heard Jenny's excited voice as she was pulling on her faded blue jeans.

"I'll be right there," she yelled back as she tucked her shirt in and stuffed her feet into a pair of sneakers. She rushed down to the living room at the same time Aunt Jane came through the door.

"Hello, my dears. Don't you both look positively healthy." She gave each of them a big hug after she placed her overnight case on the ground.

Debbie exhaled. "It's wonderful to see you."

"Aunt Jane, we've planned the coolest things to do," Jenny put in.

"Wonderful, I hope that includes a trip or two to the gambling halls. I feel lucky!" Aunt Jane had that twinkle in her eyes.

"Why don't you put your things down, and I'll get you a glass of iced tea," Debbie suggested.

"Sounds wonderful. It was a hot drive, especially through the Sacramento Valley. I think I'll sit down next to Jenny on the couch. Why don't you join me?" she asked Debbie.

"Just as soon as I get that tea." She went into the kitchen and prepared a tray with three tall, frosty glasses of iced tea and some fresh chocolate chip cookies she had picked up at the store. She heard laughter coming from the living room as she brought the tray in.

"What's so funny?" Debbie asked as she set the tray down on the wicker chest that doubled as a coffee table.

Aunt Jane smiled. "Jenny's just telling me about some of her summer experiences. It sounds like you both have adjusted well. Tell me about your job, Debbie."

Debbie proceeded to talk about working at Zak's, the people she'd met, and the running she had begun.

"I'm so proud of you, Debbie. You seem to have blossomed in adversity and taken charge of your life. If Arthur were still alive, he'd be so proud of you."

At the mention of her father, Debbie felt her eyes grow misty. She wondered what he and Mom would really think of her current situation. Would they be embarrassed by the way she had led her life? Would her impending divorce have caused them pain? Sometimes she wished desperately that they could peek down from their Camelot in the sky and give her guidance or even an affirmation that she was doing well. She was sure they'd be pleased with Jenny. She seemed to be maturing, and she had been extremely helpful and supportive throughout this entire ordeal.

"What should we do about dinner?" Aunt Jane's words broke through Debbie's silent monologue.

"I picked up the ingredients to make steak kabobs."

"Yum, that sounds good, but why don't you save it for tomorrow night. I feel like going out. My treat."

Debbie and Jenny exchanged smiles. The slots were calling Aunt Jane.

"The Crystal Bay Club?" asked Debbie.

"Sounds wonderful. I'll just go and freshen up a bit." And Aunt Jane got up and went to the bathroom.

They ended up in the steak house in the casino, and Debbie had to admit if felt wonderful to be waited on for a change. In her former life, she and Sam had gone out to dinner three, maybe four times a week. She and Jenny had only gone out once since they had moved here, and that was just an inexpensive Mexican meal. Savoring every tender bit of her delicious veal, she felt herself relax into the leather booth. The three of them chatted about everything and sipped their drinks. Jenny seemed to be animated and charged with energy. She shared information about her friends, especially a new girl she had met, Kristen, who happened to live on the next block. They were becoming fast friends, and Jenny had started to make comments about how cool it would be to stay in Tahoe through the winter, go to school with Kristen, and ski.

"What ARE your plans for the fall?" Aunt Jane probed. "When are you moving back? And I hate to pry, but have you heard about when your divorce will be final?"

"I just talked to the lawyer yesterday," Debbie explained. "All the papers have been filed, they're just waiting on the house. I haven't even thought about fall and going back, although it's in about four weeks, so I guess I'd better start thinking." She turned to Jenny. "What do you want to do, Jenny?"

"I'm not sure, Mom. Part of me wants to go home because I miss my friends, my room, and the city, but the other part of me knows my room's not going to be there, and my friends will have made new friends. Daddy seems to have forgotten I'm alive."

That hurt. Sam was divorcing her, not Jenny. How could he ignore his own daughter? "Daddy hasn't forgotten you, Jenny. He's just, I don't know, thinking with his other head."

Jenny laughed.

Aunt Jane blushed.

Debbie felt good.

The next day was glorious. Debbie awoke early to the sounds of the birds chirping. As she stretched lazily in bed, she heard noises from the kitchen, and the smell of fresh coffee made its way up to her room. It felt wonderful to have someone else there to take over the details of her life, even for a few days. She followed the smell downstairs and joined Aunt Jane for a first cup of coffee.

Debbie and Jenny had planned to take Aunt Jane to Emerald Bay for the day, and Debbie busied herself in the kitchen preparing a picnic lunch. She had baked a chicken the night before and added some fresh rolls, baby carrots, tomatoes, and luscious strawberries. She was finishing the touches on her famous potato salad when the phone rang.

"Hello."

"Debbie?" Her heart sank to her knees. It felt so good to hear his voice. Maybe, she thought, he had changed his mind, realized the mistake he had made, and was calling to ask if she'd take him back.

"Hello, Sam."

What seemed like an eternity—but in reality was only a few seconds—passed. "I'm coming up next weekend to see Jenny."

"I think you'll have to ask her if she's available. Would you like me to get her?"

The line was silent on the other end, as if Sam was taken aback by her comment. Did he think Jenny was waiting on pins and needles for his call? "Yes, please," he muttered.

"Jenny, your father's on the phone," she yelled.

"Dad?" Jenny yelled back, surprised.

"Yes, and he wants to talk to you."

"I'll be right there."

Debbie turned her attention back to the phone. "She's on her way."

Before she could place the phone down, he asked, "Debbie?"

"Yes?"

"I just want to know if you're all right. How are you surviving?"

Debbie just shook her head. He left them with almost nothing so he could go off with his young thing, and now he's concerned. Where was that concern a few months ago when her entire world fell apart? "We're fine, Sam, but no thanks to you. Here's your daughter." And she handed the phone to Jenny, who had just bounded into the kitchen.

Debbie felt agitated the rest of the day, even though the weather cooperated and there were no thunderstorms or wind to ruin their picnic and beach activities. It was a warm day, so Jenny and Kristen spent quite a bit of time in the water. Aunt Jane and Debbie sat under the shade with fat, juicy novels. Aunt Jane looked like she was devouring hers, but Debbie mindlessly flipped the pages of hers while the thoughts tumbled in her mind.

Sam had told Jenny he was bringing her, Donna, up with him. They were renting a condo for a few days, and Jenny was going to be staying with them. Debbie didn't like the idea of Jenny staying with them; she didn't think it was a good idea for a young impressionable girl to be in the same condo with a couple who was not married. But Jenny didn't seem to mind: she was just excited to be able to see her dad, in any shape that she could get him.

Why can't he just leave Donna at home? Debbie wondered. He just can't leave her alone for one weekend and devote quality time to his own daughter.

She got up, glanced over at Aunt Jane, who seemed to be enthralled in her book, and went for a walk along the beach to clear her head. The lapping of the gentle waves against the sandy beach provided soothing background music as she tried to digest her situation. The reality of Sam and Donna, an item, had finally sunk in. There was going to be no making up between Sam and Debbie, no getting back her family. Sam had told Jenny on the phone that he had something exciting to tell her. A deep sigh escaped. She scanned the beach and saw happy families laughing and playing in the warm July sun.

"Life's unfair," she muttered. "I had it all, and now there's someone else in my place. Shit!"

The next day Debbie and Jenny took Aunt Jane to visit Virginia City, an old mining town that was filled with old saloons, gift shops, candy stores, and throngs of tourists. They spent the afternoon exploring the city's stores and mines and ate lunch at the Bucket of Blood Saloon. Aunt Jane was thrilled with her win at nickel slots. Debbie was less preoccupied with Sam's arrival; the run she had taken early that morning helped her pound her frustrations out on the pavement. Jenny's favorite experience seemed to be the glass blower in one of the specialty shops. Aunt Jane purchased her a few fragile figurines to add to her collection.

Before they knew it, Aunt Jane's visit was over, and she was packed and ready to go back to the city. "Thanks so much for everything, Debbie," she said as she closed the trunk of her Mercury Sable.

Debbie smiled and gave her a big hug. "Thank you. You picked up most of the tab and made the drive."

Aunt Jane laughed. "It was my pleasure. Keep those slots warm for me. I'll be back."

Debbie and Jenny stood in the driveway and waved goodbye until she was out of sight. "It was good seeing her, don't you think?" Debbie asked as she put her arm around Jenny and pulled her close.

"She's cool. Hey, Mom! Can I go to Kristen's?"

Debbie searched her daughter's eager face. "Sure, scat, but be back by dinnertime."

Debbie watched with a smile as Jenny rushed off. She needed a break; now she had a few precious hours to herself and her thoughts.

"There he is!" Debbie watched her daughter shriek with joy as they pulled up to the condo complex Sam was staying in. Jenny turned to her. "Bye, Mom. I'll see you in a few days." She grabbed her overnight bag and tennis racket. Debbie felt her heart ache as she watched Jenny run to Sam, his face breaking into a wide grin as he scooped her up. Sam waved over to Debbie, but she couldn't bring herself to wave back. She just sat, detached from her body and emotions, and watched him stand there, looking so good in his beige chinos, white shirt, and tan loafers. His sandy brown hair now touched the collar of his shirt.

And she, the other woman, the destroyer of her family, stood possessively next to Debbie's husband, chatting with Debbie's daughter, running her hand through her long, flowing, brown mane. Donna looked quite tan for living in the city, and it seemed to Debbie that she looked even younger.

"She doesn't have to struggle to make ends meet," Debbie said bitterly as she pulled away from the happy threesome. A trickle of tears started cascading down her cheeks, and as soon as she was back on the highway and heading home, they released in full force.

That afternoon Debbie took her first really long run. As she pounded the pavement, an entire spectrum of emotions swam into her consciousness, and clarity started to come to the surface of her mind. Toward the end of the run—and she didn't know if it was from fatigue or wisdom—she came to the conclusion that she would be better off without Sam. Obviously, there had been something lacking in their marriage to have him wander, and awareness came into her consciousness that she shared some of the blame. The what-ifs started to march across her mind: What if she had not shopped as much? What if she had listened to Sam more? What if she had tried to express an interest in the ideas and activities he had been interested in? He had always been after her to take up golf, play tennis, and go sailing with him. Debbie had always put him off. To be honest, she had been too caught up in her own narrow world to make time for the things he wanted to do.

And now he'd found someone who liked to do those things.

The cabin came into view, and she wearily jogged up the driveway. Looking at her watch, she saw she had been gone over two hours. No wonder she was physically exhausted. But she felt mentally cleansed. A nice long shower and a good book awaited her. She didn't have to cook anyone dinner, and that sounded like pure bliss.

The next day she had work to take her mind off Jenny being with Sam and Donna. The restaurant was busy, which made her shift go faster, and toward the end of the day, Anne asked her if she wanted to come over for dinner.

"You want to cook tonight?"

"For you, any time," Anne replied.

"Thanks, you're a true friend." And Debbie spend a wonderful, relaxing evening with Anne and Chloe. After dinner, they sat out on Anne's porch, sipping white wine and telling each other their secret fantasies, dreams, and ambitions.

"If you keep up with the way you're training, you'll be able to run the Silver State Marathon next August," Anne said.

"Excuse me? A marathon?"

"Why not?" Anne probed. "You can do it. It'll give you something to train for, a goal if you must. I'm running it again next month, and if I could do it last year, you can do it next year. Just think, finishing twenty-six-point-two miles!"

Debbie stared at Anne in disbelief. "You think I could run twenty six miles in one day?"

Anne laughed. "Not only do I think you could, but I bet you could do it in under four and a half hours. Why, you just ran for two hours yesterday."

"Sure, and I can barely walk today!"

Anne smiled. "I didn't mean this year, I meant next year—over twelve full months of training away. Come on, what do you think? You can come and watch me this year. It'll pump you up, get you ready."

Debbie sat back on the couch. "I'd love to go with you and cheer you on, but I still don't know what I'm going to do about the fall. There's an offer on our home that sounds good, and Sam's in a hurry to sell, but I don't know if I'm going to go back to the city or stay up here. I'm uneasy about the winter. How tough is it?"

Anne broke into a fit of laughter.

"What's so funny?"

She tried to contain herself. "Spoken like a true flatlander!"

Debbie pressed her lips together. "Seriously?"

Anne thought for a moment. "Truthfully, some winters are worse than others. Last winter I was literally snowed in, and I didn't put my shovel away until Memorial Day weekend, but the winter before, we enjoyed sixty-degree days in February. But honestly Debbie, I can't think of a more beautiful, peaceful, pristine place in the world than Lake Tahoe during winter. And we do have snow plows." The sarcasm dripped from her voice.

Thoughts churned over and over in Debbie's head. Could she, a city girl, a woman who had never even held a snow shovel, make it through a difficult winter? Would the cabin be warm enough in the winter, or would she need to find a new place?

"I'll tell you the honest-to-God truth, Debbie. Living up here alone, with a child, in the winter, will teach you a great deal about yourself. You will learn to rely on yourself, and you'll become strong, physically and mentally."

"I'll give it serious consideration, Anne. Thanks."

Jenny strolled into the parking lot, suitcase in hand, with a disturbed look on her face. "Did you have a good time?" Debbie asked as she rolled down the window and greeted her child.

Jenny plopped down in the seat next to Debbie, a large sigh escaping her thin lips.

"What's wrong?" Debbie asked. She could tell by Jenny's demeanor that the visit had not gone well.

"Oh, I had an okay time. They both tried too hard if you ask me, but that's not it."

"What is it, sweetie?" Debbie asked gently.

"Donna's pregnant!" Jenny blurted out.

Debbie felt the bile rise in her throat. The oldest trick in the book! As her nausea receded, she actually felt a laugh try and escape. "She's pregnant?" she asked incredulously, trying to hold back. She could tell Jenny did not find the humor in the situation.

"Yes. She's three months along, and as soon as your divorce is final, Daddy and Donna are planning on getting married. And they want me to be there. I'm so sorry, Mom." Jenny threw her arms around Debbie and started to sob.

Debbie pulled her close and stroked her hair. Images of Sam and Donna and the new baby floated through her mind. Sam was going to have a new family. The funny thing was, he never wanted a second child with her. He had declared he only had enough love for one child, and now, by some twist of fate, he was going to have to share his limited quantity of love with two children. Debbie wondered what would happen to Jenny. Would she fade into the background like so many other kids from first marriages did?

"I'm so sorry, Jenny. I really don't know what to say. This has taken me by surprise, too."

"Can we go home now, Mom? I'm tired, and I really need to be alone to think. They were all over me, and I didn't get any breathing space.

"Sure, honey," Debbie replied as she sped home.

Jenny turned the radio to one of the stations she liked, and they drove home in complete silence, each one lost in her own thoughts. There was a message blinking on the machine when they arrived home. Debbie sat down at the kitchen table and pushed play. "The buyers accepted the counter offer," her lawyer said. "They'd like to close in a month. We are ready to finalize the divorce papers. Give me a call when you return. Good news, though. I'll be able to get you some money from the house."

Debbie now knew what she had to do.

"How would you feel about spending the winter up here and going to school with Kristen?" Debbie asked Jenny as they were eating dinner together several nights later.

Jenny looked up from the chicken she was picking at as if it were a frog on a biology table. "Really? You want to stay here permanently?"

"I don't know about permanently, but I'd like to try it for a year. What do you think?"

Jenny sat pensively and studied the dissected chicken. After a few moments she replied, "You know what, Mom? I think it would be good for us. We could be like mountain women!"

Debbie chuckled. "So I won't have to bug up about shoveling this winter?"

Jenny smiled. "I'll do my share if we can ski."

"I think that can be arranged."

"And I'd like to try snowboarding."

This might get expensive, Debbie thought. "Okay, anything else?"

Jenny grinned. "I'm sure I'll think of other things. But what are you going to do while I'm in school. Work at Zak's?"

Debbie shook her head. "I think I'm about waitressed out. I'd like to try something different. There's a real-estate school starting in a couple of weeks, and I thought I'd go and try to get a license. If I pass the test, then I'll quit working at the restaurant and find a job in that field. What do you think?"

Jenny smiled widely. "I think it's a wonderful idea, Mom. You've always loved houses, and I think you're too smart to spend the rest of your life waiting on tables.

"Thanks, honey."

Jenny's appetite seemed to pick up because the chicken and rice disappeared off her plate. "Can I call Kristen?" she asked, scooping the rest of the rice into her mouth.

"After you do the dishes."

Jenny's birthday arrived with a present from Mother Nature. On the eve of her thirteenth birthday, she became a woman. Debbie and Jenny marked the passage with a dinner at a wonderful Italian restaurant located in Tahoe City. As they sat outside, under an umbrella, and watched the colors explode in the sky as the sun gently slipped behind the mountains, they toasted Jenny's entrance into womanhood, with all its mysteries, challenges, and heartbreaks. Debbie could tell Jenny was extremely proud of herself. Many of her friends had made the leap earlier that year, and she had been patiently awaiting her turn.

The next day, her official birthday, which Debbie had arranged to take off from work, they headed down the Mount Rose highway to Reno, where she had planned to take Jenny shopping for her birthday. She needed new clothes; her legs seemed to be stretching up to her armpits.

They explored the one big mall Reno had to offer and found some success in several chain stores. Sam had sent Jenny a hundred dollars, and she had no trouble spending it all. After shopping, they took in a movie, the first either of them had seen in a theater since they left the city. They had a lovely dinner in a quaint Mexican restaurant, and as the sun was setting behind majestic Mount Rose, they headed back to the lake.

"Mom, thanks for a wonderful day. I love all my new things," Jenny said as they sped toward home.

"You're most welcome, Jenny. We did have fun, didn't we?"

Jenny snuggled down into the seat and smiled. "You know, Mom, I think I'm going to like living here. I like the way the air smells, so clean and fresh, and I like all the outdoor activities. I really don't miss the city, but I do miss Daddy and our old life."

Debbie turned and looked at her child. "Me too, Jenny." She smiled a sad smile. Jenny was all curled up, her head against the seat, and her eyes were closed. She would probably sleep the entire trip home.

Chapter 8

As the end of August quickly approached, Debbie made significant changes. She enrolled in real-estate school, signed Jenny up for the eighth grade at North Tahoe Middle School, made plans to watch Anne run the Silver State Marathon, and took a trip to the city to box up her former life. Her lawyer said Sam had already taken what he wanted, and Debbie honestly didn't think there was a great deal of stuff that would fit into her new lifestyle in Tahoe.

It was a blistery hot day when they drove down to the city. They were planning on meeting Aunt Jane around noon to go through the old house and see if there was anything else they wanted. Mixed emotions flooded her mind as she drove down the familiar street and pulled alongside the curb next to their beautiful old Victorian home. A sold sign stood in the small patch of grass that someone had mowed. She looked over at Jenny. "This is it."

Jenny just sat and gazed through the car window at the beloved home she had grown up in. Debbie could tell she was having a hard time with this. Damn Sam. "Let's go, sweetie. The sooner we get this done, the sooner we can go back home."

Jenny reluctantly got out of the car and ambled up the walkway. Debbie followed behind, gazing at her former flower beds, which desperately needed some attention.

Aunt Jane pulled up shortly after, and the three of them spent the remainder of the afternoon organizing and boxing up the rest of the stuff. Jenny wasn't much help; she was lost up in her old room, slowly boxing up her childhood. Debbie walked around the house and took a mental inventory of the items Sam had taken. She was surprised to see he had taken most of the good china and silver. They must be playing house, she decided, disgusted at the thought of Donna using the beautiful china she and Sam had picked out shortly before they were married. Finally, it was over. "Done!" she exclaimed.

She found Aunt Jane and Jenny on the back porch. They both looked worn out, but Debbie felt strong, in charge. Perhaps her running was paying off?

She took a seat by Jenny. "Did you get everything you wanted?"

"Yes, it's all in the car, Mom. I'm pooped. Do I really have to see Dad?"

Debbie smiled and gave her a hug. "Yes, you do. You won't be seeing him for quite some time. Now put a smile on your face and be the bigger person." But inside, Debbie was aching for Jenny. She didn't blame her one bit for not wanting to see her dad.

Jenny grimaced. "I'd rather have a root canal than see her."

"Honey, I'll talk to your dad, suggest that it just be the two of you tonight. How about that?"

"Would you please?" Jenny pleaded. "It's just that when she's with him, she's all over him, and he focuses on her more than me. I'd like him to pay attention to me for a change."

"I don't blame you. I'll call him now." Debbie stood up and went to find the phone. Aunt Jane moved next to Jenny and held her hand, as if for moral support.

Debbie went into her now-vacant kitchen and dug Sam's work number out of her faded blue jeans and punched in the numbers. The phone was picked up after the first ring. "Hello," said the voice she had once loved so much.

"Sam, it's me, Debbie. Do you have a moment?"

There was silence on the other end. She must have taken him by surprise. "Sam?"

"Yes, Debbie, what is it?"

Debbie politely told him that Jenny would rather just see him alone. Did he think that was possible?

"Donna will be hurt. She's planned the entire evening for Jenny."

"I'm sorry your girlfriend will be hurt, but to be honest, my only concern is Jenny, not Donna. Jenny doesn't want to see her. She just wants to spend time with you, alone."

"All right," he answered softly. "Tell her I'll be at your aunt's around seven to get her. And, Debbie?"

"Yes."

"I am truly sorry for the way everything has turned out. I never meant for you to hurt you, and I never meant to hurt Jenny. This just happened too fast."

"Not to make you feel guilty, but you did. Goodbye, Sam." And she put down the phone.

Debbie and Jenny managed to leave the city by two the next day, towing a trailer full of winter clothes, skis, Jenny's bike, Debbie's treadmill, which she had dug out of the garage, warm blankets, flannel sheets, books, and some kitchen gadgets. Debbie had stuck some of her household decorations in a storage shed, had given Aunt Jane a few expensive antiques to sell, and the rest she had boxed up and driven over to a battered women's shelter late yesterday afternoon. She honestly hoped it would help some woman in need.

As she drove through the heavy traffic, she observed the remnants of her former life with a certain detachment. It was hard to believe she had once been such a pathetic, shallow woman—a shell of the woman she was now on the way to becoming. Had she really only lived for the thrill of shopping and the fulfillment of her immediate desires? Where had her goals been?

As she sped up Highway 80 toward Lake Tahoe, her heart began to feel lighter. She smiled as she thought of the positive changes she had made and the skills she had acquired. People say growth comes from pain, and looking back, even now from this short distance, Debbie had to agree.

Jenny sat next to her in the front seat with her headphones on, listening to some new alternative group's recording she had conned her father into buying last night. She had seemed fairly subdued when Sam dropped her off in the morning, and Debbie gathered the visit hadn't lived up to Jenny's expectations. According to Jenny,

Donna wouldn't leave them alone when they returned from dinner and kept insisting to Jenny that there would be room in their family, even when the baby came. Donna told Jenny she was going to be a big sister, and wasn't she excited?

"I tried really hard not to tell her to shove it, Mom," she explained.

They reached the lake around dinnertime, and Debbie was too tired to cook, so they pulled into the Safeway parking lot, and Jenny went into the store to get take-out Chinese food, her favorite. Debbie stayed behind and guarded the trailer and all their belongings.

"Mom, hurry up! I don't want to be late for my first day of school."

Debbie laughed as she finished the touches on her makeup. They were still early as it was. Jenny took after Sam; she was early to every event and appointment. Debbie used to run on her own time, causing countless amounts of friction in their household. Working these last few months had been good for her. It had made her be on time.

"I'll be right there," she yelled back. She pulled on her clothes and grabbed her purse off the dresser. This was a big day for her, too. She was taking the real-estate exam at nine that morning. She had spent countless late nights against the backdrop of a roaring fire cramming her head with facts and figures. If she passed the test, she was planning on quitting Zak's and finding a job in a real-estate office. Debbie was tired of waiting tables, tired of whining children and their demanding parents, and she was tired of wearing food on her clothes. Anne still planned on working there through the winter; food stains didn't seem to bother her.

Dropping Jenny off at school and being told no, I don't need you to escort me in, I'm thirteen and I see Kristen waiting for me, Debbie actually felt relieved. She wanted to review her notes.

The test was hard, and she was glad she had spent all those late nights studying. Several people she had met earlier in class wanted to celebrate by going out for lunch, and since Jenny was in school all day and she had already taken the day off from work, she decided to join them. The consensus was Sunnyside, a resort on the west side of the lake, and they were lucky to snag one of the last remaining large tables on the expansive wooden deck.

It was a perfect late summer's day: cloudless, warm, and the air was calm. The water sparkled like crystals, and the sun warmed Debbie's spirits. Over ice-cold beer and deep-fried zucchini, the group toasted their efforts. The waitress brought out their orders, and Debbie's Caesar salad was fresh and crisp. Relaxed by the beer, sun, and conversation, she sat back in the deck chair and sank into the moment. Serenity and peacefulness washed over her entire body. She hadn't felt this good in a long time. Glancing at her watch, the feeling was shattered. Jenny would be home soon, and she would be eager to tell Debbie about her day.

Saying her goodbyes and promising to stay in touch, she quickly hurried to the car and prayed the traffic would be light. Jenny was waiting on the porch when she finally pulled up, and from the look in her eyes, Debbie could tell she wasn't happy.

"You forgot to put the key out!"

"Sorry, honey. Have you been waiting long?"

She glared at Debbie. "Only like fifteen minutes."

Debbie smiled gently and unlocked the door. "How was your day? Do you like your classes?"

Jenny followed her into the living room, threw her backpack on the couch, and went into the kitchen. "I have homework already, Mom. Can you believe it? It's only the first day of school." Debbie followed Jenny into the kitchen, sat down at the kitchen table, and observed her daughter opening and closing the refrigerator as if to a beat that was playing in her head. "There's nothing to eat, Mom."

"Why don't you have some cold chicken?"

"I don't want that, I want something else," she replied in her favorite two-year-old voice.

"I'll go to the store tomorrow. Please eat up what's here. I'm tired of throwing away food."

Jenny turned and gave Debbie an exasperated look and finally appeased herself with some leftover pasta salad, poured a tall, cold glass of milk, and sat down. After some food made its way into her bloodstream, she opened up and spilled out the contents of her day. Listening intently, Debbie was glad she wasn't thirteen again.

Their lives fell into a routine. Debbie trained, worked, and waited for the results of the test, and Jenny went to school, talked on the phone, and fell in love with a boy from her homeroom. Finally one day after work, when Debbie stopped by the post office to retrieve her mail, there was the letter she had been waiting for. With sticky palms and sweaty armpits, she tore open the letter. She had passed; in fact, she had scored extremely high. She now had her license.

She felt like whooping it up right there in the post office. It felt great to complete a goal, especially when she thought of where she had been a scant six months earlier. She stared at her name on the license. It was there in black ink. Included in the envelope was a list of agencies that were recruiting agents. She decided to place a few calls when she got home and see if she could arrange some interviews.

She called Anne when she got home, elated with her news, and invited her and Chloe to dinner. "Congratulations. I've got a great bottle of wine to celebrate with," Anne said. "I'll see you in a while."

Lakeside Realty was hiring, and Debbie was able to set up an interview for the following day with the manager, Beth. Beth sounded extremely efficient and business-like over the phone and answered some of Debbie's questions. They would be able to offer her a small base salary, and with Sam's child support, Debbie figured she should be able to squeak by until she started selling. Debbie had received some money from the sale of her home in Pacific Heights, but she had wisely invested it in a mutual fund for Jenny's college education and her retirement. She had vowed to herself that she was never going to rely on a man again, and if Sam helped with Jenny's college, that would be wonderful, but she wasn't going to bet her life on it.

As she sipped her coffee early the next morning, she went over her financial situation again. She had been able to save a thousand dollars over the summer from her job, and she still had fifteen hundred left from her former life. As long as the car stayed working and she and Jenny stayed healthy until she could find health insurance, they would make do. Their needs were fairly simple: rent, utilities, gas, food, and phone. Debbie couldn't remember the last time she had purchased something for herself. As she looked at the numbers on the paper, she decided she would have to budget more money for wood, and she realized her utilities would run higher in the winter.

She needed to find a doctor and a dentist. Sam had taken them off of his insurance at the end of August. It was scary having no insurance, and she hoped Lakeside Realty offered group insurance. Making a list of questions to ask Beth, she jotted insurance down. Another question that was bothering her was the fact that many real-estate agents had to work evenings and weekends. That was great if she had a husband, but she was on her own. Beth had mentioned something vague about having to work one weekend a month, and if that was the case, Debbie thought that was doable.

Her thoughts were shattered by Jenny tromping down the stairs, asking her to sign her weekly planner, and informing her she needed field-trip money.

"Good morning to you, Miss Sunshine," Debbie replied as she signed her name.

"Sorry, Mom." Jenny gave her a quick kiss on her cheek. "I forgot to have you do this last night. Good luck on your interview." And she was out the front door and off to the bus stop and the world of adolescent hormones.

Debbie stared into Beth's green eyes and tried to answer the questions as best she could. "I'm impressed with your score," Beth said. "It shows me you can perform well under pressure. Have you ever sold real estate before?"

"No, I haven't," Debbie answered. "But I have always loved houses and people. In the city I often helped many of my friends find homes. Finding the perfect home for a person is, well, like putting pieces of a puzzle together."

Beth sat back in her thick leather chair and thought for a moment. She was a petite woman; Debbie guessed she did not even reach five feet. She had short curly black hair, and Debbie imagined she was in her early forties. Debbie took a sip of her coffee, which was now lukewarm, and gazed around the wood-paneled office. Large pictures of properties hung on the walls, intermixed with hanging plants and breathtaking pictures of the lake. In the corner was a small stand that housed medals of some kind. Beth noticed Debbie's interest. "My running trophies. Do you run?"

"Why, yes, I do; in fact, I just started training this summer. There's a fun run in a couple weeks in Incline Village I'm going to run."

"Oh, sure, the Halloween Howl. I've run it several times; it's fun. Do you have a costume yet?"

"Not yet. I want to find something that'll be easy to run in. I thought about Catwoman."

Beth chuckled. "That should be fairly easy. You'll have to carry your tail, though. Are you training for any big races?"

"My friend Anne is trying to talk me into running the Silver State Marathon next summer. I watched her run it a month ago, and I'm not sure I want to subject my body to the torture. Twenty-six point two miles seems extremely long."

"It is, but it's worth it. I love that marathon, and I usually run it every year." Beth picked up one of the medals. "I got this in 1992 at the Silver Sate for placing first in my division. I'll be running it again next year." Beth gazed out the window for a moment. Debbie followed her gaze and observed several chipmunks playing tag on the tall ponderosa pines. One guy in particular certainly seemed to be a pain. He kept testing and taunting all his buddies.

As Beth continued to watch the chipmunks, she said, "I think, Debbie, you'll make a wonderful addition to our professional staff." She turned around and stared Debbie directly in the eyes. Debbie caught the twinkle of life in this woman. She was hired!

"When can you start?" Beth wanted to know.

"I'd like to give a week's notice at work if that would be all right with you."

"That would be fine, so next week."

"Wonderful," Debbie said.

Beth stood up, straightened her short black skirt, and reached across the large oak desk to shake her hand. "Welcome aboard, Debbie. You're going to fit in nicely around here."

"Thank you, Beth," Debbie said as she shook her small, dainty hand. She followed Beth out of the office and was introduced to the young secretaries and several other agents. She noticed a few of the people had running shoes on, there were posters of races on the walls, and some had running plaques by their desks. It looked like she was going to have to run that damn marathon now!

Later that day, after a particularly long shift at Zak's, she decided to push herself and go for a long run. She was discovering that running allowed her the time and space to think her problems through. And today Jenny was at Kristen's doing homework, so she had several hours to think and run.

As she headed off down the trail, she drank in the scenery with more interest. The leaves on the aspens were a brilliant golden color, and the sunlight danced off the red and yellow bushes that ran along the small babbling creek that followed the trail. The trail was quiet; her only companions were the occasional squirrel or quail that ran across her path. The air had a distinct chill to it, but rather than make her feel cold, it invigorated her and gave her the extra energy she needed to push herself faster and faster up the hill. As she pushed, she struggled with the limited oxygen available at sixty-three hundred feet.

Finally she reached the mountain peak, which overlooked the entire Lake Tahoe basin. She felt she was on top of the world, up where only the eagles dared to soar. She took a much-needed break, had a swig from the water bottle that was strapped to her belt, fixed a loose shoelace, and headed along the top of the ridge. Glancing at her watch, she noticed it had only taken her an hour to reach this point. She was definitely improving. The run back would not take as long. It was much easier on her stamina to go down the mountain, but harder on her quad muscles.

Feeling like she was one with the universe at that moment, she headed back down the mountain. It was getting darker earlier and earlier each day, and soon the time would change, snow would fall, and she would have to do a great deal of her training on a treadmill. She was going to miss her mountain runs when the snow came, but she had promised herself she would take up cross-country skiing.

In her former life, the only type of skiing she had done was the occasional run on an easy slope at Squaw and then a quick rush to the bar, where she sat sipping white wine or hot buttered rums in front of the roaring fire, dressed in a designer ski outfit, waiting for Sam and Jenny to come in from their day of exertion. But it was different now. Debbie was into exercise, and she was looking forward to cross-country skiing, even though it was extremely strenuous. Anne had sung the praises of the sport, and Debbie was eager to give it a try. Jenny had her heart set on snowboarding, and Debbie had begun to look around for a used one; it would make the perfect Christmas present.

Before she realized it, she was back down the mountain, and her house was in sight. She pushed herself harder, even though her legs were screaming "walk," and sprinted in. Whew. Done. She looked at her watch. One hour and fifty-three minutes. Not too bad.

Her last day at Zak's was bittersweet. After her shift ended, the crew had a small cake and a present for her. Touched, Debbie opened the gaily wrapped box to find a leather organizer. "To keep all your new appointments in," Anne said. "We don't want you being late."

Debbie chuckled. "Thanks everyone. I appreciate your thoughtfulness, and if you're ever in the market for a house or condo, please call."

That brought laughter and promises. "Are you ready for the Halloween Howl?" Anne asked as they walked out of the restaurant.

"I think so. I've just never done anything like this before. I'm nervous."

"That's to be expected. Think of it this way: you're running for you. Think of it as running from your old life and to your new life."

Debbie thought for a moment. She liked the sound of that. It gave the run a symbolic meaning. "Maybe I will. Thanks, Anne."

They stood next to Anne's Jeep. Anne gave Debbie a hug. "I've got to rush and get Chloe. Have a wonderful first day at work tomorrow. Call me."

"I will, and thanks again." Debbie watched Anne climb into her Jeep, pull her long hair into a ponytail, and start the engine up.

Finally the morning of the race arrived. Debbie had slept little the night before, her stomach tied up in knots and her mind trying to talk her body out of it. She pulled her Catwoman costume on, got Jenny out of bed—she was to be Debbie's cheering section— and they headed over to the race. Glancing around as she stood near the starting line stretching, she observed the various costumes and the good cheer among the runners. It looked like all the Super Heroes were there, and the sponsors had even gotten into the spirit of the holiday and had dressed up as Star Wars characters. Jenny stood off to the side taking pictures and smiling at all the runners. Debbie turned around and saw Wonder Woman staring at her. "Is that you, Anne?"

Wonder Woman smiled. "Yes, do you like it? I wore it several years ago." Anne twirled around, showing off her muscular legs and body. She looked phenomenal in that getup.

Jenny came up and took a picture of the two of them. "Great costumes, guys. I'll see you at the finish line."

"Are you nervous?" Anne asked as they walked over to get in their starting positions.

"A little. My stomach keeps flipping, and I really don't know why I bothered to shower this morning."

"Relax and have fun. This is for a good cause. Right?"

Debbie took a deep breath. Anne was right. It was just a fun run, and all the proceeds did go to breast cancer research. The run was dedicated to a woman who had died several years ago from the disease. Her husband had started the Halloween Howl in her memory. According to local gossip, Halloween had been her favorite holiday, and even when she was in the last stages of the disease, she had to dress up and give out treats to the neighborhood children. "You're right. I'll try and relax. This isn't the Olympics."

"On your mark . . . get set . . . GO!" yelled Han Solo. And they were off. Debbie paced herself for the first few miles with Anne, but as she started to tire, Anne sped up and left her. She followed the rest of the pack and limped across the finish line. Six miles at full speed. She had done it! Princess Leia shouted out, "Forty-four point three." Anne and Jenny were waiting for her. Jenny handed her a carton of orange juice. "Way to go, Mom. That was cool," Jenny said.

"You did it," congratulated Anne.

Debbie struggled to catch her breath, gulped down the juice, and walked around slowly to cool her body down. Anne came back up to her, laughing and talking with a tall, muscular man who was dressed in what looked to be a Daniel Boone costume. "Debbie, I'd like you to meet Bill Howard."

Debbie felt she couldn't have looked worse if she had tried. Her makeup was smeared all over her face, and she smelled awful. She managed to wipe the sweat from her brow and said, "Nice to meet you. Great costume."

He laughed and put down his musket, and Debbie stared into his brilliant blue eyes. He pulled his hand through his black curly hair, which was flecked with gray. And what a body! Debbie felt weak in the knees. "First race, Debbie?" he asked in a deep, masculine voice.

"Yes, it was, but it was easier than I thought. I worked myself into a panic last night over it and didn't sleep well."

"First-race jitters; I know them well," he explained with a wide grin that exposed his perfect white teeth. "Would you like to go and get some more juice and perhaps some fruit?"

Debbie looked over at Jenny and Anne, and they both encouraged her with their nods. "I'd love to. I'm starved." She followed him over to a table that was full of refreshments. Anne and Jenny had disappeared. This was a set-up!

Bill retrieved two more orange juice containers, grabbed a couple of bananas, and led her over to a large rock that was in the sun. The sweat was beginning to dry on her body. He leaned against the rock, opened the juice, and drank it down in one gulp. "So, Debbie, Anne tells me you're from the Bay Area, and you're going to spend your first winter in the high country. Do you ski?"

She finished the juice in several gulps, hoping he wouldn't notice, and she thought to herself that if she saw Anne right now, she'd wring her neck. How much had her friend told this dashing, sweaty Daniel Boone who she was swigging orange juice with? "I've skied somewhat before. I guess you could say I'm a snow bunny, but I plan to try it again this winter. My thirteen-year-old daughter, Jenny, loves to ski. What about you? Do you ski?"

Debbie could see his beautiful blue eyes light up. "Yes, I guess you could say I love to ski. I'm a ski instructor at Squaw Valley."

"Interesting. Maybe I should take lessons from you."

"It would be my pleasure, Debbie. What line of work are you in up here, or do you work?"

Debbie sighed and played with the dirt with her running shoes. "Oh, I have to work. I don't know if Anne mentioned to you that I'm in the process of a divorce, and my soon-to-be ex left us without a great deal of money."

"I'm sorry. Were you married long?" His face showed a general look of concern.

"Fourteen years, but don't feel sorry for me. It seems to be working out for the best. I just received my real-estate license, and I started work at Lakeside Realty last week. Before that I waited tables at Zak's. What do you do in the summer when there is no snow?"

"I teach tennis at a racket club and I lead kayaking trips."

Debbie smiled. Bill certainly was a mountain man. That explained how he still had a dark tan so late in the year. "So, I'm in the company of a real Daniel Boone."

Bill laughed, and she suddenly felt weak in the knees again. "I love the outdoors," he explained. "I'm not the kind of guy who could be cooped up behind a desk in some stuffy office all day. My spirit soars in the fresh air."

"How long have you lived up here?" Debbie asked.

"I arrived in Tahoe in the late seventies after graduate school. I wanted a six-month break from my studies, so I gave myself a season to be a ski bum. As you can see, I'm still one to this day."

"So," she finished for him, "you got a job teaching what you loved and picked up tennis and kayaking to support your passion in the off-season."

Bill beamed. "You got it! And you know what? I've never regretted it once. I built my own home around ten years ago, which saved a great deal of money, and I've never married or had any kids, so my expenses are few."

Never married? What was wrong with all the women up here? This man was intelligent, kind, and a hunk!

"There you two are," interrupted Anne as she rushed up to them. "I've got to get going, and I told Jenny I'd give her a ride back, so you two can visit as long as you like. I'll see you tonight at the party." And she was off.

Bill and Debbie just looked at each other. "I think she did that on purpose; what about you?" he chuckled.

"I think you're right."

"Do you think you can give me a ride back?" he asked. "I came with a friend, but I don't see him," Bill said as he scanned the crowd.

"I'd be happy to," she said, and they walked over to Debbie's car. Bill gave directions to Debbie, and as they drove along, they chatted about all kinds of topics. Debbie discovered Bill was easy to converse with. He was well-versed on a number of subjects and he had a passion for reading.

"I'm in my Hemingway mode right now," he explained. "Several of his books are stacked on my nightstand for rereading. He brings out the adventurer in me. Who's your favorite author?"

He caught Debbie completely by surprise. "I hate to admit this, but I haven't read anything of substance since Jenny was born."

"And how old is she again?"

Debbie felt her cheeks turn red and her palms grow sweaty as she gripped the wheel. Embarrassed, she answered, "Thirteen last August."

Bill looked surprised, but he kept his eyes forward. Debbie desperately wanted to impress him, but she felt she had turned him off. She tried to rescue her credibility. "I read quite a bit in college. Whom would you suggest I read?"

Bill thought for a moment. "Have you read any of Mark Twain's works? He's sort of a regional writer; he spent quite a bit of time in Virginia City during its heyday."

"I just read *Huckleberry Finn* in junior high."

"How about if I lend you one of his books; *Roughing It* is one of my favorites. It has a great deal to do with the Tahoe basin."

If it would mean she could see this gorgeous man again, she'd agree to read Tolstoy.

"Sure, I'd love it."

He looked pleased. "I need to search for it. I could bring it over tomorrow."

"That would be wonderful." She gave him directions to her house.

She pulled up alongside a wooden A-frame house, and he got out. "I'll be over around noon tomorrow, if that's okay with you."

"That'll be great. See you tomorrow, Bill." She played a mental tape of the day in her head as she drove home. Every muscle in her body felt stiff and the sweat had dried, but she felt elated. Not only had she finished the race, but she had just met the most amazing man.

There was a note from Jenny on the kitchen table informing her that she was over at Kristen's practicing their lip-sync routine. Time to myself, she thought. She decided to make the most of it and soak in a hot bath. Turning on some Kenny G, she filled the bath with soap crystals and lit the candles around the tub. Leaning against the bath pillow, with the bubbles up to her neck and the pleasant smell from the candles filling the air, she drifted off to another space.

Chapter 9

THE DAYS BEGAN TO GROW COOLER, and the consensus among the locals was that snow was coming. Never having spent a winter in the snow, Debbie followed everyone else's lead and prepared for its arrival. She and Jenny stacked several cords of wood she had ordered next to the porch one chilly, clear November day. She also hired a man to help her prepare the cabin for the winter, and she broke down and purchased a used snowblower for the mounds of snow everyone said were on their way.

"Mom, can we quit? I'm tired."

Debbie looked behind her; there was still a huge pile of wood to be stacked. "Not yet, Jenny. When the wood's all stacked neatly."

"But, Mom! Kristen's expecting me."

"Sorry, honey. We need to get that wood stacked now, in case it snows."

"Can I call her and see if she wants to help?"

"Be my guest."

As Jenny raced into the house, Debbie continued stacking and thinking about her life. Work was going well. In fact, she had just sold a condo. Jenny was thriving up in the crisp mountain air; she had made several friends and even had a boyfriend, a cute kid if you were attracted to boys with earrings and baggy clothes. Bill had dropped off several books for her to read the day after the race. They had chatted for a while, then he said he had to go. She hadn't seen him since, but Anne had said he was interested, and he was just biding his time until she was divorced.

Speaking of being divorced, her lawyer had called the other day and said she should receive her papers in about a week. She no longer feared the big D; she realized it was a reality.

She found herself thinking of Bill quite a bit. He was so different from Sam it was almost comical. Why on earth she was attracted to a Grizzly Adams she had no idea, but she was. He was everything Sam wasn't.

And Sam! She no longer even thought about him, and sometimes she almost wanted to thank Donna for leading him away. Her life had taken a direction she had never dreamed of, and she now found it exhilarating. She loved being on her own, taking care of herself and Jenny, and working. A year ago, if someone would have told her she would be stacking logs on a Saturday afternoon instead of socializing or shopping somewhere, she would have told them her she was crazy.

But here she was, stacking her own wood, building her own roaring fires, fixing her own toilet, and cleaning her own house, and she loved it. She had even recently learned how to change a tire, which was certainly easier now that she didn't have to worry about breaking a nail.

Jenny came back out. "Kristen's on her way over to help so we could get going.

"Whatever. I do have to go and show a house at three. I want you home by dark."

"Okay, Mom, but I'm not a baby."

Debbie smiled. "You'll always be my baby."

A soft, light snow fell during the night the second week in November. Jenny was ecstatic when she awoke to find the world covered with a fluffy white blanket. The only sounds that could be heard were those of their neighbor's shovel. Debbie ventured outside with her steaming cup of coffee, wearing her heavy down parka and snow boots. The sight was breathtaking. It looked as if a good six inches had fallen. This would be her first experience driving in the snow, and she quickly gulped down the rest of the coffee, hoping the caffeine would give her the skill she so desperately needed to maneuver her car down the steep hill to the highway below.

"Hey, Jenny, get your coat on and come help me clear the walkway!"

"Right here, Mom." Debbie turned and saw Jenny, who was dressed in her new ski attire. "Isn't this cool, Mom! It's so beautiful!"

Debbie smiled and handed her a shovel, hoping her enthusiasm would keep up until the walkway and deck were cleared. Luckily Jenny was thrilled to be playing in the snow, because Debbie was running late. She had to get Jenny to school and herself to the office.

Work was slow; snow seemed to keep potential house buyers indoors. Beth told Debbie to leave early and make sure she had enough food in the house in case this was a powerful storm and they got snowed in. The entire office seemed to be praying for massive amounts of snow, which would open the ski resorts and bring the tourists, many of whom would fall in love with Tahoe's winter beauty and want a second home or condo.

She stopped off at the store and loaded up on winter foods: soup, marshmallows, crackers, hot cocoa, wine, and cookies. She gathered ingredients to make the bread and stew they used to enjoy in the city. The mountain air would make them taste even better, she decided as she stacked her cart with magazines, candles, a flashlight, and a few videos.

The post office was on the way home, so she decided to pick up the mail. She hadn't been in a few days; she had few bills and little correspondence. It seemed all her former "friends" had forgotten her, and she had come to realize they most likely hadn't been real friends, just mere passers-by on the bumpy road of life.

Opening the box, she could see it was jammed with a large manila envelope. She carefully nudged it out of the tiny box, along with her power and phone bills. Her stomach sank as she realized what it was. She decided to open the envelope in the privacy of her own car. Mixed emotions crushed like a giant tidal wave over her body as she carefully read the decree—first elation, then realization, and then the tears flowed. It was final, over. She and Sam were no longer, and Jenny was the child of a broken home. She didn't remember how long she sat in the car crying, but when she finally had no more tears left in her, the windshield and windows were covered with snow.

She drove to Jenny's school and waited for her. The buses usually had a difficult time in the snow, and Jenny and Debbie had a standing arrangement: if the weather was bad, Debbie would pick her up.

School was dismissed, and the students left the building with elation on their faces. Many of them picked up snow and flung it at others. The teachers had a difficult time keeping order. Debbie smiled and shook her head. Why couldn't they just let them be kids instead of trying their hardest to turn them into miniature adults?

Jenny saw her, and Debbie waved her and Kristin over. As she drove them home and listened to their chatter, she felt better. Jenny didn't seem to notice her silence; she and Kristin were talking about the upcoming dance and the boys they thought were so fine.

"What's wrong, Mom? You seem awfully quiet," Jenny finally asked after they pulled up to the cabin.

"It's nothing, honey. I just had a bad day."

"Why don't you take a nice long soak? Kristen and I'll take in the groceries and put them away."

Debbie gaped at her daughter. "I'd appreciate the help. Thanks."

Later that afternoon, when Jenny and Kristen were upstairs working on their math homework, she pulled out the divorce papers and reread their final words. Sipping her hot herbal tea in front of the blazing fire, she read word by word and let their resonance sink into her fragile being. She was still granted a thousand dollars a month for Jenny's support until she reached eighteen, and Sam had been ordered to continue paying for Jenny's medical insurance. The proceeds from the house had already been divided between Sam and Debbie, and instead of paying her alimony, he had picked up her hefty lawyer's bill as she had requested. There was nothing left from her former frivolous lifestyle except the house money, which she had put into a mutual fund a while ago. I'm not going to make that mistake again, she thought bitterly. I'm determined not to let my spending get out of hand. She had gone to an investment counselor, and he had shown her how to make the money grow safely for Jenny's college, wedding, and her own retirement. Their lifestyle was fairly lean now, and she planned on keeping it that way.

The phone rang, but she didn't move to get it; usually it was for Jenny or Kristen, who often had her calls forwarded. "Mom, it's for you!"

She put down the papers and picked up the phone. "Hello."

"Are you snowed in up there?" Aunt Jane asked.

Debbie suddenly relaxed and felt better. "Not yet, but we're on our way," she observed as she looked out the window at the snow-covered winter wonderland. The snow was coming down quickly.

They shared the events of the past weeks, and then Debbie told her aunt that the papers had arrived. Aunt Jane grew silent on the other end. "Well, Debbie, what's done is done," she finally said philosophically. "It's time to forge ahead, my dear. There's no time for you to sit on the pity pot."

"You're right. It's just so, so final."

"It is, Debbie, but it's also time for you to grow."

"I'm sure you're right, but I feel like I've grown ten years in the last few months."

"I'm sure you have," Aunt Jane said, and then she changed the subject and talked about the weather and the upcoming holidays and Debbie's trip to the city. Debbie shook her head as she listened to Aunt Jane's plans. Part of her wanted to go, but the other part didn't. It was too painful, but she didn't want to worry about Aunt Jane driving on the snowy highways to see her.

"I'll call you next week, Aunt Jane."

"Bye, dear."

As soon as Debbie hung up the phone, it rang again. This time it was Anne, and Debbie found herself pouring out the day's events.

"You poor dear, you shouldn't be alone. Chloe and I are on our way; open the wine."

"But, Anne . . . it's really snowing out there."

Anne laughed. "And that is why I have four-wheel drive. See you in a few."

Anne and Chloe were over shortly, snow covering their hair. Debbie popped some popcorn and made hot chocolate for the girls and hot buttered rums for the adults. Jenny and Kristen were kind enough to take Chloe with them after they finished their snack, and Debbie and Anne sank back on the couch and watched the snow gently swirling down outside the living room window. Anne was a wonderful listener as Debbie poured out her deepest feelings on the divorce. She just sat patiently and held Debbie's hand as her feelings tumbled out and the tears followed. "Thanks for coming over, Anne. You're right, I do feel better."

"You're welcome, Debbie. That's what friends are for."

"Then I'm lucky to have such a good friend like you. I guess I have to let go of feeling like a failure. I just never pictured myself divorced."

"You're not a failure, Debbie. You should be proud of yourself; just look at the way you've changed your life around."

Debbie thought for a moment, then smiled through the tears.

"Guess who I ran into yesterday?" Anne asked.

"Who?"

"Bill."

"Bill Howard?"

"Do you know another Bill?" she teased. "He asked about you."

"And what did you tell him?"

"Oh, that you were fine, and also that your divorce should be final soon."

"Why would you tell him that?" Debbie asked surprised.

"Because he asked."

Debbie was puzzled. "Why?"

"He'd love to take you out, but he won't get involved with a woman who's still legally tied to another man. He had asked me earlier to let him know when you were free."

Wow, Debbie thought. What a guy! He has morals, convictions, and he's handsome.

"Would you like me to say something, Debbie? Do you want to go out with him?"

Debbie didn't even hesitate. "Yes, I would. He's such a nice guy, but I haven't been on a date in a long time. What do I do?"

Anne chuckled. "It's like riding a bike. Once you get back on, it'll all come back to you."

The snow stopped sometime during the night, and Debbie awoke the next morning to the brilliant sun bouncing off the snow-covered landscape. She glanced at the alarm clock, which she had forgotten to set, and saw she had overslept. "Jenny, get up, we're late," she yelled as she made a dash to the shower. She had no idea what kind of condition the roads were going to be in, although she thought she had heard the plows in the middle of the night.

"Take the bus home tonight," she told Jenny as she dropped her off at school. "I'm probably going to be late. Call me when you get home."

She inched her way to work. The roads were plowed but slick, and she hadn't had much practice driving in adverse conditions. People zoomed by her in their four-wheel drives, but she plodded along, tortoise-like. Work was busy, and she showed several condos to buyers and arranged a few vacation rentals for people from the Bay Area. On her lunch break, she decided to head over to the Kings Beach Library because she needed some new books to read.

She walked in and scanned the building. The library was small; in fact, it was one large room with books shelved neatly, the shelves almost reaching the ceiling. The librarian was a small older woman, somewhere in her late fifties, with graying brown hair that was tucked neatly into a bun and glasses that hung around her neck on a shiny gold chain. She asked if she could help Debbie find anything, and Debbie told her that she was looking for something good to read on these long, winter nights. The librarian smiled and showed her where the current bestsellers were and also where the fiction area was located.

Debbie thanked her and went to look at the current bestsellers. The shelf was pretty well picked clean, so she ventured over to the fiction section and perused the shelves. To her amusement, the shelves were filled with many of the famous authors Aunt Jane and former teachers had tried to get her to read when she was younger. She used to laugh when they tried to impress upon her the merits of reading Hemingway, Faulkner, Fitzgerald, Emerson, and Thoreau. As she looked at all the wonderful books she, in her ignorance, had decided she didn't need to read, it clicked inside her that now was the perfect time to make their acquaintance. She chose four books: a Brontë, a Hemingway, a Bradbury, and an Austin.

"Wonderful books, my dear," the librarian said as Debbie placed them on the check-out counter and fished out her library card. "You should enjoy these immensely."

"Thanks, I hope to," Debbie replied as she left the library with her homework in hand.

Running outdoors was posing a problem now for Debbie with the darkness that crept across the basin as early as four-thirty in the afternoon. She reluctantly plugged in her treadmill, turned on the TV for mental distraction, and ran her five miles in the comfort and warmth of her own home.

Bill called a few days later and asked if she was free to join him for dinner Friday night. Jenny stood right next to her mother mouthing that she should accept and volunteering to go to Kristen's while Debbie tried to make up her mind. As Debbie finally agreed to Bill's invitation, she felt her heart leap into her mouth. She trembled like a lovesick teenager.

"Well?" Jenny probed as Debbie hung up the phone. "Where are you going and when is he going to pick you up?"

She turned around and was greeted by Jenny's smiling face, her arms crossed in front of her chest. It seemed as if Jenny was playing the role of the parent. "He's picking me up at seven, and he's taking me to Hugo's," Debbie answered.

"Cool, Mom. What are you going to wear?"

"I hadn't really thought about it. Would you like to help me pick something out?" When Jenny was a little girl, she loved to help Debbie pick out her outfits when she and Sam were going out.

"I think you'd better dress warm, Mom," she laughed. "I don't think it'll be a night for high heels."

Bill showed up promptly at seven Friday evening. He looked gorgeous standing there on the snowy porch dressed in a huge down parka, a red V-neck sweater, and navy blue dress slacks. "You look beautiful, Debbie," he said as she ushered him in the front door after he stamped his snowy feet on her welcome mat. "These are for you." He handed her a dozen red, perfect roses, and her knees almost gave way. She couldn't remember the last time she had received flowers from a man for no particular reason. Sam used to bring flowers when they were first married, but as the years went by the flowers were delegated to birthdays and anniversaries.

"Thanks so much. I'll put them in water. Can I get you something to drink?"

"A beer would be nice, if you have one."

Debbie went into the kitchen and found a vase to put the roses in. She grabbed a Corona out of the refrigerator, poured herself a glass of white wine, and arranged some crackers and cheese on a pretty blue platter. She noticed Bill had worked on the fire as she came out to the living room with her tray. She set the tray down, and he joined her on the couch. The wine began to loosen her tongue, and Debbie found Bill easier and easier to talk with. They discussed all kinds of topics, politics, movies, books, and, of course, skiing. He seemed impressed when she told him she had been reading Hemingway's *For Whom the Bell Tolls*.

"One of my all-time favorites," he said as they discussed the book. He glanced at his watch. "We should be going. Our reservations are at eight."

"Just let me get my purse," she said as she cleared the glasses. Bill checked the fire again, and they put on their heavy coats and headed out into the crystal-clear, cold November night.

They were ushered to their table by a tuxedo-clad maitre d' and given tall, thin menus. Their table overlooked the lake, which was sparkling like a jewel from the lights on the shore. Bill ordered champagne, and they sipped the drink and discussed their lives. He asked about her divorce, and she told him that it was final and she was a free woman. That seemed to relax him even more. They both ordered steak Diane, which was prepared beautifully at their table and elegantly served alongside perfect string beans and a baked potato. Over coffee by the roaring fire in the bar after the delicious meal, she noticed his arm had finally made its way around her shoulders.

Later Bill walked her to the door, leaned over, and kissed her on the cheek. "I'd love to see you again. Would you and Jenny be interested in going into Reno on Sunday and seeing a movie and having some dinner?"

"I'd love to, but I'll have to ask Jenny. Can I call you tomorrow?"

"That'll be great." And he kissed her cheek again, turned, and walked down the snowy driveway to his car.

Debbie entered the cabin, closed the door, leaned against it, and sighed. Smart man, she decided. He knows he has to court my daughter as well as me.

Bill arrived bright and early Sunday morning. Debbie was ready, but it was taking Jenny multiple outfit changes to find that perfect look. When she finally came down—in her seventh outfit yet—Bill found it amusing. "You remind me of my kid sister, Claudia. She changed her clothes at least five times every morning before school, was always tardy, and I would be late with her because I had to drive both of us."

Jenny just glared at Bill and got into the back seat. Debbie tried hard to suppress a smile, and Bill handed Jenny the newspaper and told her to pick a movie. That seemed to get her mind off his comment, and she poured over the movie listings.

"What are you doing for Thanksgiving," Bill asked Debbie.

"We've been invited to Anne's. What about you?"

He smiled at Debbie. "Then I guess I'll see you there. She gives a wild Thanksgiving." As he drove over the majestic Mount Rose, he asked Jenny if she found a movie she wanted to see. Jenny discussed the merits of several of the movies she was interested in seeing, and Debbie found her thoughts drifting back to last Thanksgiving.

It had been one of those perfect San Francisco days—clear sky and a mild temperature. The wind had blown all the pollution out to sea, and the city stood sparkling on its hills. Debbie had slaved half the night before preparing a gourmet feast for Sam's entire family, who arrived early, hungry, and full of cheer. Debbie spent the majority of Thanksgiving day working in the kitchen, with only an occasional offer of a hand from a relative, but she didn't mind. She loved serving delicious food and loved having people in their home. Over dinner, Debbie, Sam, and his parents had discussed spending several weeks together at Lake Tahoe during the summer. Funny how things work out, she thought. I was the one who ended up here. Sam's parents had never even made the effort to come and visit; it was as if she no longer existed.

She sank back into the seat and sighed. She had always gotten along with Sam's parents, even though they had snobby tendencies. Graciously, they had welcomed her into their family, and when Jenny was born, they had lavished gifts and attention on her. Now, Jenny didn't even rate a phone call.

She wondered if Sam had been seeing Donna then. He had never been totally honest about when he took up with her. For all she knew, it could have been going on for years. And this Thanksgiving, Donna would have her place at the table. Bitch! And soon Jenny would be squeezed out by Donna's child.

A "friend" had called last week to tell Debbie about the society blurb in the paper announcing Sam and Donna's engagement. The article said there was to be a small wedding next fall, but, if Donna was pregnant, Debbie wondered why they were waiting so long to get married. The divorce was final, so what was stopping them?

She picked up the newspaper Jenny had placed on the front seat and looked at all the Thanksgiving ads. As she scanned the ads—many for kitchen gadgets to prepare that perfect turkey—she shook her head, realizing that this Thanksgiving would certainly be different. She wouldn't be cooking, she wasn't married any longer, and she was seeing this gorgeous man who was driving Jenny and her to Reno for a movie and a early dinner. Things Sam used to do, she lamented, but now things he did for Donna and her fetus. Life was funny.

"What do you think of the movie Jenny decided on?" Bill asked her, bringing her back to the present. She looked at the two of them and realized they seemed to have hit it off.

"What movie is that?" she asked.

"Mom, weren't you listening to a thing we said," Jenny asked.

"Sorry, honey, I was day-dreaming. Whatever movie you picked, I'm sure it will be fine.

They had a lovely afternoon. The movie, a comedy, was very funny, and the three of them howled along with the rest of the audience at the antics of Kevin Kline. They had an early dinner at a Mexican restaurant in the mall, and then Jenny pleaded with them that she "had to go shopping." They indulged her, and Bill and Debbie strolled the mall hand-in-hand and looked at all the stores dressed up in their Christmas finery. As they headed back home, tired but happy, Debbie decided that it had been a perfect day. It was as if they were a family again, only this time, Bill was playing the part of Sam.

Chapter 10

"A STRONG STORM FROM THE GULF OF ALASKA is on its way for the Thanksgiving holiday," warned the TV announcers. "We suggest you stock up on staples and make sure your snow shovel is handy."

"Did you hear that, Mom?" Jenny shouted from the living room, where the news was on. "Cool. We might be snowed in."

Debbie came in from the kitchen, where she had been preparing a pumpkin pie and a vegetable dish to take to Anne's. As she wiped her hands on her apron, she stared at the potentially powerful storm on the TV screen. "You're right, Jenny," she concluded. "It looks like we better get to Safeway and stock up. That looks like a nasty storm." She quickly cleaned up the kitchen, and they piled into her four-wheel drive and headed to the store.

Thanksgiving morning arrived snowy as predicted. Debbie stirred the fire that had died down overnight, made fresh coffee, and sat on the couch watching the large, fat, wet snowflakes come down hard and fast, covering the world outside in a fluffy white comforter. Inside, she was cozy and warm. She knew she needed to run, but Mother Nature had other plans, so after she finished her coffee, she stretched, and plugged in the treadmill and ran in the warmth of her own home. She would have rather been outside, with the fresh, clean mountain air filling her lungs, but the snow was already piling up quickly, and visibility was poor.

Jenny finally dragged her teenage body from the warmth of her bed around ten, and Debbie prepared a delicious Thanksgiving breakfast of scrambled eggs, blueberry muffins, orange juice, and grapefruit. "Anne's serving dinner around three, so make sure you eat up, because this has to last you until then," she urged her daughter, who seemed to be playing with her food. They spent the rest of the morning cleaning up the small cabin, doing laundry, and watching the snow come down harder and harder. Debbie turned on the radio and listened intently as the announcer spoke of the massive amounts of snow that had already fallen. Around one, Donner Summit, the main artery between the lake and the Bay Area, was reported to be closed. Two feet had fallen since last night, and several more feet were predicted before the storm would be over.

Jenny gazed anxiously out the living room window. "Do you think Bill will make it up here to get us?"

Debbie joined her at the window and looked at her watch. He was already fifteen minutes late. "I'm sure he'll make it. He's been driving in the snow a long time."

Bill pulled up ten minutes later. "I'm sorry I'm late. There was a big accident on the highway, and they were holding traffic," he explained as he stomped his feet on her front porch.

"How bad are the roads?" Debbie asked. She had never seen snow come down this hard and fast. "Are we going to make it to Anne's?"

Bill chuckled. "It's not that bad. Nothing my trusty old truck can't handle," he said with a grin. "Let's go."

He helped Debbie carry her offerings out to his truck. "Ski season is here!" he exclaimed. "Ready to ski, Jenny?"

Her young face lit up. "I'm ready."

As they got in the truck, he asked Jenny if she would like to go skiing with him one day soon. "And I'd like you to come too, Debbie. I'll personally give you a lesson." And he winked at Jenny.

Debbie climbed in the truck, beside Bill. She was nervous to ski with him. All she had heard from others was how smooth and elegant he was gliding down even the most treacherous terrain. She, on the other hand, seemed to cross her skis even on the bunny hill. She and Bill were getting along well; she just didn't want to jinx their relationship by having to get off the chairlift gracefully with him.

Thanksgiving at Anne's was a far cry from all the holidays Debbie had shared with Sam. There was no rhyme or reason to Anne's table arrangement, menu, or the diverse people she had gathered. In reality, it seemed to be one big mishmash, but it worked. People were scattered all around the living room, sitting on whatever they could, wine flowed, food was enjoyed, and stories were told. A blazing fire kept them all cozy and warm, while outside the snow continued to pile up.

Later, helping Anne clean up in the kitchen, Debbie stacked the paper plates and cups to be taken out to the trash. "This was wonderful, Anne. The people were interesting, and the food! Thanks for inviting us."

Anne smiled as she placed the trash in large black trash bags. "Thanks. I always enjoy doing Thanksgiving this way, gathering up all the people I know who are without families, or between families, and bringing them together for one afternoon to make a new family. It's sort of like what the Pilgrims did the first Thanksgiving. They gathered up all their neighbors, who were so far from home, and gave one hell of a party. Only they were celebrating a harvest and the survival of the previous year, and we are celebrating the holiday and the first big snow of the season."

Debbie grinned as she wiped down the counters and thought back to the conversation during the meal. Snow had certainly been the topic, with bets being placed on how much the final total of snowfall would be from this storm.

"How's your training going, Debbie?" Anne asked as she put the remainder of the food into containers.

"I was up to almost eight miles a day, but since the snow has arrived, I've had to resort to my treadmill."

Anne grinned. "The downside of training in the Sierras. There'll be days when you'll be able to run outside, but you might want to think about getting some cross-country skis; that's an excellent alternative to running."

Debbie chuckled as she remembered how she used to scoff at the people who participated in that sport, with all their funny-looking gear and perspiration-soaked bodies. "Isn't it harder than running?"

"No. Once you get the hang of it, it's actually quite easy. And you are able to take off and go places you wouldn't be able to get to otherwise in the dead of winter. There's a ski swap next weekend.

How about if we go? I need some new boots, and it's a good place for you to find some reasonably priced equipment."

Debbie thought it over for a moment. "Sounds good. Maybe I can find Jenny some things also."

Debbie had to work the reminder of the Thanksgiving weekend, and luckily for her, Kristen had asked Jenny if she would like to go skiing with her family. The ski resorts opened with a record amount of snow for the end of November, and the plows worked all through the night to clear the roads so the skiers could come. "Have a wonderful time," she told Jenny as she watched her daughter lug her skis out to Kristen's brother's car. "Be sure to wear sun block." The storm had moved through and the snow was shining brilliantly on the several feet of fluffy white powder.

Jenny turned back and shouted, "I will. Don't work too hard, Mom. I'll call you tonight."

Debbie smiled and closed the front door. She needed to hurry and get ready for work. She was already running late.

Later that day, she had to show condos to a fiftyish-looking couple from L.A. who wanted to purchase one before the Christmas holidays. Tim and Jan were in a hurry to find the perfect condo so their entire family could spend the holidays skiing. Debbie lined up a list of potential condos, several located next to ski resorts. Jan, a blond, plump mother of four, wanted one that could sleep ten comfortably, while Tim's only concern was that the condo be located near a ski resort. Debbie showed them what felt like hundreds of condos, none of which fit their tastes. Finally, as the sun was slipping behind the mountains and the cold started to grip the air, Debbie brought them to one of the last ones on her list, an older condo, built in the late seventies.

"Look, Tim, this would be perfect," Jan exclaimed as she walked around the living room. "How many bedrooms did you say there were?"

Debbie looked at her sheet. "There are two downstairs and three upstairs."

Jan looked at her husband, who seemed to be getting tired of the entire process. Every condo he had liked, she had shot down. This was the first one that had grabbed her attention, but it wasn't that close to a ski resort. Tim walked around the living room, checked out the massive fireplace, went upstairs, came back down, and ambled into the kitchen with Jan at his heels and Debbie close behind. The kitchen had dark cabinets and white-tiled countertops. There were four bar stools next to the large counter, a dark brown refrigerator, double ovens, and the kitchen sink had a view of the mountains. There was a laundry room, already equipped with a washer and dryer, off to one side and a small alcove off to the other side that could function as an office.

Debbie left them alone in the kitchen to talk and went into the living room and sat down on the worn velvet couch. She could hear them discuss the property. She usually left buyers alone so they could have some privacy to make a decision without her breathing down their backs. Debbie could hear them back upstairs, opening and closing doors and closets. After a few minutes, Jan and Tim ventured back down to the living room. "Does the condo come furnished?" Tim asked as he walked over to the slider that opened up to a large patio and a view of the homeowners' beach.

Debbie checked her notes. "Yes, it does, and it looks as if the owners are anxious to sell."

Jan walked over and stood next to her husband. "This is perfect, Tim. It has enough room for the kids, and the beach is so close they can walk down in the summer."

Tim asked her, "Are you sure this is what you want? It's not that close to the ski resorts."

She turned to him with excitement in her eyes. "Yes, I do. We can drive to the resorts and walk to the beach in the summer. Let's make an offer."

They joined Debbie on the couch, and she laid all the information on the condo out for them on the glass coffee table. Tim and Debbie discussed the condo for a few minutes, while Jan just sat back on the couch with a satisfied smile on her face. Then Tim suggested a price, and Debbie wrote up the offer. Tim took out his leather checkbook and gold Cross pen and wrote a check.

"I'll be in touch after I present the offer to the owners," Debbie said as she dropped them off at their car in the real estate office's parking lot later. "Have a good evening."

Jan and Tim went back to their hotel, and Debbie went back to her cabin, alone, where she was greeted by the chill of the empty house and her loneliness. She quickly turned on the electric heat and started to build a fire. A few minutes later, warmth began to circulate through the cabin, and she felt her body slowly begin to thaw. Damn, it was cold. She went into the kitchen and put the teakettle on. As the water heated, she checked her messages. She listened to Jenny's excited voice telling her she had a great day skiing, no broken bones, and she'd be home sometime tomorrow. "I'll call you in the morning, Mom."

When Jenny's message ended, Debbie felt sorry for herself. Another long, cold, winter's night alone, with nothing to keep her company but her own thoughts and perhaps a good book, unless there was something on TV. She flipped through the three channels her TV offered—she had decided against cable to cut costs—and seeing there was nothing on that interested her, she decided to read. As she glanced through the stack of books she had checked out at the library, a book by C. S. Lewis caught her eye. Hmmm, she thought, this looks like an interesting book. She made herself a cup of tea, curled up on the couch, covered herself with a thick, warm blanket, and dove into the book. Around eight, she began to notice a hollow feeling in her stomach. She realized she had forgotten to eat, so she went into the kitchen, opened a can of minestrone soup, pulled herself up to the kitchen table, and continued to read.

Once, during her reading marathon, she got off the couch and looked out the window. The moon was full, and as it cast its light upon the winter wonderland, the snow glistened in its wake, and there seemed to be a hush upon the world. She pulled on her heavy down parka and went out and stood on her front porch and took several deep breaths of the pure, crisp air. Millions of stars twinkled above, and she felt a sense of peace as she wrapped her arms tightly around her body and went back into the warmth of her home.

The weeks before Christmas were very busy in the office. There were many bookings for condos for the upcoming holiday, and Debbie showed quite a few properties to potential buyers. Beth seemed to have taken a liking to her, and she passed on some great leads. Debbie's running was going strong; she often ran during her lunch break and then showered in office bathroom. Quite a few of the other agents were runners, and there were a several times when Debbie had to stand in line and wait her turn for the shower.

She found that running in the sparkling daytime sun was exhilarating. Even though the temperature hovered around the forty-degree mark, it still felt warm enough to run in a short-sleeve top. The sun reflecting off the snow was so bright, she found if she didn't wear her sunglasses, she was blinded.

Debbie had begun to add some free weights to her training program, and in the evenings, in front of the fire with Jenny, they both pumped some iron. She was beginning to feel strong—which was good because the two of them were going to San Francisco for the holidays, and she needed her strength. There would be some old friends to see, and the places she and Jenny used to go with Sam would be there to haunt her.

One night, a week before Christmas, Debbie and Jenny went to a tree lot to pick out their Christmas tree. Debbie had never done this task alone before; Sam had always taken charge of the tree when they were married, and before that, Aunt Jane and Debbie's father had seen that a tree was always there in the living room for her to decorate. She felt her eyes grow misty just thinking about last year's beautifully adorned Christmas tree. Jenny and Sam had lovingly picked it out together, while she had stayed at home getting all the decorations out and putting the finishing touches on her home.

"Mom, here's the perfect tree," Jenny shrieked. Debbie made her way over to a small but perfectly shaped tree.

"It would look good in the corner by the window," Debbie agreed. "And it's not too big. I forgot to bring up the ornaments—they must be in the storage shed, or I got rid of them—so we're going to have to make our own."

"Cool," replied Jenny as she picked the tree up and took it to the cashier.

"How much is it?" Debbie asked, following behind Jenny.

Jenny looked at the price tag. "Twenty-five dollars."

"Ouch," Debbie said, rummaging through her purse for her checkbook. "I wonder how much your father used to pay."

The next evening, Debbie popped several huge bowls of popcorn, and she and Jenny sat on the braided rug in front of the fire and started stringing a popcorn garland.

"Jenny, if you keep eating it, we won't have any to string!"

Jenny laughed and popped a big white kernel into her mouth and followed it with a sip of her hot chocolate. "We'll just have to pop more, Mom," she answered with a chocolate smile. Debbie smiled widely at her daughter, who looked totally contented, and popped a few kernels into her own mouth.

A few hours later, the tree stood gaily decorated with popcorn strings, some red glass ornaments Debbie had picked up at the grocery store, and gold bows. "Let's take a picture, Mom. The tree looks so cool." Jenny ran upstairs to get her camera. They took turns snapping pictures of each other pointing to the tree. Suddenly, Debbie felt contented as she captured her daughter's essence on film. They were going to be all right!

Debbie awoke early the morning of Christmas Eve and padded down to the kitchen to put on some coffee and listen to the weather report. She looked out her kitchen window and saw the skies were clear. Since moving to the mountains, she had gotten used to listening to the weather reports because the weather was extremely unpredictable; one minute it could be sunny and warm, and the next minute a fierce storm could blow into the area closing roads and canceling life.

"Clear and cold with highs in the thirties," droned the forecaster's voice. "This afternoon a low-pressure system is expected to move into the area, and it is predicted to leave several feet of snow in the higher elevations. If you have holiday travel plans, we suggest you leave early."

Debbie glanced at the kitchen clock: it was eight. Maybe she should get Jenny up so they could leave earlier than they had planned. She glanced out the window again: the sky was clear, but a wind had picked up, and the treetops were swaying. She finished her cup of coffee and went to wake Jenny. "It's too early, Mom. Can't I sleep longer?"

"No, we've got to leave by ten. Another storm's coming, and I don't want to get stuck on the hill, so get going."

They managed to get on the road by ten-thirty, and already the clouds were moving swiftly across the sky and into the basin. Jenny fiddled with the radio dial until she found a station that was playing Christmas carols. Debbie and Jenny sang along to all their favorites as they made their way over the summit and down the mountain. The snow started to fall as they drove past the Soda Springs exit. Thoughts floated through Debbie's mind about the impending holiday. She would have to see Sam tomorrow when he came to get Jenny at Aunt Jane's. Even though they were divorced and he had scorned her by having an affair with another woman, there were still some feelings for him that she had buried deep down in and that she needed to come to terms with. A part of her still ached for his embrace, even though on the conscious level she knew that would never be a reality. She acknowledged to herself that she was still hurt, hurt by the way he had betrayed her, and hurt by the way he had used her money.

She glanced over at Jenny, who seemed to be sleeping. I wonder if he was more attracted to my trust fund than he was to me, she mused. Does Donna have any money? That would make sense if she did, Debbie decided. Sam had always seemed like such a pretty boy, someone whose tastes ran to the finer things in life, things that were much more expensive than he could afford with the salary he drew at the architecture firm. Sam had always been a fairly good architect, but he had never seemed to want to push himself to be the best. He was satisfied with being mediocre.

Debbie decided she was tired of listening to Christmas carols; in fact, she was tired of Christmas, and it wasn't even over yet. She flipped through the stations until she came to a news network and listened to the stories of the day. Even on Christmas Eve the news was the same: murders, car accidents, bombings, and that reminder that people had only one more day left to shop. The city finally came into view, and Debbie felt a familiar tug—home.

"Jenny, we're almost here," she said, gently poking her sleeping daughter. "There's the city."

Jenny slowly opened her eyes and stretched. "She looks beautiful, Mom. I certainly have missed her."

Debbie had to agree; even in the pouring rain, San Francisco looked inviting. "Me too, sweetheart, me too."

They pulled up in front of Aunt Jane's apartment building as the rain began to get heavier. Aunt Jane stood in the window and waved anxiously when she saw them emerge from the car. Debbie and Jenny raced for the door to avoid getting wet.

"You made it safely," exclaimed Aunt Jane as she opened the door to the building. She had a large apartment on the second floor of a twelve-family apartment building. "On the news they said I-80 was closed on top of Donner Summit."

Debbie gave her a big hug, and she and Jenny followed Aunt Jane up to her apartment. "We must have made it over before they closed it. We didn't have any trouble."

Jenny took off her coat and hung it on the hall tree. "Look, Mom, look at her Christmas tree."

Off in the corner of Aunt Jane's spacious living room stood a tall, sweet-smelling evergreen that was decorated entirely with angels. Jenny walked over and examined them. "These are so beautiful, Aunt Jane."

Aunt Jane beamed. "I've been collecting angels for years, and this year I had enough to do an entire tree. I'm glad you like them. There's one on the tree for each of you. Can you find them?"

Jenny eagerly searched the magnificent figurines and found two delicate creatures with the names "Debbie" and "Jenny" carved on them. "These are for us?"

"Yes. You may take them with you when you leave. Now, how about some refreshment after your long journey?"

"Great, I'm thirsty," Jenny replied, and the three of them went into the kitchen. Debbie and Jenny sat at the counter while Aunt Jane bustled around in the kitchen, preparing a snack. Debbie exhaled deeply and glanced around her aunt's kitchen. Not much had changed since she had been Jenny's age; the same appliances and knickknacks took up space. Aunt Jane had installed a window greenhouse, where she had a variety of healthy green plants growing.

Aunt Jane placed a small platter of snacks in front of them, opened Jenny a soft drink, and poured Debbie and herself a glass of a local California white wine. She took the third stool and offered up a toast. "Merry Christmas, girls! I'm so glad you're here." And they all clinked glasses and took a sip of their drinks.

Aunt Jane had prepared a wonderful Christmas Eve feast. They dined on roasted pumpkin bisque, a fresh salad, and pan-roasted quail with a bourbon and molasses sauce. "This is absolutely divine, Aunt Jane," Debbie exclaimed. "You made this?"

Aunt Jane chuckled. "Sure I did. I made the phone call that arranged for all this to be delivered."

Debbie and Jenny laughed. "It's wonderful," Jenny added. "What's for dessert?"

"Just you wait." Aunt Jane got up and brought in a covered cake dish. She set it down in front of Jenny and took off the cover. "This is chocolate cake with chocolate sauce and a chestnut filling—the woman at the bakery guaranteed it to be divine."

"Yum," Jenny said as her mouth watered.

I had better run twice as far when I get home, Debbie thought. This cake looks like it'll stick right to my thighs.

Aunt Jane got three plates from her china hutch and took her cake knife out of a drawer. "You do the honors, Jenny, while I pour us all a glass of champagne." She handed Jenny the knife.

"Can I have a glass?" Jenny asked Debbie with her eyes wide.

"Just half," Debbie replied. "Only because it's a special occasion."

After the cake was devoured, they took their drinks into the living room and sat around the Christmas tree, sipping the champagne and watching the twinkling white lights on the Christmas tree.

"Are you ready to open your presents, Jenny?" asked Debbie. Jenny was spending Christmas Day with Sam and his family. Debbie would accompany Aunt Jane to church and then brunch. Christmas would be different this year, and Debbie was secretly hoping it would pass quickly and they could just go home. She had also been invited to an open house at their former neighbor's, which she was dreading. Why she had said yes escaped her, but it had seemed the right thing to say at the time.

Jenny's excited voice brought her back to the moment. "Yes, let's open them." She quickly scoured the packages for one with her name. The three of them spent the next hour opening the gaily wrapped packages and squealing with delight.

"It's just what I needed, Aunt Jane. Thanks." Debbie lifted out a beautiful hand-stitched purple sweater with a black turtleneck. Also inside the box were several pairs of wool socks and an elegant pair of leather gloves. "This will definitely keep me warm." She gave her aunt, who sat there with a wide smile on her face, a big hug.

She held the sweater up to her body, taking in the smell of new clothes. How long had it been since she had purchased something new for herself? Outside of a few pair of jeans and some running gear, a long, long time.

Aunt Jane loved her watercolor of Lake Tahoe. "I have the perfect spot for it. Now I can look at it every day and visualize where you two are."

Debbie finally handed Jenny a small box. "What's in here, Mom?"

"Open it and see."

Jenny gingerly opened the box and saw a picture of a snowboard. "Thanks, Mom! Just what I wanted."

"It's waiting for you in my office, honey. We'll get it when we get home."

After the wrapping paper had been cleared away, they all curled up on the couch and turned on the TV. *Miracle on 34th Street* was playing, and they all felt enchanted with by its beautiful message.

Aunt Jane woke Debbie and Jenny up Christmas morning with the smell of a Christmas blend of coffee and the sounds of carols playing on the stereo. Debbie opened her eyes slowly and saw Jenny staring at her. "Merry Christmas, Jenny. What's wrong?" One glance at the look on Jenny's face, and Debbie could tell something was amiss with her daughter.

"I don't want to leave you alone today, Mom. I'm worried about you."

Debbie wrapped her arms around Jenny and pulled her young, thin body close. "I'll be fine, honey. I have Aunt Jane, and I'm going to stop by Kevin and Mary's. Don't worry. You just have a good day with your daddy." Jenny hadn't seen Sam since late August. He called once a week and made a few noises about coming up to see her but never did.

"Are you sure, Mom?"

Debbie could tell Jenny was excited to see Sam, but she knew her daughter's loyalties were with her. She looked at the clock. "You better get ready; he'll be here in about an hour."

When Sam arrived, Aunt Jane answered the door. Sam entered the apartment, handsome in a navy blue wool blazer. Jenny ran up and gave him a huge hug. "Daddy! It's great to see you!"

Sam's face lit up as he scooped his daughter up in his arms. "Wow, you've grown!" He stood back and gazed at Debbie, who stood off to the side. "Merry Christmas, Debbie. You're looking well."

Debbie pulled her robe tighter around her body. "So are you, Sam. Merry Christmas." She quickly turned to Jenny, gave her a big hug. "Have a wonderful day, sweetheart. I'll see you bright and early tomorrow."

"I'll have her back by ten, Debbie. Get your stuff, Jenny, the day's waiting."

Jenny bounded off, and that left the two of them alone. Debbie felt nervous standing in the foyer with Sam, a man she had shared a life with for fourteen years. "How are you really doing, Debbie? I think of you often."

Sam's guilt was plastered all over his handsome face. There's no way, bud, I'm ever really going to tell you how hard it's been and give you the satisfaction of knowing that you wrecked my life, she thought to herself. What had initially attracted her to Sam, she didn't remember. She smiled sweetly at him. "I'm doing fine, Sam. I have a good job, Jenny's adjusted, and I've met some great people. But thank you for asking," she graciously answered and then quietly left the foyer and went to her room, where she threw herself down on the bed and let the tears flow. It hurts when you really see people for who they are and not the fantasy you once concocted, she thought as she cleansed her feelings.

Later that day, after church and brunch with Aunt Jane and several of her widowed friends, she went over to visit her former neighbors, Kevin and Mary Dodd. They were holding their annual holiday open house. They were some of the few people Debbie still kept in contact with. Jenny used to babysit their twin five-year-old daughters.

"Debbie, how wonderful to see you!" boomed Kevin's loud voice a he opened the door for her and gave her a hug. "You look terrific." Kevin was a large man with graying brown hair, a mustache, and a stomach that broadcasted he loved to eat.

Debbie returned his hug. "Thanks, Kevin, it's great to see you." Kevin led the way to the kitchen, where Mary was busy filling platters with food. Her large brown eyes twinkled and her face lit up when Debbie came in.

"Debbie, thanks for coming," Mary exclaimed, wiping her hands on her apron and giving Debbie a warm hug. Mary was a petite woman with thick, shoulder-length brown hair. "You look wonderful, Debbie. The fresh mountain air must agree with you. You have rosy cheeks, and they don't look like they're from make-up."

Debbie smiled. She couldn't remember the last time she had worn blush. "Thanks, Mary, and thanks for inviting me."

"Let's sit down and catch up," Mary suggested. She turned to the maid. "Could you please put these out," she said as she pointed to several filled trays. "And check what we're running low on."

"Yes, Mrs. Dodd," replied the young maid.

"Let's go sit by the fire, Debbie. I want to hear everything." Debbie followed Mary through the crowded hall and family room, stopping to say hello to people she hadn't seen in a long time. While she had never been particularly close to Mary, they had always gotten along well as neighbors, accepting deliveries for each other and picking up the newspapers and mail while the other was gone. Debbie followed Mary's lead over to the immense stone fireplace and took a seat next to her in one of the vacant club chairs.

"Your house looks wonderful, Mary," Debbie said, scanning the gaily decorated family room.

"Thanks, I had the same professional service as last year. They do a marvelous job," she added.

Debbie smiled and thought back to last year. She had come over with Sam. Was it really only a year ago? It seemed like an eternity. Mary seemed to be chattering about something, and Debbie struggled to bring her mind back to the present. Mary was talking about the latest fundraiser the Junior League had undertaken, a project Debbie would be heavily involved in if she still had her former life. "We miss you so much, Debbie. It's not the same without you. Are you coming back next year?"

"I don't really know. I'm just going to take it one day at a time. Jenny and I are nicely settled, and I have a job I like now."

That seemed to surprise Mary. "Oh, I heard someone say you had to work now. What are you doing again? A travel agent?"

"No, I'm a real-estate agent, and I really enjoy it. Jenny's made some good friends, and I've taken up running."

Mary looked amazed. "So, that's how you lost the weight. I thought it was from the divorce." Then she whispered, "You do look wonderful, but isn't running a hard way to take it off? Wouldn't liposuction be easier?"

Debbie grinned. Mary hadn't changed a bit, and somehow her naiveté was refreshing. "I enjoy running, Mary, especially up there, and besides, I don't have the money for that kind of cosmetic surgery. It felt good to take the weight off myself."

Mary seemed intrigued. "But isn't it too cold up there right now to run? And what do you do at night? Is there opera or the theatre up there?"

Debbie would've laughed, but the woman was serious. "After working and running, I'm usually pretty tired. Most nights I crawl in bed with a good book."

"Hmmm, interesting," she said. "Well, Debbie, it was wonderful seeing you. I've got to circulate and see how all my other guests are doing. I'll see you later," and she was off, leaving Debbie sitting alone.

She just sat there, contemplating the situation. She really didn't belong anymore; she didn't have much in common with the people she used to socialize with. It was as if they were caught on a merry-go-round, spinning through the same boring, mundane activities—dinners out, concerts, opera, etc—and Debbie had somehow gotten off, broken free, and was blazing new territory. It was time to let go of the past, she decided, and she got up and went into the kitchen, where she found Kevin and Mary listening attentively as a couple talked about their recent trip to Europe.

"And we dined at the most wonderful restaurants in London, and the prices, they were absurd. I'm so glad we don't have to worry about money," the elegantly dressed woman said to Mary.

"I'm sorry to be interrupting you," Debbie said as she touched Mary's shoulder. "I've got to be going, Mary. Thanks for inviting me."

"Wonderful to see you again, Debbie. Do keep in touch. We'll do lunch when you come again," Mary replied sweetly.

"I'll walk you to the door," said Kevin, remembering his host manners.

"Thanks, but I'll see myself out. Merry Christmas." Debbie left the house, glad to get away from the superficiality of the situation.

"Thank God!" she exclaimed as she shut the heavy oak door behind her. "What did I ever see in those people?" She got in her car and took off down the street, not even looking at her old house. She wasn't due back at Aunt Jane's until five, so she had a couple hours of to kill. She didn't want to show up early because she didn't want her aunt worrying any more about her, so she decided to drive over to Golden Gate Park to take a walk.

The park was fairly deserted, so she didn't have any difficulties finding a parking place. She zipped up her coat, stuck her hands into the pockets, and headed off. A brisk wind was blowing off the

Pacific, but the rain had stopped. Heavy, dark storm clouds still hung in the air. She kicked dead leaves and rocks with the toe of her boot, lost in the world of her thoughts. She was ready to go back to Tahoe tomorrow; in fact, she felt no attraction to staying in the city at all. The only person she would miss would be Aunt Jane, who also had informed her that she was going to Australia for several months with a friend after Christmas. She had told Debbie that Australia was a place she had always wanted to go to, and now that Debbie and Jenny were settled, and the opportunity had arisen, it was the perfect time for her to go.

On the one hand, Debbie wished Aunt Jane would stay, just in case she needed her for something, but on the other hand Debbie realized that was incredibly selfish. Aunt Jane had literally put her own life on hold when Debbie lost her parents, and since then she had acted as a surrogate parent. Aunt Jane wasn't getting any younger, and she needed to follow her own bliss while her heart was strong. Debbie walked and thought for quite a while, finally noticing that the sun was sinking lower and lower in the horizon. She glanced at her watch. It was late; she'd better get back before Aunt Jane worried.

Sam dropped Jenny off the next morning, heavily laden with gifts. Guilt, Debbie concluded as she watched Sam lug several loads to her car. Jenny placed all her presents in the back of the car, closed the door, and gave Sam a hug. Sam seemed to hold on to her, as if he didn't want to let go.

Debbie met Jenny at the door, and they said thank you to Aunt Jane, wished her a wonderful trip to the Outback, and headed to the car and back to their lives.

"Drive safely," Aunt Jane warned as she waved them off.

"I will. I'll call you tonight," Debbie shouted from her car.

"Well, tell me," she said to Jenny, who seemed to be staring out the window as they pulled away. "How was it?"

Jenny turned and looked at her. "It sucked, Mom. It didn't feel like Christmas. Donna was all over me, and they got me all that junk," she said in a disgusted tone as she pointed to the back of the car. "Who do they think they're kidding? Do they think I don't know they're trying to make me forgive them by giving me all that stuff. Stuff I know Daddy didn't pick out. She must have."

"I'm sorry, Jenny. I did hope you would have a wonderful time with your father. Did you see your grandparents?"

"Yes. They came for Christmas dinner last night, which by the way, was horrible. Donna burnt the turkey."

Debbie tried not to laugh. "What did they get you?" She was curious. In the past, Muffy had always called her and asked for suggestions. She hadn't called Debbie this year.

"Clothes," Jenny said with a sigh. "And not clothes I would ever wear! They're pink and purple. What does she think I am, six!"

"Just clothes?" Debbie was surprised. Usually Jenny's grandparents were very generous with their gifts at Christmas and on her birthdays.

"Oh, they got me some gloves, hats, scarves, things like that. Don't they think we have that stuff already? We've only had snow for, like, almost two months now." Jenny shook her head and plopped against the seat.

Debbie kept her eyes glued to the road. Damn Sam, she thought bitterly.

Chapter 11

"ARE YOU READY, MOM? It's really snowing outside," Jenny yelled from the living room. Debbie sighed, grabbed her gloves, and tromped down the stairs, part of her reluctant to go on this adventure.

She met Jenny at the front door. "Okay, I'm ready, let's do it," she told her eager daughter. She opened the front door, and the two of them left the warmth of the cozy cabin for the frigid outdoors, where their cross-country ski equipment stood patiently waiting for them on the front porch. Debbie inhaled the cold, invigorating air, pulled her woolen hat down over her ears, and struggled with her gloves. The Tahoe area had recently been dumped with over five feet of snow from a powerful storm out of the Gulf of Alaska. Roads were still unpassable, and schools and businesses had been closed for several days. It seemed as if the world they lived in had come to a screeching halt. "Let's ski down to the beach and along the water," Jenny had suggested to Debbie on their second morning of being snowed in. "Wouldn't it be cool to ski to the grocery store and get our groceries?" Debbie had agreed; cabin fever had begun to set in and, she had found herself ready to climb the walls.

They strapped on the skis they had picked up at a ski swap and headed out into the pristine winter wonderland. The snow continued to fall silently as they made their way down the road. The world was undisturbed except for their ski tracks and the tiny footprints left by animals most likely looking for food. The towering pines stood quietly, while the snow softly piled on their branches. The smell of wood smoke from the houses buried deep in the snow filled the air. As she glided along, Debbie discovered she enjoyed making tracks through the heavy powder. She struggled to keep up with Jenny, who was ahead of her, charged with youthful energy.

"Mom, isn't this the coolest!" Jenny exclaimed.

"Wait up, Jenny. My boot laces are coming untied."

Debbie came up to Jenny, who stood with her mouth open, catching snowflakes on her tongue. She joined her daughter, sticking her tongue out for fat, wet snowflakes. "Isn't it amazing, when you come to think about it, Jenny, that there are no two snowflakes alike?" she asked as she tied her laces tightly.

Jenny smiled, turned, and headed down toward the highway, with Debbie fighting the deep snow to keep up. As they made their way down the steep hill, she noticed the plows hadn't come yet. It was strange to see the world covered in a thick white blanket, and Debbie took in the breathtaking sights of a world held hostage by Mother Nature. Snow makes you realize how little control you have over things, other than your own reactions, she mused as she followed Jenny's lead.

As they trekked along the road, Debbie noticed that few other people were out, no businesses had yet opened, and the snow was becoming heavier. She felt energized by the renewal and rediscovery of the wonder of winter, a season that had previously escaped her.

Jenny stopped, and Debbie skied up to her. "Mom, it's so quiet, so peaceful. I love it here!"

Debbie smiled. "Me too. This was a great idea. Thanks for dragging me out against my will." Debbie looked around her. "Don't you think we should be going back? The visibility is getting worse."

Jenny nodded. "I think you're right. I'll race you!"

"Jenny, it's all uphill," Debbie protested. But Jenny had taken off, and Debbie did her best to follow her daughter's lead. It was much harder skiing back up the hill, and Debbie felt her legs ache as she inched her way toward the inviting thought of a warm fire, dry clothes, and a cup of hot cocoa.

Several hours later, she and Jenny lay sprawled before the roaring fire, dressed in dry clothes, their energy spent on the physical exertion they had endured. Debbie felt her eyes grow sleepy as the warmth of the fire lulled her into an altered space. Before she faded off, she managed to glance over at Jenny, who was listening to her music through headphones and smiled. I'm so blessed, she thought, drifting off to sleep.

Debbie glanced at her bedside clock when she awoke, and the thought of having to get out of her nice, warm bed to make a fire was extremely unappealing. But she had to get up because she had promised Jenny she'd go downhill skiing, even though it was against her better judgment. As she stretched in bed, she felt the familiar ache in her right knee. Pain throbbed in it quite often lately, especially when she ran on her treadmill. Nothing a few Advil won't take care of today, she decided as she got out of bed, threw her robe on, and stuffed her feet into her fuzzy, warm slippers. I don't want to disappoint Jenny, and we haven't spent that much time together lately. She hobbled to the bathroom, took the pills along with her daily regimen of vitamins, and headed downstairs to bring the fire back to life. Brrr, it was cold. She gazed out the window and noticed the sky was clear and the wind calm. As soon as the sun came over the mountains, it was going to be a sparkling, sunny day. I guess it's as good a day as any to try downhill again, she decided as she stoked last night's embers into an awakening state and added more wood and newspapers to the fire. I'm going to have to clean this out tonight, she concluded as the fire began to roar and warmth started to circulate downstairs. Cleaning out the fireplace was a chore she detested. She always managed to get ashes and soot all over herself and the hearth. This would've been Sam's job, she thought. But Sam was cleaning out someone else's fireplace now, and that someone was due to have his baby in a few months. Maybe the kid will have colic, and Sam won't get any sleep, she thought bitterly. It would serve him right!

As the fire began to roar, she got up and straightened the living room. Books, newspapers, mail, and magazines were strewn about. She glanced at a postcard Aunt Jane had sent from Australia. "The weather's warm, the people are friendly, and I'm having the time of my life," it read. "Wish you were here."

Sometimes Debbie did wish she was there, or anywhere else that was warm. The novelty of winter had begun to wear off. She found it was a chore living in the high Sierras, a chore she was becoming less fond of with each heavy snowstorm. Everything took longer to do in the snow, and she always seemed to be shoveling, bringing in wood, and building fires. Also, she had begun to grow weary of wearing sweaters, turtlenecks, long underwear, and wool socks. She had told Anne this recently when she was over for dinner, and Anne had laughed and said she'd better just relax and get used to it, because it was only the beginning of February, and they had at least three more months of winter left.

Would Debbie make it until the end of winter? Sometimes she just didn't know. Her shoulders ached from lifting the heavy amounts of snow, her right knee throbbed, the real-estate market was slow, and she had begun to grow weary of having no social life. She longed to go out to dinner, see a movie, and treat herself to a new outfit. But her financial situation was bleak. She hadn't closed a property in a month.

But today she had promised Jenny she'd go skiing with her at Squaw. Bill was going to meet them for lunch and, hopefully, if he could get away, ski with them in the afternoon. This sport has way too much gear, she decided as she went to the laundry room to gather up her ski equipment. Unlike running, which only required shoes. And speaking of running, she hadn't done that in a long time, only the treadmill. There was too much snow; she'd have to wait until some of it melted.

But Jenny had fallen in love with skiing. Actually, it was snowboarding that held her interest, but she had to go every weekend, and it was getting expensive. I better close a house soon, Debbie thought as she went upstairs to wake Jenny and get herself ready.

"I'm ready, Jenny," she said an hour later.

"Finally, Mom. Hurry, we'll miss the best snow."

It was a spectacular drive over to the resort. The azure blue sky was intensified by the mounds of pure white glistening snow the plows had carefully stacked on the sides of the road. Debbie felt like she was driving through a long white tunnel as she maneuvered mounds of snow left in the middle lanes. When they arrived at the ski resort, traffic was lined up for about a half-mile just to get into the already-jammed parking lot. "I told you, Mom," Jenny scolded. "We should have left sooner."

"I'm not in a good mood today, Jenny. I really don't need this. I'm doing the best I can." She felt tears start to fill her eyes, and she didn't want Jenny to see her upset, but it was all getting to her. Single parenthood was the pits!

Jenny just sat back in her seat and glared ahead. "I'm going to miss my friends, Mom. They're waiting for me."

That comment got under Debbie's skin. "Jenny," she began patiently, "if you would have helped me a little more around the house this morning, I would've been able to leave sooner. I'm tired of being your maid." Jenny seemed to ignore the remark, and she turned the other way.

Lately, it seemed to Debbie, Jenny was preoccupied with something. It was as if she was lost somewhere in the clouds. She spent a great deal of time listening to music, talking on the phone, or just lying on her bed and vegetating. Debbie had picked up some books at the library that dealt with teenage behavior and read up on what she could expect in the coming years. From all indications, it didn't look good. Maybe it had been her own naiveté, but she had honestly thought her own beautiful daughter would escape the horrible creature stage of adolescence. At least Jenny had not dyed her hair purple or pierced every orifice of her body. Well, not yet anyway.

It took quite a while for Debbie to find a parking spot, and finally they were on their way, lugging their equipment. Debbie was lucky to snag a vacant locker to store their gear in, and she stood in line to buy the tickets while Jenny anxiously scoured the crowd for her friends. Ouch, Debbie thought as she forked over the enormous expense for two lift tickets. Hamburger Helper this week, she decided, giving Jenny her ticket and hooking her own to her parka.

"Mom, I see them. Can I go?"

"I thought you were going to ski with me first," Debbie said.

"I'll meet you right here in an hour. Just let me go and do a few runs with my friends first."

Debbie's heart sank. She had known that this day was coming, the day she would be left for friends on an outing the two of them had planned, but as much as she had prepared herself for this situation, it still hurt. "One hour," she replied firmly. And she trudged over to the quad chair by herself and stood in line. It didn't take long for the line to move, and Debbie suddenly found herself on a huge chair lift with three other skiers, charging up the massive mountain at full speed.

She managed to get off the chair without taking anyone else down, stood high atop the mountain, and looked down the hill Jenny had told her to try and ski first. "It's an easy hill," Jenny had insisted. Well, it didn't look that easy to Debbie. But there was no other way to get down, so she slowly traversed her way down the hill, careful not to fall, and careful to avoid the multitude of skiers who flew right by her. "Whose bright idea was this?" she muttered. "Now I remember why I spent so many afternoons in the ski lodge. I don't like this!"

At that instant, a young man on a snowboard plowed right into her, sending her tumbling over her skis and face-down in the thick powder. She swore she heard a pop, and then her right knee began to scream with intense pain. She couldn't move. "Shit!" she yelled.

"Are you all right? I'm sorry, I didn't mean to run into you, but you turned before I could avoid you. Can I help?"

Debbie stared into the green eyes of a young man with a punk haircut, earrings in his eyebrows and ears, and baggy pants. She grimaced with pain. "I don't think I can move this leg. Can you call for help?"

The young man looked scared. "Sure, I'll ski down and find the ski patrol. Wait right here."

Debbie grimaced again and thought, Where does he think I'm going in this condition? She lay back in the snow and held back the tears. This was perfect! Now she was going to be laid up with a bum leg. She tried to move the right leg, but the knee refused to budge. Ouch! It really hurt.

A few minutes later, the ski patrol came upon her. "Are you hurt?" the man asked. His partner, a young woman, skied up to Debbie, took off her own skis, and began to check Debbie out. "Where does it hurt?" she asked.

"It's my right knee. I heard a pop when I fell."

"Have you ever hurt it before?"

"It's been bothering me lately. I thought it was the cold weather."

"Let's get you down the hill and to the clinic, where they'll check it out." The ski patrollers carefully loaded Debbie on to the stretcher, tied her down, and the man pulled her down the hill while the woman skied behind with Debbie's skis. The young man who ran into her skied up to them.

"Is she going to be all right?" he asked with a worried look on his face. "I'm the one who ran into her."

"We really don't know. She says her right knee hurts, and we're going to take her down and have it checked out," the man answered. "You can follow us if you want."

The procession went down the hill, and before Debbie knew it, she was whisked into the clinic and the doctor came over. "What do we have here?" he asked.

The ski patrol guy gave him a description of what had happened, and then he and the woman left to go out and patrol the slopes. "Good luck," they said. "We hope you feel better."

A nurse came in and helped Debbie take off her pants. Her right knee was indeed swollen, especially the back of the knee, which was almost twice its size. "Ouch," exclaimed the nurse. "That must hurt."

Debbie's knee was killing her. Suddenly she was exhausted. All she wanted to do was lie back and go to sleep, but that wasn't going to happen. The doctor, who didn't even look old enough to be shaving, began to poke and prod her knee. "I think she needs to have it x-rayed," he advised the nurse. He turned to Debbie. "We're going to have to get you to the hospital so you can get that done. We don't have that kind of equipment here in the clinic. Do you have someone here who can drive you?"

"No," she answered. "I'm here with my thirteen-year-old daughter, Jenny, who is up somewhere on the slopes. I do know Bill

Howard, one of the ski instructors. I was supposed to see him at lunch."

"We'll try and find him, but meanwhile, we need to get this done right away. Do you have anyone else you can call? Husband? Mother? Father?" he asked.

Debbie grew anxious. No! she wanted to scream. My parents are dead, my husband left me for another woman, and my aunt, the one person I could always count on, is halfway around the world. So, I guess you could say I'm shit out of luck. Instead she said, "There is another person, Anne Montgomery. I'll try her."

A half-hour later, Anne and Chloe flew into the room where Debbie was waiting. Anne threw her arms around Debbie. "How bad is it? I'm so worried about you. Where's Jenny?"

"They're trying to find her. I was supposed to meet her an hour after we started skiing, but I bet when she discovered I wasn't there, she went off and skied with her friends again. Oh, Anne, my knee is killing me. I hope I didn't do anything too bad to it?"

"What do they think is the matter with it?"

"The doctor said he thought I stretched my ACL. But he won't know until they x-ray it, and the clinic doesn't have any x-ray apparatus; that's why I need to get to the hospital."

"Well then, let's get you to the hospital. I'll leave a note asking Bill to look for Jenny and tell her what happened and not to worry. We'll pick her up later."

Chloe gave Debbie a hug. "I hope you feel better, Debbie."

"Thanks, Chloe. Sorry to ruin your stay-at-home day."

"It's okay." And Chloe went back over to stand by Anne and hold her hand.

A few hours later, at the hospital, after the X-rays had been taken and the doctors had conferred, one doctor, a balding, friendly man who looked to be in his late forties, came into Debbie's room. "Well, Debbie, we have good news and bad news. The good news is that you didn't break anything, but the bad news is that you stretched your ACL pretty bad, and you're going to have to lay off it for a while. No skiing, no running, and no driving for a while. We're going to give you a brace and a list of places you can go for physical therapy to get it stronger, but you're out of commission for a while."

Debbie lay back on the cot and sighed. Well, it wasn't as bad as she thought. No broken bones, but what was an ACL? She had never heard of it, but come to think of it, she had slept through anatomy. "Thank you, Doctor. I'll be a good patient and do the physical therapy and lay off the running. Promise. By the way, what is an ACL?"

The doctor stood up straight and began to give Debbie a lecture on the knee. He finished by saying, "The ACL is your main ligament. And you've stretched yours." He patted Debbie's hand. "The nurse will be back in a few minutes. She'll give you a brace and some medication for the pain. You'll need to stop by Admitting before you leave and fill out some papers."

Shit, she thought. I forgot. I don't have any insurance. I wonder how much this is going to cost. "Thank you, Doctor."

She looked over at Anne, who was sitting next to Chloe and reading her a book. "Well, at least it's not broken; that's the good part," she sighed. "Now I wonder how much this escapade will set me back."

Anne closed the book and put her arm around Chloe. "It's not going to be cheap. I know from personal experience. I broke my ankle a few years back, and it took me a long time to pay off the bills. If you need any money, let me know. I have some set aside."

The last thing I'd do is take Anne's money, she decided. I'll have to go into my savings and really hustle selling some houses. "Thanks, Anne. But I'll manage."

They were in Anne's car driving back toward Squaw a while later. Debbie just sat in the back seat with her right leg extended and stared straight ahead. The medical bill was over three thousand dollars, and her knee wasn't even broken, and that didn't include physical therapy or the doctor's bill. This would put a big dent into her financial situation. Suddenly she wished she was still married. She was tired of doing everything by herself.

It was three o'clock when they finally reached Squaw. Anne had been able to get in touch with Bill, who had managed to find Jenny at lunch. She was anxiously waiting for them with both sets of skis when Anne pulled up. Anne turned around. "Bill and I will come over here later tonight and get your car, so don't worry." She rolled down her window and yelled to Jenny, "Put the skis in back and hop in. Watch your mom's leg."

"Are you okay, Mom? I'm sorry I ditched you. I feel so guilty. This wouldn't have happened if I had stayed and skied with you," she said as she gingerly got into the back seat, careful not to disturb Debbie's leg.

Debbie gave her a smile. "No, Jenny, don't beat yourself up. It just happened. A snowboarder ran into me. I really don't know whose fault it was. Maybe I went into his space, I don't know. I just want to go home and rest. I'm suddenly very tired."

Jenny leaned over and gave her a hug. "I'm here to help you, Mom. I'm truly sorry."

Anne, Jenny, and Chloe helped get Debbie into the cabin and out of her clothes and into pajamas. They propped her up on the couch, Anne made a fire, and Jenny prepared some soup and crackers for dinner. Bill came over to get Anne, and the two of them went back over to Squaw's parking lot to get Debbie's car. When they returned, Bill stacked some wood inside the front door and told her he'd check up on her in the morning. "You did all this to get out of skiing with me," he teased and kissed her lightly on the cheek.

Debbie spent the night on the couch, the pain pills numbing the throbbing in her knee, and slept deeply. She opened her eyes and was surprised to see broad daylight streaming through the windows. She glanced at her watch: 9:10. Unbelievable, she thought. I've been asleep almost twelve hours. She stretched and felt her knee scream with pain. It's still there, she told herself. It wasn't a bad dream.

After an interesting breakfast fixed by Jenny—pasta and grapefruit—she decided to call her boss. "Beth, it's Debbie. I hate to bother you at home, but I tore my ACL yesterday skiing at Squaw, and I'm going to be bedridden for a few weeks."

"Oh, Debbie," replied the voice on the other end. "How terrible! I know people who have done it, and they really had a hard time with it mending. Can you drive?"

"No, it's my right knee, and the doctor said I have to have two weeks of no pressure on it, so that rules out driving and selling houses. I'm sorry. I hope it won't hurt the company if I take the time off work."

"No, Debbie. Don't think that way. You just take all the time you need. How about if I stop by tomorrow with your mail and any work you left on your desk. Perhaps, when the pain dies down, you can attend to it."

"Thanks, Beth, I'm sure I'll be able to soon. Right now I'm taking some pretty strong pain pills, so it's hard for me to concentrate. I'll start physical therapy next week."

"Can I help get you there?"

"That would be wonderful. My friend Anne has graciously volunteered to help shuttle me, but if she can't, I'll definitely call you."

"I hope you feel better, Debbie, but I've got to run, literally. A group of us are going on a long run down in Washoe Valley. See you sometime tomorrow. I'll call before I come."

Debbie hung up the phone and sank back against the pillows Jenny had lovingly propped up for her after their interesting breakfast. A nice long run on dry pavement, she thought. That sounded good. But that wasn't going to be happening for a while. How was she going to handle being laid up for so long? She was going to have to rely on other people to help her with the necessities of life. Shit, and just when she was starting to get her life in gear.

Jenny came in a few minutes later. "Can I get you anything, Mom? I'm going over to Kristen's to try and get this social studies project done. It's due on Tuesday. I'll be back in a few hours."

"I'm fine, Jenny. You go right ahead. I think I'm going to rest for now. Those pain pills knocked me for a loop."

She heard the front door close, and she drifted off into a wonderful space, with the help of the pills. Awakening a few hours later, she glanced at the fire, which had died down. A chill lingered in the air. She had been trying lately to keep the electric heat down to save money. She put her brace back on, dragged herself from the couch, and hobbled over to the fireplace, where she added a few logs and newspapers. Shortly after, the fire began to roar. The warmth felt so good she just plopped herself down on the braided rug, stretched out, and soaked in the fire's heat.

How did I get myself into this pickle? she thought. How did I end up here, at almost forty, in this old drafty cabin, alone in the dead of winter, divorced, without any money, and, to top it off, with a bum knee? Now she couldn't even work for the time being. She'd have to dig into her limited savings, and what's more, she'd have to pay for physical therapy. And to think she used to pay a personal trainer. She should've saved that money instead of spending it on something that frivolous.

And what about all her training for the marathon? It was the one thing that had become a symbol to her, a symbol of her inner and outer strength. Was it all for nothing? Would she be able to run it at all? Or was that dream gone also. Shit! Never in a million years would she have predicted this!

The phone rang. She looked around for it and saw it was back on the couch. She scooted over on her butt to get it. "Hello," she said on the fourth ring.

"Mom, are you all right? What took you so long?"

"I'm fine, Jenny. I was just over fixing the fire. What's up?"

"Can I stay at Kristen's longer? We're not done with our project, and her mother has invited me to stay for dinner. They'll take me home."

"Sure, honey. You have a good time."

"Are you sure, Mom? I can come home."

I could use the time alone, she decided. "I'm fine. I'll see you tonight."

The next couple of weeks dragged by for Debbie. She was housebound, the weather was lousy, and all she had were her thoughts and books for company. Anne came over frequently to get Debbie's grocery list and to help her with the chores, Kristen's mom took Jenny to activities and school, and Bill came over once with several books for her to read. He stayed, and they chatted for a while, but she found that whatever it was that had enchanted her about him earlier had disappeared. They seemed to be going in different directions. While she enjoyed his company, there was nothing else there.

She wished Aunt Jane were in the country for her to talk with, but she wasn't due back for several more weeks. Jenny seemed very involved in her own life, and even Anne, who always seemed to have time for Debbie, was preoccupied with something in her life.

Debbie dragged herself around the cabin for the first few days of her confinement, watched all the TV she ever cared to, and then suddenly decided that it was time to stop feeling sorry for herself. She woke up one bright and sunny morning, tired of being depressed, and jump-started her energy with a moment of truth. Suddenly, a light bulb went off in her heard. This injury had happened for a reason, she realized. She needed this time to think and grow; she had become so busy with the trivialities of life, she hadn't had the time she needed to process the last year. Obviously, her spirit thought differently than her head. She needed to break away from the leftovers of her former life and claim her own new life. In her former life, she had given away a great deal of her personal rights. Granted, she had a pretty good life on the outside—a beautiful house, a handsome husband, a beautiful daughter, the right friends, the right groups and activities—but something was missing.

She instantly realized that she and Sam had lacked the intimacy that a real marriage demands. Both of them had been too preoccupied with other people's opinions, material possessions, and networking. Maybe they had shared the same bed for fourteen years, but they had never shared their goals, dreams, and aspirations with each other. Maybe that was what Sam went looking for.

I hope he finds it, whatever it is that he needs, she decided. Because I don't wish him harm any longer. I'm just as much to blame for the lack of intimacy in our marriage as he is. I'm not a failure because I'm divorced, she realized. The breakup of my marriage is allowing me the opportunity to grow, to change, to reinvent myself, and if I don't try, then I'm a failure. I'm not a child any longer. I've got some experience, and I've learned a great deal, but there is much more out there for me to learn.

Suddenly, she realized she was not searching for love with a man; she was searching for herself.

I really don't know who I am, she decided. I have always been someone's child, niece, wife, or mother. But I need to find me.

I wonder if I would have had a better sense of self if my parents had lived. She reflected back to her high school years and the intense feeling of loneliness she had endured. She ached when she thought of her parents, especially her father. He always seemed to have time for her, while her mother spent all her energy on herself and her husband. Aunt Jane had been wonderful, but an aunt wasn't the same as having your parents watch you complete all of life's milestones. They never got to see her graduate from high school and college, attend her wedding, or meet their only grandchild.

She thought back to her college years and the wildness she had enjoyed: parties, dates, shopping, and beaching—activities with no substance. She had been an average student, only doing what was the minimum. In fact, she conceded, up until this point, she had never really done anything of real substance. Even her committee work had been done with the wrong objective. She had wanted to be seen in the right circles, not help humanity.

I suddenly feel freer, she decided, free from many things: people's opinions, having to look a certain way, entertain and decorate in a certain way. Come to think of it, she mused, Sam had been overly critical and aloof at times. What had she ever seen in him, other that his being a "pretty boy"?

Yes, she decided, it was time to enlist in Serenity 101, take time out of her life, pause and take a big breath, and concede that real growth starts within. It was as if her soul had just let out a long sigh of relief, and her head agreed that it was time to listen to the inner yearning of her creative muscles. Time to transform the negative into the positive, and if she was laid up for a few months with a bad knee, so be it. There was a great deal of training she needed to do on the inside before she went back and trained her outside.

Yes, it was time.

Finally, the doctor allowed her to drive and begin her physical therapy. She was to be returning to work shortly and was thrilled with the idea of working again. In all, she had been laid up for three weeks, but those three weeks had been productive and refreshing. She had meditated, contemplated, read, written in a journal, spent time with Jenny, and written some new goals. She had begun to create her own reality, and she was free at last to think and act the way she wanted to, not the way she someone else thought she should.

She had decided that it was fine she was single; in fact, she had begun to actually feel comfortable with the situation. She concluded that she enjoyed selling real-estate, and if she wanted to achieve more financial independence, she was going to have to try harder. And she still had the marathon as a goal to achieve. She prayed she would be able to run it because it would prove many things to her, especially by revealing her inner and outer strength and her ability to complete a huge task.

So she threw herself into her physical therapy, went the prescribed three times a week, and diligently performed her exercises at home. Slowly but surely, her knee began to heal, and slowly she felt the inner strength she so desperately desired begin to grow. Patience began to grow where intolerance used to lie. She shed her off former illusions and opinions of others and started listening to the whisper of her soul.

One day, after she had been in physical therapy awhile and had just sold a house, as they were eating breakfast, Jenny asked, "Mom, do you feel all right?"

Debbie smiled. "Yes. In fact, I never felt better. Why do you ask?"

"I don't know. I'm confused. You really don't seem like yourself. You're so calm and serene. Is there something wrong you're not telling me?"

"No, Jenny. There's nothing wrong. I've done a great deal of thinking, and I've changed some of my opinions about ideas I used to hold."

Jenny seemed confused. "What was wrong with the way you thought before, Mom?"

"Well, nothing really. I guess you could say I was pretty limited in the way I thought. I think I had blinders on to what was truth."

"And what is truth, Mom?"

"Well, Jenny, that depends. Truth is different for everyone, and as you grow and mature, you will define your own truth. But truth for me is living my own life, my own way, and not worrying about what anyone else says or thinks about me or what I do. It's about having the freedom to do what I want and to leave the world a little better off when I depart. It's also about managing my own responsibilities and not being in such a panic to have the best of everything."

Jenny chewed her toast thoughtfully. "That sounds pretty good, Mom. I like that. Am I too young to develop my own truth?"

"Never!" Debbie exclaimed. "Maybe if you start now, you won't have such a hard time when you're my age."

Jenny thought for a moment. "I think I might do that, Mom."

Chapter 12

"How's it going today, Nan?" Debbie asked the older woman she had befriended during her many trips to the physical therapist's office.

Nan glanced up from the glossy magazine she was reading and gave Debbie one of her dazzling smiles. "How nice to see you again, Debbie. I feel wonderful. How's that knee of yours? Are you doing the exercises like you're supposed to?"

Debbie sat down next to Nan and undid her knee brace. She flexed her leg a few times. "Yes, and you'd be proud of me. I've been doing them in the evenings, and I think the knee is getting stronger. How about you?"

"Oh, my ankle is improving, but the cold isn't helping my old bones. I can't wait for spring this year. I'm thinking about spending next winter with my sister in Arizona. I don't think I can take another heavy snow year."

"I agree. It's been a rough one." Debbie replied. This year the weather phenomenon El Niño had pounded the West Coast with one fierce storm after another. Even many of the natives were becoming disenchanted with snow. As they waited for their appointments, Debbie resumed their conversation from last week. "You know what, Nan? I did some thinking about what you said last week and it's starting to make sense."

"What's that, Debbie?"

"When you shared the story about your experiences and told me one can react negatively to the demands placed on oneself, or one can choose to transform the negative into positive. 'Gratitude is an attitude,' I think is how you put it."

Nan smiled. "One of my favorite sayings. I used to tell that to my children when they were young and would whine about the things they didn't have. Especially Jimmy, my youngest. He still hasn't learned that lesson yet, and he's almost forty-five." She shook her head and smiled at the memory.

Debbie smiled and patted Nan's thin, veined hand. "I also took your suggestion and went to the library and checked out some of May Sarton's works. I had never heard of her before, and I fell in love with her works and her life. She has so much to teach me."

Nan looked contemplative for a second, closed the magazine, and ran a hand through her short, white, curly hair. "I too gave myself a period of solitude, like May Sarton. After I divorced my husband of thirty years and moved up here over twenty years ago, I was completely alone for the first time in my life. My children were raised, my marriage was over, and I had just sold my business. I felt totally adrift, alone in the sea of life, but then something exciting happened. I discovered my life had begun to take off in a marvelous direction that I never in my wildest dreams could have envisioned. I thought that when I turned fifty, I was going to be old and used up, but in reality, I started to discover who I really was and what I really wanted. For the first time in my life, I started to live how I wanted to and not how others thought I should. I also read May Sarton's works and began to keep a journal of self-discovery like she did, and it was through the act of writing that I began to find out a great deal about myself. So, Debbie, I guess my lesson is don't despair, you're just beginning. Pretty soon your daughter will be on her own, and it will be your time to live, to really live for yourself."

Debbie sat back in her chair and smiled. "I'm beginning to come to that conclusion too. Funny, I'm going to be forty on my next birthday, and while it used to scare me because it was that much closer to fifty—which I had also deemed was death—now I'm actually looking forward to it. For some reason, I had imagined fifty was old age, sitting in a rocking chair, with nothing to look forward to but losing my hair and teeth, and no energy left to try new things. But thanks to you, and authors like May Sarton, I see that isn't the case. It's up to me. I can make the second part of my life anything I want it to be."

"You're right, and the exciting thing is that midlife will be your time. I wake up every morning excited to start the day. I have too many projects to do, too many things I want to accomplish to listen to people tell me I belong in an old people's home. It's all in your head, Debbie. Don't listen to anyone else."

"I won't. You've shown me that." Debbie smiled. Nan had broken her ankle going over a jump on skis.

The receptionist called Nan's name. "I'll see you next time, dear," she said and she limped off.

"God, I want to be like her when I grow up," Debbie sighed. She picked up a magazine from the coffee table and mindlessly flipped through the pages, waiting for her own name to be called.

Several weeks later, Debbie found herself in the doctor's office, the weeks of physical therapy completed. The doctor looked at the X-rays and checked out her knee. "The stretch looks healed. I'm going to give you the okay to assume your normal activities, but I'm going to advise you to take it easy for a while. No marathons this week," he said with a twinkle in his eyes.

Debbie smiled. "Thanks, Doctor. I promise I'll take it easy."

Doctor Lemons smiled and pushed a stray strand of graying blond hair away from his dark blue eyes. "Remember, Debbie, you're going to have to wear that brace whenever you run or do any other type of physical exercise. Your knee is vulnerable, and I encourage you to continue your knee exercises."

Yuk, Debbie thought, I hate that brace; it restricts me. But she felt the itch to run and had no desire to go back to square one. "I promise, Doctor, I'll wear it."

"Even if you run the marathon? It's that important. I can't stress that point enough."

"Yes, Doctor, even if I run the marathon."

I wonder if I'll even be able to run the marathon this year, she pondered as she exited the doctor's office, got in her car, and headed toward the grocery store. When she thought about it, she had really only missed three months of training. But it had felt like an eternity! Even though the race was at the end of August, and the calendar only said April, she had some doubts about whether her body would be ready.

While she drove along and observed the scenery, she flashed back to springs in the city. Flowers would be blooming, the smell of freshly mowed green grass would fill the air, and she wouldn't be wearing these damn pesky wool sweaters. There was still several feet of snow covering the ground, and it would be at least June before she could plant some flowers.

Easter vacation for Jenny started after school, and Debbie was sending Jenny down to visit Sam and Aunt Jane. She couldn't afford to miss any more work, so she had decided to stay and try to sell a few properties. She was driving Jenny down to Reno in the morning to catch the United Express flight to San Francisco. In one way, Debbie was looking forward to having the time alone. Jenny's hormones had been fierce lately, and Debbie wanted the space to concentrate on her work. The plan was for Jenny to split the visit between her father and her great aunt. Donna recently had the baby, a little boy they had named Sam Junior, and Jenny was anxious to meet her half-brother. Sam and Donna had still not tied the knot. For some anal reason, Donna could only be married in October, and last October Sam had still been married to Debbie, so they had to wait until the following year. The date was not final, but Sam had told Jenny he wanted her there.

The following day, a windy, cloudy, early spring day in Reno, Debbie saw her daughter off on the 9 A.M. shuttle. "Have a wonderful time, Jenny, and I'll see you next Saturday at five."

Jenny looked a little worried. "Are you going to be all right, Mom? I'm sorry about last night."

Debbie gave her a hug. "That's okay. You're forgiven. It would be easier on me if you would just do what you're told." Last night Debbie had lost it, snatched Jenny's boom box from her room, and told her to go to bed. Jenny had slammed the door after her and called her some ugly words. "I'm not here to be your best friend," she had reminded her daughter.

"I'll try. Are you going to be lonesome spending Easter all by yourself?"

"I'll be fine. I've got some work to do, and I need to start training. Hey, maybe I'll sell that house I've been trying to for so long!"

The announcer called Jenny's flight, and Debbie gave her a final hug, held back the tears, and let her only child board the plane.

Easter week proved to be a warm respite from winter's relentless storms, and as the snow began to melt and spring tentatively tried to enter, Debbie started to run again, slowly at first, one step at a time. The pain seemed excruciating, and her lungs screamed for more oxygen when she began a light jog. She found the brace uncomfortable, but she remembered the doctor's words and told her mind to focus on something else. Gasping for breath, she stopped when she reached the highway. What happened to all my training? she wondered. All my strength and conditioning is gone. Tears began to fill her eyes and she wondered if she would ever be in shape to run the marathon.

She wiped her eyes, adjusted the brace, and jogged down to the beach, where she spent the next forty-five minutes alternating between running and walking. Frustrated with herself, she felt the tears come back and finally gave in, sitting on a bench and feeling sorry for herself. Why me? she asked the universe. Why did I have to hurt myself? Why am I back to where I was in July?

She watched the waves on the lake for a while and began to feel soothed by their rolling motion. It was a breezy, cool day, with temperatures hovering in the low fifties. The ground was mushy, the snow was melting, and the sky was a brilliant blue. She let go of all the thoughts that had been floating around in her mind and sank into the moment. Time seemed to stand still, and she began to gain some perspective on her situation. If she still wanted to run the marathon, and she thought she did, she was going to have to buckle down, focus, and just do it—quit her bitching and moaning and push herself through the pain. I can do it, she decided. She stood up, stretched, and began the jog and walk back to the cabin.

"Hey, Anne, it's Debbie. Do you have a moment?" she asked several hours later after she had showered, eaten, and relaxed.

"Sure, Debbie. What's up?"

"I just need someone to talk to. I went for my first run today, and I became terribly frustrated. I'm so out of shape, the brace is like an anchor, and I seem to have lost my capacity for breathing. Do you have any suggestions?"

"What did the doctor say?"

"He said I could run if I took it easy and didn't push myself too hard at first. But, Anne, I didn't push myself. I just started jogging, not even running, and my body wouldn't hold up. I guess I'm just frustrated, and I wonder if I'll be able to run the marathon."

Silence for a moment on the other end. Finally, "Debbie, you have to realize that you had an injury, and it takes the body a while to recover. You need to be slow and steady with yourself and allow for some pain at first. It's easy to get out of shape quickly, especially as we get older. The body doesn't bounce back as quickly as it did when we were younger."

"That's for sure," Debbie agreed. "I guess I just feel so frustrated. I was doing so well with my training before the accident, and now I feel it was all for nothing."

"Debbie, are you sure you want to run the marathon? Is it that important to you?"

"I've thought about it, and yes, it is. I need to do this for me. I need to prove to myself that I have the inner and outer strength to accomplish this feat."

"Then, Debbie, you'll make it happen. One step at a time, just like you rebuilt your life after Sam left. You can do it if you put your mind to it. Overcome your body's limitations, push yourself, yet be gentle with yourself at the same time."

Debbie processed her friend's wisdom. "Thanks, Anne. I guess I just needed encouragement. Sometimes I feel so alone. Thank you."

"You're welcome. Remember, I'm here for you. How about dinner tomorrow? Chloe's going over to a friend's for the night."

Debbie smiled. Anne was such a good friend. "That would be wonderful. I'll call you after work. Thanks."

After she hung up the phone, she sat back on the couch and

decided there was no other option. She'd get herself back in top running form. Just focus and do it, she reminded herself.

Debbie anxiously scanned the passengers disembarking from the plane. Finally she saw her daughter emerging, backpack flung over her shoulder and packages in her arms. "Jenny, over here!" Debbie yelled.

Jenny saw her mother and pushed her way through the crowd to get there. "Mom!" she exclaimed. "Boy, did I miss you." Jenny put her packages down and threw her arms around Debbie.

"What do you have here?" Debbie asked after she hugged her daughter.

"A few of these are for you from Aunt Jane. She thought you could use some new things. And Daddy bought me some new shoes and an outfit."

Debbie helped Jenny gather up her belongings, and they began to walk over to the baggage claim area. "Tell me about your week. How's Aunt Jane, and how did your visit go with your father and the new baby?"

"Aunt Jane's cool. She said she's coming up in June. The visit with Daddy was okay, but the baby cries a lot! I had to share a room with him, and he kept me up at night."

"How are your dad and Donna dealing with the new baby?"

"If you ask me, Donna needs to take a chill pill. She's a nervous wreck. She fusses over Sam Junior all the time, and Daddy tries to help, but to be honest, he's useless. Was he a help when I was born?"

Debbie reflected back to when she had brought Jenny home from the hospital. Sam had seemed overwhelmed when she had placed the pink bundle in his arms, and he had quickly given the baby back to her. Motherhood had come easily to Debbie, and Jenny had been a good baby. "Your father didn't know what to do with you when you were little. I think you scared him because you were so tiny. But as you got older and could sit up and make noises, he began to take more interest in you. But that was a long time ago, Jenny. I'm sure this baby thing is much harder now on your father."

Jenny thought for a moment. "Who helped you when you came home from the hospital with me?"

"Aunt Jane was there, and she was wonderful. She took care of the cooking, the laundry, and the cleaning. All I had to do was focus on you. She made it very easy for your daddy and me. Who does Sam Junior look like?"

"Mom, he's just a little baby. It's too early to tell. But Daddy seems to think he looks like I did when I was a baby."

"Well," Debbie replied, her mind flooded with images of Jenny as a baby, "you were a beautiful baby."

They made their way to the luggage area and waited quite a while for the baggage handlers to get the luggage on the carousel. "I should have carried my bag," decided Jenny. "This is taking forever."

Finally, they made it to the parking garage, loaded up the car, and headed up to the lake. Jenny chatted about all kinds of things while Debbie skillfully drove along the mountain highway. If Debbie had learned one thing about being a mother, it was that if you were a good listener, you could find out a great deal about your child. Jenny talked about several of her friends she had seen and things that were going on in their old neighborhood. "Oh, Mom, I heard from Penny that Jan and her husband have separated. Penny said Jan found him and another woman in her bed when she came home from shopping one day, and she snapped and kicked him out. You two were good friends, weren't you?"

"Yes, we were, but when your father left me, she didn't want anything to do with me. Maybe she thought divorce was catching. That's too bad. Perhaps I'll call her and offer her some support," she thought out loud.

"That would be nice, Mom. I like the way you treat people. You don't do the same things they did to you. You always treat them with respect."

Debbie smiled. "I try, Jenny. Thanks."

Over the next month, Debbie was able to devote a great deal of her spare time to training. She gradually increased her mileage and felt her body and mind growing stronger and stronger. Slowly her pace began to pick up, and she found herself enjoying her runs once again. It didn't seem as hard this time to get herself in shape, and before she knew it, she was able to run ten miles.

"Mom, you look pooped," Jenny exclaimed when she saw Debbie drag her body up the driveway.

"Ten miles, Jenny. I'm back. Let's go out for Mexican food tonight to celebrate."

"Congratulations, Mom. That sounds wonderful."

"Debbie, do you have a moment?"

Debbie looked up from her desk to see Beth standing there with a manila folder in her hand. "Sure, what can I do for you?"

Beth handed her the folder. "I have a very important client coming into town next week who is looking for a house to rent for the summer. I'll be on vacation, and I'd like you to handle this. I've been very impressed with your job performance. You're doing extremely well, and I'd like to show my appreciation by giving you this client. There's a hefty bonus if you can satisfy his wishes. He's very particular."

Debbie beamed. She knew she had been doing well, but it was nice to hear it from her boss. "Thank you for the lead. I'll get the job done."

"That's what I like to hear," Beth replied. As she started to leave Debbie's office, she turned and said, "Debbie, have you sent in your registration for the Silver State Marathon?"

"No, not yet. I still have time, don't I?"

"You'd better hurry. Registration closes soon. Don't forget."

"Thanks, I won't."

Luckily, for Debbie, she was able to satisfy Mr. Palmer's wishes and found him the perfect vacation rental on the beach in Incline Village for the month of July. She must have shown him fifteen high-rent properties, but the fleshy, balding movie producer found fault with many of the exquisite homes. Finally, he fell in love with a beautiful, six-thousand-square-foot home with a private dock, gourmet kitchen, and maid's quarters. The owner was adamant about a two-month rental, and Debbie was able to convince Mr. Palmer that he could come up to Tahoe during the weekends throughout the month of August to escape the heat in Southern California.

"You're right, Debbie," he finally decided as he took out his gold pen and wrote the check for the hefty down payment. "My family will love it here. Maybe they'll want to stay on during the month of August. I know I've been difficult, so I want you to have this." And he pressed a hundred-dollar bill into her hand.

Debbie was stunned. "Thank you, Mr. Palmer. But I can't accept."

"Nonsense, dear. You treat yourself to something fun." He shook her hand and made his way out to the car.

As she drove home later, she processed the day. Coupled with the bonus from Beth, this would turn out to be a fairly profitable day. Lately she had closed several houses and listed several more. Business was going well for her. The hundred-dollar bill was tucked into a pocket in her purse, tempting her. She had been so good lately. It had been so long since she had purchased anything. Why not? Didn't she deserve something?

She found herself turning into the shopping mall that housed several boutiques she had browsed in before. Maybe, she thought, exiting the car, I'll find something I like, something that'll look beautiful on me. She entered the first boutique, looked around, and found a few dresses she liked, but when she saw the price tags, she cringed. Her hundred-dollar bill wouldn't cover even half the price. But in the second boutique, there it was, a dress that had her name on it. She looked at the size—perfect, a six—then she looked at the price tag: eighty-nine dollars. Not too bad. Carefully, she took the dress off the rack and went over to the full-length mirror and held it up to her body. She observed the denim dress and contemplated the situations in which she could wear it. The dress had a scoop neckline, and it was gathered loosely in the front and again in the back, where a fabric band added the finishing touch.

"Would you like to try that on?" the young sales clerk asked.

"Please."

Walking out the door a short time later, the dress lovingly packed in a shopping bag, Debbie felt marvelous. This was a good investment, she assured herself as she got into the car. I can wear it in the winter with boots or on summer evenings with sandals. Thank you Mr. Palmer!

A few days later, Debbie decided to go to the local running store and pick up an application for the marathon. There was a display in the corner of the store along with a stack of applications. Debbie picked one up and read the information. It said that if she signed up early, the event would only cost her twenty dollars. She was also informed that all finishers in all events would receive a precious medallion and a T-shirt. Several other races were being offered that day: a half-marathon, a 10K walk, and a 10K run. Debbie took the application and brochure and sat down and read it again word by word. Do I really want to do this? she asked herself. I could run the half-marathon. That's only three more miles than I ran last week. Am I up for the entire twenty-six-point-two miles? The application described the route the race would take. Runners would start at six in the morning from Bowers Mansion County Park and follow a scenic loop around Washoe Lake—which mostly consisted of paved roads, some with gentle hills—then they would run through the tall ponderosa pines along Franktown Road and back to the starting line. Maybe if I went down there and drove the loop it wouldn't seem so overwhelming to me, she thought.

Just then a good-looking man around her age with a tight, chiseled body and two earrings in his left ear came up and took an application form and started to fill it out. He caught Debbie's gaze. "Thinking of running the race?" he asked.

"I've thought about it for a long time, but for some reason I'm hesitant to fill out the application form."

"Have you done your training?" he asked as he filled in his form.

"I was in good shape up until several months ago, when I stretched my ACL skiing. I had to take time off, do a great deal of physical therapy, and now I have to wear a brace when I run. I've been running again for over six weeks, and I'm up to ten miles again."

The man smiled. God, Debbie thought, he's gorgeous. "My name's Ed," the Greek god said. "I would say that if you're up to ten miles now, you should be fine by the end of August. But if the marathon gets close and you're still uneasy, you could always run the half-marathon."

"No," Debbie said. "That's not an option for me. I told myself I would run the marathon, and I'm determined to do it. I don't want to wiener out. I've failed at many other things during my lifetime, and this is something I have to complete."

Ed smiled and flashed his perfect white teeth. "I understand. I've run a few marathons, and if I were to offer any advice, it would be not to worry about the other guy and don't get hung up on your time. Twenty-six miles is a long way, and most of us hit the wall at some point. It's your race, run it your way."

"Thanks for the advice, and by the way, I'm Debbie. Maybe I'll see you at the race." She took out a pen and started filling out the form. Ed finished before she did and flashed her another smile as he turned the form, along with his money, in to the clerk .

"Good luck, Debbie. I'll see you around."

I hope you do, she thought as she got up and wrote a twenty-dollar check and turned in both items.

On her run later that day she felt her knee twitch, but she chose to ignore it, adjusted the brace again, and pushed herself harder than she ever had before. God, I feel so good, she exclaimed as she limped into the house. I'm going to do it!

June arrived at the lake and with it, finally, pleasant weather. Jenny was going to be out of school soon, and Anne had asked her if she would babysit Chloe again for the summer. "Anne pays well," she had confided in Debbie, "and I like Chloe. This year Anne said I can take Chloe to the beach, so that should be pretty cool."

Debbie looked up from the tacos she was eating for dinner. "That's wonderful, honey. Remember, I need to send you to your dad's for a visit. When would you like to go?"

Jenny crinkled up her nose. "Do I have to, Mom? There's nothing to do, and they'll make me sleep with the baby again."

"I'm sorry, Jenny, but according to the divorce decree, I need to send you for two weeks in the summer."

Jenny put down her taco. "That's not fair. Why didn't the judge ask me what I wanted? Does he know that I have to hang out with a wacko-almost stepmom and a little baby when I visit my father because he's not there. He's always working."

"I'm sorry, Jenny, but sometimes life isn't fair, I agree. Unfortunately, this is one of those things I can't do anything about. So after dinner, why don't we pick out a time and let Anne know so she can arrange something for Chloe during those two weeks."

Jenny burst into tears and ran upstairs to her room. Debbie heard the door slam, and she imagined her daughter had flung herself on the bed and was sobbing about the inequities of life. Not that she blamed Jenny. She wouldn't have wanted to go and stay with a father who wasn't around much, his almost-new wife, and a new baby. Jenny was almost fourteen, and she wanted to be out with her friends. Debbie shook her head and cleared the dishes. Damn you, Sam. Obviously, you weren't thinking about your daughter when you got involved with Donna and became a father again.

Aunt Jane was coming up for a visit next week, and this time she was going to stay a week. It will be good to have her, Debbie decided as she wrapped up the taco Jenny hadn't eaten. Jenny will be out of school in a week, and maybe I can send her back with Aunt Jane. That will save me airfare, she mused.

Debbie, exhausted from the morning's activities, sank into the chair by the kitchen table She had gotten the house and yard ready for her aunt. She had tirelessly planted brilliant colorful petunias in the large oak barrels she had picked up last week at the local hardware store. She had swept the porch, taken the wicker chairs out of their winter storage, placed a new patio table and chairs on the porch, and decorated the table with a red-and-white-checked tablecloth and a pitcher of carnations. Then she had taken her energy into the kitchen, where she had prepared an entire refrigerator full of foods so she wouldn't have to cook. Luckily for her, Jenny was at Kristen's and wouldn't be home until later that day. She glanced at her watch and saw she had an hour before she had to be at the office. Aunt Jane was due in around five, later that day.

Debbie spent the afternoon cleaning up her desk, returning phone calls, and setting up her schedule for the next week. She was looking forward to seeing Aunt Jane, and she and Jenny had planned several activities. Jenny would be returning with Aunt Jane. No matter how much Jenny had protested, Debbie had held firm in her decision. "You're visiting your father for two weeks, then you'll be done for the summer. This works out well for them. It won't be too bad, Jenny. I promise. Try to look at the visit as an adventure. Just think you'll be able to see some of your old friends."

Several hours later, she heard Aunt Jane's car pull into the driveway. Debbie had just returned from the office, and she rushed out to see her beloved aunt. "Aunt Jane, it's so wonderful to see you," she exclaimed, throwing her arms around her aunt's wrinkled neck. Aunt Jane returned the hug.

"Let me look at you, Debbie." She examined Debbie closely. "You look wonderful, dear. Clean fresh air and hard work must agree with you."

Debbie picked up her aunt's suitcase and led her into the cabin. "I agree, it must, because I'm really happy, and I can't wait to tell you all I've learned. Why don't you stretch your legs a minute, and I'll run this up to the bedroom."

"That'll be great, Debbie. These old legs do tend to get cramped during the long drive." And she wandered around the living room, picking up photos and glancing at Debbie's books.

When Debbie returned, she found her aunt in the kitchen. "How about some iced tea? I just made some. We could take it out to the porch and wait for Jenny to come home."

"Sounds wonderful. My mouth is dry."

"That's common in the altitude. I find I drink so much water here." Debbie poured two tall frosty glasses with raspberry sun tea and added a slice of lemon to each for garnish. She placed them on a yellow wicker tray and arranged some crackers and cheese to nibble on. She led her aunt out to the front porch and her newly created outdoor dining room.

"This is nice, Debbie. When did you get this?" Aunt Jane eased her body into a chair, propped her feet up on the porch railing, and took a thirsty drink of the iced tea. "Ah, this hits the spot!"

Debbie took a drink of her tea. "I just purchased this set the other day. I missed eating outside last summer, and finally my finances are smoothing out."

Aunt Jane smiled. "Business is going well, I take it."

Debbie breathed in deeply. "Yes, it is. I'm starting to see the light at the end of the tunnel. I've sold quite a few properties, paid off my medical bills, and I even have money saved toward the purchase of my own home. As much as I like this cabin, I'm getting ready to own my own home again. Something small and hopefully not as old." She chuckled. "I'd like reliable heat in the winter."

Aunt Jane looked confused. "Doesn't this have heat?"

"If you want to call it that. Last winter I used the fireplace most of the time and only used the electric heat for backup. I won't lie to you; it was damn cold in the mornings. It just took so much time to keep the fire going. So, I've been thinking of looking for a house, or a condo for that matter. One that's newer and not as hard to maintain."

Aunt Jane took another drink of her tea, scouted out the perfect piece of Brie cheese, and placed it on a wheat cracker. She thought for a moment. "So, you think you're going to stay up here for another winter, Debbie?"

"I've been thinking about it. Jenny and I are settled, we've both made friends, and I do like my job. Jenny starts high school in the fall, and she's fallen in love with snowboarding. After all we've been through, I guess I don't have the heart to move her again. And to be honest, I've come to like the lifestyle up here. It's not as fast paced as the city, people seem to be more down to earth, and I really enjoy the outdoors. I don't know if I could go back to living in the city. Furthermore, besides you, there's nothing to go back to in the city. Sam doesn't seem to have much room in his new life for Jenny, and my friends have seemed to have moved on."

"I had a feeling you would make that decision."

That comment startled Debbie. "Why is that

"I've really seen you grow this past year, Debbie. I agree, if you moved back to the city you would lose much of the ground you have gained. Of course I miss you, but to be honest, I feel your being up here is for your own good. And if Jenny's happy, then I say stay."

Interesting, Debbie thought. "I haven't made my mind up for sure, Aunt Jane. I do need to talk it over with Jenny, who, by the way, is not looking forward to seeing her father."

"Not that I blame her! She's been displaced by a new baby and a new woman. When are they getting married?"

"Not until October. Donna has some superstition about getting married in any other month."

Aunt Jane shook her head. "And what does that teach the child! Thank goodness it's still a baby."

Just then, Jenny rode up on her bike. "Aunt Jane!" she squealed when she saw her beloved aunt sitting on the porch. She jumped off her bike, threw it to the ground, and galloped up to the porch, where she smothered her aunt with a tremendous hug.

Aunt Jane's visit flew by. Debbie had arranged her schedule to take a few afternoons off, and she took Aunt Jane on long, luxurious hikes through green meadows filled with intoxicating wildflowers. It was wonderful to have her aunt there to listen to her, to keep her company at night, and to bounce her ideas and goals off of. Jenny accompanied them on several outings, but she wanted to be with her friends whenever possible. Jenny's graduation from eighth grade came at the closure of Aunt Jane's visit. Graduation proved to be a bittersweet evening for Debbie. Now her daughter was a high school freshman, and before she knew it, Jenny she would be off to college. Aunt Jane took them out to an elegant seafood restaurant to celebrate the event, and then they dropped Jenny off at a slumber party for the night.

Sitting outside later that night, wrapped tight in their warm sweaters, they were finally able to have some quiet time alone.

"It's been a busy week," Aunt Jane exclaimed. "You've worn me out, dear."

Aunt Jane was going back to the city in the morning, and she was taking Jenny to Sam's. Two weeks of solitude awaited Debbie. She touched her aunt's hand. "I hate to see you go. I've really enjoyed the week."

"Me too, dear, but I've got some things to do back in the city. And, of course, I have to deliver Jenny to her father."

"Yes, you do, and I appreciate you taking her. It saves me air fare. I wish he could have come up for her graduation. I'm sure it hurt Jenny."

Aunt Jane rocked back and forth in the rocker. "Yes, I imagine it did. I remember how I felt when my father left us. My poor mother had a hard time coping with us kids alone. I wish he would have gotten in contact with me. I'm sure he's been gone for a long time."

Aunt Jane didn't often revisit her past. When she was younger, Debbie had loved listening to her aunt tell stories about her youth. "That must have been difficult for you and my father. Do you think of my father often?"

"There's not a day that goes by, Debbie, that I don't think about Arthur in some way. It might be something I see that reminds me of him, or someone will say something that he would have, or I glance at one of his pictures in my house and suddenly wish he was around so I could talk to him."

Debbie gazed out into the night. "I do too. I wish he were still here."

"But he his, dear Debbie. I often feel his spirit close. I'm sure he watches out for you."

"You and my father were really close, weren't you?" Debbie knew the answer, but she wanted Aunt Jane to talk about her father.

"Yes, Arthur and I were extremely close because when our parents divorced, I was forced into caring for him so our mother could work. Even though I was seven years older, and acted more like a mother figure, we became inseparable. Especially when our mother started to have a series of one-night stands." She thought for a moment. "Perhaps that's why I never married."

"But Dad did. Your mother didn't scare him out of marriage."

"No, but look who your father married. Don't get me wrong, dear, Claire was a wonderful mother to you, but she was a strange duck. I often felt Arthur fell for her because she was so young and vulnerable and he could take care of someone else for a change. Perhaps I over mothered him," she laughed.

"Tell me what you remember about my mother. I don't remember a great deal about her."

Aunt Jane seemed to fall back in time. "Your mother was a beautiful creature, and your father spoiled her like one would a small child. From what I remember, she had a strange upbringing. Her father had also left, her mother found a new beau, and when Claire graduated from high school, the very next day, her mother boxed all Claire's belongings, put them on the front porch, and told her to have a nice life. Stunned, Claire fled to the west, where she met your father, and the rest is history."

"Mom never had a job or anything, did she?"

"If I remember correctly, your mother waited tables for a while, and after she married Arthur, she never worked again. She had you when she was barely nineteen. Remember, Arthur was a good ten years older than she was, and he had already established himself in his career when he met her."

"Didn't Dad meet her at a coffee shop?" She seemed to remember a story her father had told her about falling in love with her mother over fried eggs.

Aunt Jane nodded. "Yes, she waited on him, and I guess it was love at first sight, or something like that. How she ever was a waitress is beyond me! Your mother was scared of life, and that is why I think she was attracted to Arthur. He controlled her."

"I do remember Daddy made all the decisions."

"Yes, but your mother allowed it. She was incapable of making a decision on her own. She had a high school education, but never read a book that I can remember, and never seemed to have an opinion or thought that she could call her own. But your father loved her deeply. It's hard to judge others, Debbie. We all carry around our own hurts in our hearts. Claire never saw her family after she left the east, and she took her past to her grave. All I do know is that your parents loved you dearly, and Debbie, as I told you earlier, they'd be extremely proud of you if they could see you now."

Debbie stared, smiling at the fingernail moon that hung in the starlit sky. "You think so?"

"I know so, Debbie."

The following day, with tears and hugs, Debbie saw her aunt and daughter off. While it had been a remarkable visit with her aunt and she would miss her daughter terribly, she was looking forward to the time alone to work, train, and think. "I'll see you in two weeks at the Reno airport," she yelled to Jenny as Aunt Jane began to pull away. "Have a good time with your father, and I'll talk to you tomorrow."

Chapter 13

With Jenny safely in San Francisco with Sam, Debbie was able to focus on her training and work. The second day of her "holiday" she met Anne for a long run. Anne was standing by the trail marker patiently waiting for her when she pulled up. "Sorry I'm late," she told her friend as she jogged up to where Anne was stretching her Achilles tendon. "I had to show a house at the last minute."

"No problem." She checked her watch. "I just have to watch my time today because Chloe's at the neighbor's. She's really looking forward to Jenny's return."

The two of them started out at a light jog. "What are you doing with Chloe for these two weeks?" Debbie asked.

"I put her in the Summer of Fun program, but so far she hasn't really liked it. I thought it sounded good when I signed her up: field trips, the beach, arts and crafts, and cookouts."

"Maybe it'll be better when she meets a few more kids," Debbie suggested, remembering how Jenny used to respond to new situations when she had been younger.

"I hope so. Chloe's always been shy and not very good at making friends. I thought this would be good for her."

As they jogged, Debbie thought back to the summers she had gone to camp. She had loved the feeling of independence, the activities, and all the friends she had made. Camp for her stopped after her parents' deaths. She had sent Jenny to several camps when she was younger, but camp for Jenny had stopped when Debbie and Sam had divorced.

As she followed Anne down the trail, she remembered the first time she had gone running with Anne last year and how hard it had been to keep up with her. This year seemed so much easier. She realized she must have gained confidence along with her new fitness level.

"You're running really well," Anne yelled back to her. "You'll do fine in the marathon."

"You think so? It's still two months away."

"Just keep your mileage up and make sure you eat correctly and get enough rest. You'll finish."

Debbie followed Anne for the next hour, staying far enough behind so she wouldn't have to breathe the dust kicked up off the path. They stopped to take a water break. "You lead the way back, Debbie. I'll follow," Anne encouraged. Debbie pushed herself faster on the way back.

"Great run, Debbie," Anne uttered, almost out of breath when they finished. "I've got to go and get Chloe. See you."

"Mom," Debbie heard the voice on the other end of the phone say, "I've tried to call you several times, but you're not home when I call. Where are you?"

Debbie chuckled to herself. "I've been working, honey, and I've been putting in quite a few miles. I miss you, Jenny. How is your visit going?"

She heard Jenny sigh. "It's all right, but I'm ready to come home now. Do I really have to stay these last few days?"

"I've already paid for your ticket and it costs money to exchange it. Try and make the best of the situation, Jenny. Has your father and Donna set a date for the wedding?"

"Yeah, it's October twelve at the Yacht Club. I have to be in it and wear this stupid, ugly dress Donna took me to get. You should see it, Mom!"

Debbie laughed and thought back to all the friends' weddings she had been in. "And I bet she told you that you could wear it again!"

Jenny laughed. "I don't think so!"

Debbie glanced at her watch. It was getting late, and she had to get up early the next morning. "I need to get to bed, Jenny. I've got an incredibly busy day tomorrow. I'll call you tomorrow night. Sweet dreams, sweetheart."

"Good night, Mom. I love you." And she heard the phone click.

Debbie felt depressed as she hung up the phone. So they'd set a date. October twelve. Funny, it still hurts somewhat, she decided. I thought I'd be over him, but I guess there is still a part of me that cares for him. Poor Jenny. I don't think I would have liked to have seen my father with another woman. She got up and went to bed. Sleep came swiftly.

She picked Jenny up several days later at the Reno airport. "I swear you've grown," she laughed as she hugged her daughter.

"Boy, have I missed you. I'm never going to have children! Sam Junior is cute, but he's a lot of work! All he does is eat, sleep, and poop his pants. And the drools that come out of his mouth! Disgusting!"

They walked out into the intense desert heat. "Did you take care of him?" Debbie asked.

"Almost like every day. Donna has relaxed since the last time I was there, and she is anxious to get back to work. She and Daddy are looking for a nanny, and they left Sam Junior with me so they could go out to dinner and to several parties."

Debbie felt angry. How unfair to the baby, she thought. If I could do it all over again, I wouldn't have had a nanny, and I would have focused my energies on Jenny and my marriage, not my social pursuits. I thought Sam would have learned from the failure of our marriage, she thought as she started up the car. "I'm glad you're back, Jenny. Now let's get back to the lake and out of this oppressive heat."

As they began the drive to Tahoe, Jenny said, "Mom, I'm hungry. Sam and Donna didn't have any good food. Do you think we could stop somewhere? Maybe McDonald's?"

"Sure, Jenny. Look for a place."

It was good to have her home.

With less than two months before the marathon, Debbie immersed herself with vigor and enthusiasm into her training. She pushed and inspired herself with daily meditations and upbeat music on her headphones while she traversed the mountain trails behind the cabin. She ran several local races to prepare herself mentally for the race.

The housing market was booming at the lake thanks to the gain in the stock market and the drop in interest rates. Debbie found herself incredibly busy and managed to squirrel away much of her earnings. The owners of the cabin indicated that they were going to put the property on the market soon and asked if she was interested in purchasing it. She thought about it but then decided that it was a little too rustic for ownership. Last winter had been a challenge, but she decided that if she and Jenny were to stay another winter, they would need more of a house, with heat. She began to search for a place of their own.

Jenny was busy with babysitting Chloe and hanging out with friends. Debbie began to notice subtle changes in her daughter. The kids she had befriended seemed to lack the parental supervision that Debbie imposed on Jenny, and the two of them had more and more disagreements. "But, Mom," Jenny would protest when Debbie wouldn't allow her to do a certain activity. "Everyone else's parents are cool. Why can't you be?"

Jenny began to see less and less of Kristen and more and more of two girls named Tiffany and Destiny. Debbie could swear she smelled cigarette smoke on the two girls' clothes much of the time, and often they seemed to be in an altered state. The only words that seemed to come out of their lips were "Hey, Debbie" and "Cool, that sounds awesome." Debbie continued to smell Jenny's clothes and suggest that she hang around Kristen more, but Jenny brushed her off with "Kristen's such a baby. She does not want to do anything."

"Hey, Mom! Tiff and Destiny are going to this really cool party tonight at Tiff's brother's friend's house, and they'd like me to go. Please!" Jenny pleaded.

Debbie glanced up from the paperwork she had strewn all across the kitchen table. She had several properties closing soon, and she had to go back to the office after dinner. "Are there going to be parents there?"

She glanced up at Jenny, who turned her back to her and replied, "Of course, Mom. The party's going to be in their back yard and this guy's band's playing. Please can I go, Mom? Tiffany said I could spend the night at her house, and that way I won't bother you, and you can get your paperwork done in peace."

A nagging voice in her head told Debbie something wasn't right, but she was too busy to listen. She had all this work to do, and how terrible could it be if the parents were there? She thought it over for a moment and decided that she really needed the time to get this work done and with Jenny out of the house and the phone silent, she could accomplish this task. Besides, it was time to start trusting her. Right?

"Well, all right. As long as you promise you won't do anything you're not supposed to."

"Sure, Mom. No drinking, no drugs, no sex. I got it." And she rushed to the phone.

In retrospect, Debbie would remember that Jenny never made eye contact.

"Bye, Mom," Jenny yelled when Debbie dropped her off in front of Tiffany's house.

"Are you sure you don't want me to take you kids over to the party? I'd be happy to."

"No, Mom, that's okay. We're not going to go over quite yet, and we'll catch a ride with Tiffany's brother."

Tiffany sauntered out of the house wearing jeans with the knees cut out and a fringed long-sleeved top. "Hey, Debbie," she said as she came up to the car.

Jenny looked worried. "Bye, Mom." She hooked arms with Tiffany, and the two of them walked back into the house. Debbie shook her head and thought Tiffany looked right out of the summer of '67. She headed over to the office, still ignoring the nagging voice in her head that said something wasn't right. After she finished her business and faxed the papers that needed to be faxed, she dropped by Anne's for a beer. They sat outside on Anne's porch and talked about the upcoming marathon. Debbie told her about Jenny's new friends. Anne was quick to point out that Jenny was a good kid and that she too went to parties when she was Jenny's age. Debbie glanced at her watch and, noticing the time said, "I've got to go, Anne. I've got an early appointment in the morning."

Anne walked her to her car. "I'll see you tomorrow for our long run. Sleep tight and don't worry about Jenny. She'll be fine."

"Thanks, Anne." And she headed for home.

The message light was blinking on her answering machine when she returned. "Debbie, this is Jason, Tiffany's brother. I think you'd better come and get Jenny. She's pretty sick." He gave her the address of the party. Puzzled, Debbie played the message a second time and listened intently. Confused, she called Tiffany's number, but no one answered. That's strange, she thought. You'd of thought her parents would be home. She got in her car and headed over to the address Jason had given her.

She pulled to a house that had music blaring. Looking at the address on the paper, and not finding a house number on the house, she figured this must be the place. She walked up the walkway, almost tripping over several wine bottles, and entered through the open front door. Glancing around, she saw the house was filled with teenagers; no adults seemed to be present. Beer cans lay scattered around the kitchen and living room, and Debbie could see the band playing their loud noise in the back yard through the livingroom windows. She stopped a shirtless young man with bleached blond hair who was wearing a nose ring, an eyebrow ring, and two nipple rings. Ouch, she thought. "I'm looking for my daughter, Jenny Burke. Do you know her?"

He gazed at her with a dazed and confused look, thought for a moment. "No, man. You might want to see Todd. He's in charge." And he wandered out to the back yard and the blaring music.

Debbie looked frantically for Jenny or Tiffany. Dismayed, she saw a few young girls around Jenny's age heaving in corners and groups of others chugging what looked like some kind of punch. Finally, she saw someone who looked like Tiffany bending over another girl who was vomiting. She came upon the two, went to tap Tiffany's back, and to her chagrin saw that the young girl gagging over her vomit was Jenny.

"What's going on here?" she asked. "Why are you sick, Jenny?"

A very sick-looking young girl turned her head and saw her mother. "Oh, Mom," she wailed. "I feel so sick. It must have been the hot dog I ate." At that instant, she turned her head and barfed. *That's no hot dog,* Debbie decided.

"Please move out of the way, Tiffany. Jenny, what did you drink?"

Jenny's tear-stained face looked up. "Nothing, Mom. I told you it was the hot dog."

"Hot dogs don't smell like that. What did you drink?"

Debbie turned around to ask Tiffany, but she had mysteriously disappeared. "Jenny, this is me, Mom," she said, wrapping her arms around her shivering daughter. "Talk to me. What did you drink?"

Jenny started to cry. "You'll hate me!"

Debbie held her close. "No, I won't, but I can't help you unless you tell me the truth."

Jenny sighed. "I just drank some punch Todd made. He said there was just a little bit of alcohol in it, and I wouldn't be able to taste it. So I tried it."

"How much did you drink?"

"I don't remember, Mom. We played a chugging game, and I just took a big drink every time the jug came around." She turned and heaved again.

"Jenny, I'm going to take you home now. With some Tylenol and some rest you'll feel a lot better. Then we'll talk about it in the morning." She helped Jenny to her feet and led her shivering daughter out of the party and drove her home, stopping several times for Jenny to heave by the side of the road. By the time they arrived home, Jenny had fallen asleep. She dragged her child up to bed, took off her shoes, and covered her small thin body with a comforter for the night. She was not going to feel good in the morning.

Sleep eluded Debbie that night. *What have I done wrong?* she chastised herself as she tossed and turned. *Why would Jenny do such a thing?* She realized that Tiffany and Destiny were not the best influences on Jenny, and she probably shouldn't have let her go to the party without talking to the parents. But why would Jenny lie to her? *Damn you, Sam. You're not here to help me with this.*

You're two hundred miles away, tucked safely into bed with your new family, and you've left me alone to handle these nasty teenage hormones. Finally sleep came. Vivid dreams rose up from her subconscious where Jenny threw up all over Sam and Donna while Debbie stood in the background and clapped.

She called the office early in the morning and told them to reschedule her appointment for the following day. She had to deal with Jenny, and she wasn't going to leave her alone. She puttered around the house, waiting for her daughter to get up. Finally, around ten, she heard the bedroom door open, the toilet flush, and the stairs creak as she came down.

"How do you feel this morning?" she asked as she met Jenny at the base of the stairs.

Jenny rubbed her eyes and avoided Debbie's glare. "My head hurts, and I still feel sick to my stomach."

Debbie led her to the kitchen and poured her a glass of orange juice and gave her two Tylenol. "You're going to feel like this for a while, Jenny. This is called a hangover, and it comes from too much alcohol in your system. Can you tell me why you drank? You know the rules."

Jenny swallowed the juice and pills and thought for a moment. "I really don't know, Mom. Everyone else was doing it, and I guess I just wanted to be cool. Jason said a little bit wouldn't hurt me."

"I don't think you drank just a little, Jenny. That was quite a lot of heaving last night."

"I don't remember how much I drank. Am I in trouble?"

"What do you think?"

Jenny shrugged her shoulders. "I don't know."

"Why did you do this, Jenny? You know this is unacceptable behavior."

Jenny swirled the juice around in her glass. "I don't know. I guess I just wanted to be accepted by the cool kids."

Amazing, Debbie thought, Tiffany, Destiny, and those boys are the cool kids. "And Kristen's not cool?" Debbie probed gently.

"Kristen's okay sometimes. It's just that Tiffany has a really cute older brother, and her parents let her do anything she wants."

"Is that what you want, Jenny? You want me to let an almost

fourteen-year-old girl run wild and get into who knows what kind of trouble?"

Jenny continued to stare at the table as if there were something fascinating in the wood. "No, I guess not. I just don't want to be treated like a baby."

"I wasn't under the impression that you were. I thought I treated you like a young lady, gave you some freedom and independence."

"Yeah, I guess so." She thought for a moment, then angrily spat at Debbie, "You're never here, Mom. You're always working or running. Sometimes I get lonely. I miss our family, and Daddy has no room for me in his new life." She burst into tears. "I'm sorry, Mom. I promise I'll never do it again."

Debbie put her arms around her daughter and hugged her tight. So that was it. The stress of the divorce and Debbie's working had finally caught up with Jenny. "Jenny," she gently whispered, "help me out here. I have to work, and I need to run the marathon for me, to prove to myself that I can do it. After the race, I promise I'll cut way back on the running. I love you, honey. I'm sorry if you think I'm not here for you, but I'm doing the best I can."

Jenny released first from the tight embrace. "What's going to be my punishment?"

"I'm not sure right now. I'm going to have to think about it, but you do realize the dangers of drinking, don't you?"

Jenny made an awful face. "I guess so. Will my head ever stop hurting?" She laid her face on her hands as if to cradle the pain.

"Yes, Jenny, I can tell you that by tomorrow you'll feel better. Now, would you like something to eat?"

Jenny made a face. "I'm not hungry."

"You need to get something in your tummy to settle it down. How about some toast?"

No response from Jenny.

"Please, Jenny, you need something."

But Jenny had made a mad dash to the bathroom.

Jenny spent the rest of the day in bed sleeping and finally reemerged around six. Debbie was out in the living room watching the news. She looked up from the crossword puzzle she had been struggling over. "Feel better, sweetheart?"

Jenny yawned and lazily stretched her arms. "Yeah, I do. Do you think I could eat something? I feel hungry."

Debbie put her crossword puzzle down and got up off the couch. "Sure, let's go into the kitchen and have some soup and crackers. That should sit nicely in your stomach."

Over soup and cheese and crackers, they discussed the situation again. Debbie had had the afternoon to stew over the situation and had come up with several punishments. A few were too radical—housebound for the summer, grounded until she was sixteen—but when they discussed the situation, Jenny decided on her own that she needed to find some new friends or go back to Kristen. "I guess I let them influence me to do things I knew I shouldn't have. You're right, Mom. I need to be stronger."

"I've thought about your punishment, and I feel you should be grounded for a week. I'd ground you more, but I feel you punished yourself enough by throwing up so much. So one week of no friends and no phone. Fair?"

Jenny thought for a moment. "Fair," she agreed. "Did Tiffany call at all today?"

"No, she didn't. I'm sorry."

Jenny took her punishment with grace and didn't once complain. Tiffany called on the third day of her confinement, but Debbie told her Jenny was grounded from the phone and friends for a few more days. "Tell her to call me when she's off grounding," she asked.

I don't think so, thought Debbie.

"Mom?" Jenny ventured at the end of a warm summer's day in the middle of August. "I've been thinking. Maybe I should start running. It would be fun to run with you, and I think I need to get in shape. I haven't done much this summer but lie on the beach, babysit Chloe, and watch TV."

Debbie looked up from the book she was reading on the porch. "That sounds like a wonderful idea. I agree, it would be fun to run together. If you're serious, we'd better get you some good shoes. It's very important to have the proper footwear."

Jenny sat down in the chair next to Debbie. "Could we go out tomorrow and get them, Mom? I'd like to start as soon as possible."

"Sure, but why the rush? I'm just curious."

"I've been doing some thinking, and I want to get in shape and firm up my thighs, especially before high school starts. Also, I've been thinking of trying out for the soccer team. Kristen says she's going to be playing, and I thought it might be fun."

"Are you and Kristen friends again?"

Jenny rocked back and forth in the white wicker rocker. "Yeah, I've seen her a few times, and we've been talking on the phone lately. You know, Mom, Tiffany and Destiny never called me after that party. I'm pretty hurt about that. I thought they were my friends."

Debbie nodded her head and wondered if she should tell Jenny that Tiffany did call once, but then decided against it. She didn't want Jenny to have any further contact with those two. "I know firsthand how it feels to have a friend betray you. But to be honest, I think you can pick healthier friends."

Jenny rocked for a moment. "You're probably right. It's just that I felt so grown up when I was with them, and Jason was so cute."

"Don't you think Jason was a little too old for you?" Jason would be a senior in the fall.

"Yeah, probably. Hey, Mom, I've been wondering. When can I date?"

Date? Weren't you just in diapers! We can't be having this conversation!

"Mom!"

"Sorry, Jenny, but you caught me off guard. Date? I haven't really given it a thought."

"When did you start dating?"

Debbie scoured her mind for the information. "I really don't remember. Probably somewhere around my sophomore year. You'd have to ask Aunt Jane."

"You didn't date your freshman year?"

"I don't think so, but you have to remember I had lost my parents six months prior, and I still was grieving." Debbie breathed in deeply. "Jenny, how about we don't assign a particular age for dating and see what comes up. If a boy your own age asks you to a dance, I don't see a problem. But if a boy Jason's age asks you out, I'd have to say the answer would be no."

Jenny smiled. "That seems fair, Mom. I'm going to go in and watch some TV. Do you want to come?"

"Thanks, but I think I'll sit out here and enjoy the warm air. Winter will come soon enough."

Jenny stood up and then bent down and placed a kiss on Debbie's cheek. "I love you, Mom. Can we get those shoes tomorrow?"

"Sure, it's a date."

Later that evening, Debbie took a long, hot bath with lit candles around the tub and classical music playing softly on the radio. After drying herself off, she wrapped a thick terry-cloth bathrobe around her body and padded out to the kitchen, where she poured a glass of lemonade. Jenny had already gone to bed because she had to be at Anne's at nine the next morning, and Debbie had the downstairs to herself. She sat down on the couch and reflected back to their conversation earlier. She conjured up a picture of herself in her mind when she had been Jenny's age. Had she been young-looking or what? So many questions about dating, boys, makeup and sex had run through her brain, and she had sought the answers in magazines and slumber parties. Aunt Jane had tried her best, but she used to blush crimson red when they discussed the "dirty deed."

Her own mother had missed that part of Debbie's youth, and Debbie wondered how her life would have been different if her parents had lived. As a parent now, she realized how important parents are in a young person's life, and she wished that Sam would take more of an interest in Jenny's life, especially since the two of them had once been so close. She had tried to call him several times after the drinking incident, but either he never got the message from Donna, or he was that busy. You didn't divorce your kid, Sam, she thought bitterly. Your daughter could use some fatherly attention. Sometimes she wondered if Jenny's drinking experience and rebellious friends were just her way of getting attention.

In a way, she thought, Jenny and I are similar. We both lost our fathers around the same crucial age, thirteen. At least Jenny has me, and I'm going to try even harder to be a better mom. Once this damn marathon is over, I'll be able to devote more time to her.

Debbie and Jenny found a pair of running shoes the following day, and Debbie was surprised to see her daughter take off and run by herself for a half-hour. "I'll run with you when I'm stronger," she had told Debbie. "I want to do this on my own."

I can respect that, Debbie thought as she took off in a different direction for her hour-long run. She was participating in a twenty-mile run on Saturday with Anne and some other runners to help prepare herself mentally for the marathon, and she planned on pushing herself today, followed by a couple of days off so her muscles could rest for Saturday. The marathon was three weeks from Sunday, and how well she ran the twenty would indicate her time in the race. She was nervous every time she thought of the marathon, and hoped the twenty-mile run would put her mind at ease.

It was damn hot the day of the twenty-mile run. Anne picked her up and dropped Chloe off for Jenny to watch. "Do you have enough water?" she asked Debbie as she kissed Chloe and handed Jenny some money. "It's a hot one today."

"I hope so," Debbie replied. She held up a belt with two water bottles strapped in. "I thought it didn't get this hot up here."

Anne pulled a couple of sweat rags out of her pocket and gave one to Debbie. "Here, you might want this. Yeah, this heat is really rare. Let's hope it breaks before the marathon." She turned to the girls. "You two have fun at the beach, and Jenny, please watch Chloe when she's in the water. We'll probably be back in about five hours."

"Good luck, Mom," Jenny said as she led Chloe back into the house.

During the ride over, Anne prepped Debbie on what she could expect during the run. The farthest Debbie had ever run was twelve miles, and twenty miles would certainly put her body to the test. "Conserve your energy, Debbie. You don't want to start out too fast. And don't worry about how the other person is running. Run at your own pace." The others they were meeting were all experienced marathon runners.

A man and two women stood patiently waiting for them. After introductions were made and the course was explained to Debbie, they all encouraged her, then headed off. The couple, Stuart and Connie, sprinted ahead, while Anne and the other woman, an operating room nurse named Julie, hung back with Debbie for a while.

"I think I'm going to open myself up," Julie relayed to Anne. "I'm warm and ready," and she began to run faster.

"Debbie, do you think you'll be all right if I push myself a little faster?"

Debbie, who had been taking it slow, replied, "Go for it, Anne. I don't want to hold you back."

"Thanks, I'll see you at the finish." Anne took off in a cloud of dust, and Debbie was left by herself to plod the course. For the next several hours, Debbie ran by herself, one foot in front of the other, and tried to concentrate on her breathing. Several times she stopped to walk because of a pain in her right side and because her knee brace needed adjustment, but as soon as the pain subsided, she took off running again. She watched her water intake and stopped once to eat a few raisins she had put in her running pack for energy. She glanced at her watch. It seemed like she had been running for days, when in reality it had only been three hours. Would she ever be done? According to Anne, it would take her at least four hours. Would she make it?

Doubts began to fill her mind. You can't do it, Debbie. You're not strong enough. Your knee will give out. At that thought, she stopped and adjusted the brace again. Be strong, knee, she told it. Don't let me down.

As she trudged along and the hot sun beat down on her, she realized that she could give in to her fatigue, or push herself through the pain. I can do it, she suddenly realized. I can do anything I set my mind to. I will finish this! And with that thought in mind, she felt the adrenaline rush through her body and plodded the rest of the way in.

The rest of the group was waiting at the finish. "Way to go, Debbie!" screamed Anne when she saw Debbie's weary body turn the corner in the trail. Anne jogged up to Debbie and ran the rest of the way in with her. "You did it." She congratulated Debbie with a pat on the back.

"Whew," exclaimed Debbie when she finally stopped running and walked around. She suddenly felt dizzy and grabbed a fence rail for support.

"Debbie, have something to eat to help your blood sugar, drink some water, and don't sit down yet," Anne warned. Debbie heeded her friend's advice and slowly her body began to feel better. Anne came up to her, gave her a smelly hug, and thrust a bottle of Gatorade into her hands. "Drink this. I'm so proud of you, Debbie. How do you feel?"

Debbie smiled. "I did it, Anne. Maybe I didn't have the fastest time, but I did it. I'm pretty proud of myself, too."

"You should be," insisted Julie, who didn't even look like she had broken a sweat. "Tim should be here any second to take us down to our cars." Stuart and Connie came up to congratulate her, and Stuart offered her some trail mix.

"Thanks, this tastes wonderful." As Debbie limped to the car, she suddenly felt ravenous. *I bet I can eat whatever I desire tonight. A bowl of Ben and Jerry's would certainly hit the spot!*

Later that night, after a long, luxurious soak in the tub, many glasses of Gatorade, and a huge pasta dinner—and, of course, the Ben and Jerry's cookie dough ice cream—Debbie sat down on the couch and reflected back to her accomplishment. She had done it, she had run the twenty miles, she could move, talk, and in all sincerity, she didn't feel that bad. Even with the marathon looming in only three short weeks, she was no longer scared. She could do it. Hell, if she only ran twenty miles like she did today, she could walk the last six-point-two-miles in. She flexed her knee. It didn't feel too bad, even though it was cumbersome to wear the brace when she ran.

What a far cry she was from the woman who had fled to Tahoe a little over a year ago. Look what she had done! She knew now that she could and would finish the marathon.

Chapter 14

"I SHOULD BE THERE AROUND SIX TONIGHT, unless I get hung up in Sacramento's traffic."

"Okay. I'll be waiting, Aunt Jane. I'm looking forward to seeing you. I'm just so nervous about the marathon."

Debbie could hear Aunt Jane's grin over the phone. "I'm sure you'll do wonderful. You've been training for this for such a long time. I'll be at the finish line to cheer you on."

"I'm counting on it. See you tomorrow." She hung up.

Debbie sat down at the kitchen table, lost in her thoughts. The race had crept up so quickly, and tomorrow she had to go down to Reno to check in at the race headquarters and pick up her packet. The marathon began the following morning in Washoe Valley at the godawful hour of six. She rubbed her quads, glad she had taken off the last several days from running to prepare her body for the grueling run. She was going down with Anne very early that morning, and Aunt Jane and Jenny would follow later. Debbie was praying that she could finish the marathon in under four and a half hours.

The phone rang again. It was Anne. "Hey, Debbie. I'll pick you up around one to go and get our packets. I picked up some wonderful sauce to go with the pasta you're fixing tonight."

"Sounds good. I'll see you soon." Debbie went into the kitchen and looked over the ingredients she had for her pasta feed tonight.

It was a warm, later summer's day when Anne and Debbie headed over Mount Rose to the Peppermill Hotel and Casino to pick up the packets that contained their race number, T-shirt, and important information. Reno was hot, and they quickly raced into the climate-controlled gaming environment and stood among the throngs of other runners. The atmosphere was charged with excitement as people chatted about the race, anticipating the times they would hopefully break.

Finally, Debbie made her way to the front of the line and gave the young girl her information and was handed a packet.

"What's your number?" Anne asked as Debbie examined the contents of her package.

Debbie took out the paper with the number "117" on it.

Anne smiled. "Lucky numbers in craps, perhaps they'll bring you luck in the race. Now, let's see what my number is." She plowed through the manila envelope. "Hmm, sixty-three, and what else do we have here," she said as she pulled out several drink coupons, a certificate good for five dollars at the buffet, several gaming tokens, and a T-shirt. She held the shirt up to her and examined it. "Cool design," she decided as she surveyed the shirt, which read "Silver State Marathon, 1997" in red letters on a white background. On the back was a list of all the sponsors.

Debbie pulled her own shirt out of the envelope and held it up. "Wow, now I am a full-fledged marathoner!"

Anne broke her thoughts. "Are you ready to get back?"

Debbie thrust her shirt, number, and coupons back into the packet. "Sure," she answered, and they left the air-conditioned casino.

Aunt Jane arrived around six, heavily laden with all kinds of grocery bags. "I thought you could use some energy food," she relayed as Debbie came out of the cabin to greet her. "I have some special fresh pasta you can only get in civilization, some French bread that was baked this morning, a bottle of your favorite wine, and some prawns."

Debbie felt her mouth drool as she took some of the bags from her aunt. It was a good thing she was going to run twenty-six miles tomorrow. "Thanks, Aunt Jane. Looks good."

They brought the bags into the kitchen, and Debbie unloaded

them while Aunt Jane stretched her legs. To her surprise, Aunt Jane had tucked in several other treats: fresh ground coffee, chocolate chip cookies, a peach pie, and chocolates. "Aunt Jane," Debbie exclaimed, "with all this, I might have to run two marathons!"

She smiled and gave Debbie a warm hug. "I just worry you're not eating enough, especially with all that running. Look how thin you are."

That comment took Debbie by surprise. While she had noticed that her jeans were a little looser, she really hadn't paid much attention to her body. She had left the scale behind in the move. "Thanks. I assure you, I do eat." And she popped a chocolate into her mouth and felt its velvety essence slide down her throat. God, it was so good. She quickly unwrapped another one.

Aunt Jane laughed and gave her another hug. "You don't want to ruin your appetite."

"Not to worry. I now seem to eat enough for several people. I'll have to watch it after the marathon."

Aunt Jane walked over to the kitchen window and observed the tall majestic pine trees. "Are you going to keep running after this, or is this it?"

Debbie started to put the groceries away. "I'm sure I'll keep running, but I don't know if I'll train for another marathon. It consumes a lot of time, and with Jenny and work, I really don't know if it's feasible."

"And speaking of Jenny, how is she?"

Debbie glanced at her watch. "She should be home any minute. She's fine, looking forward to high school, and starting to test the limits." She then went on to explain the drinking incident, her choice of friends, and how she had dealt with the situation.

Aunt Jane gave a snort. "Sounds like you've had your hands full. Sorry I wasn't around to help you. Have you told Sam any of this?" Before Debbie could answer, Jenny burst into the kitchen, and, seeing her aunt, rushed up to her and threw her arms around her white, wrinkled neck. "It's so wonderful to see you!"

"It's great to see you. I've been having such a nice visit with your mom. Look how nice and tanned you are!" Aunt Jane exclaimed, observing Jenny's body. "Why don't you sit down and tell me all about your life." And while the two of them chatted, Debbie got up to start dinner. Anne, Chloe, and several other runners were going to be over soon.

The pasta feed went well, and after they were all contented and lay sprawled around the living room, several of the other runners shared their wisdom about the race. "And Debbie," warned Matt, a tall, thin, balding runner who had to be in his late forties, "don't start off too fast. That gets novices every time."

"Ditto," agreed Angie, his wife, who was also running the race. "Be sure to pace yourself."

"Debbie will do fine," Anne said. "She's been training with me for quite some time, and she's ready."

"You did tell her to make sure and bring her shoes," added Matt.

"Very funny," Anne replied.

"What happened?" Debbie asked.

"Oh, nothing really."

"Tell, Anne," Matt teasingly said.

"Tell me." Debbie's interest was piqued.

"Well," Anne began, "several years ago, when I was a novice runner, I signed up to run this race, trained hard, and did everything else I was supposed to. I dropped Chloe off at the babysitter, and rushed over to Truckee, where the race was to be held. I was late when I got there, and when I looked in the back of my car for my shoes, they weren't there. I panicked and frantically searched the entire car. Then I realized that they must be back at the house. There was nothing I could do. No stores were open, and the only shoes I had were the sandals on my feet—not proper foot attire for an eight-mile race! So I had to drop out of the race. But I did learn something."

"What was that?" Debbie asked. What a bummer it would be not to be able to run a race you had trained for because you did something so careless as forget your shoes!

"I always keep a spare pair in the car."

Later that night, before Debbie turned in, she took an old pair of running shoes and placed them in her car. Even though Anne was picking her up in the morning and she had planned on wearing her running shoes down to the race, she wanted to be safe, if only for the next time, or to appease the running gods.

She fell asleep quickly that night but was awakened around two in the morning by an urgent need to use the bathroom. She found it difficult to fall back to sleep—nerves and anxiety seemed to grip her soul. Would she be able to finish the race? Would her knee suddenly act up? Would she be able to push herself through the pain?

She rubbed her knee and silently sent it love and healing. You can do this, Debbie, she told herself. You have been training for this for a long time, and you're ready, she championed her doubting self. You have to do this!

She got up again and went down to the kitchen and poured herself a glass of milk. She glanced out the kitchen window and saw the full moon bathing the world below with its mystery and beauty. She inhaled and it felt as if she were being nourished by its magic. She stood in the moon's iridescent light, soaking up the extraordinary power.

You can and will run this, she told herself, and she climbed the stairs back to her bedroom and fell asleep.

The alarm clock blasted her awake with a country-western tune. She got up and stood under the shower for energy, made herself a cup of coffee, and tiptoed quietly out to the porch and waited for Anne's headlights to come up the driveway while she munched on a Power Bar. Okay, Debbie, she told herself, this is it. The day of reckoning. Twenty-six-point-two miles or bust! And as she saw Anne's headlights approaching, she stretched again and told herself, "You go, girl!"

Anne was fairly animated during the ride down, while Debbie just sank back against the seat and tried to hold her Power Bar and coffee down in her churning stomach. She glanced over at Anne, clutching her stomach, but Anne continued to blabber about all kinds of things, oblivious to Debbie's discomfort. Debbie shifted in the seat.

"You're awfully quiet," Anne finally said. "Are you okay?"

"I'm just somewhat nervous."

Anne flashed a brilliant smile. "First-marathon jitters. You'll do fine. Just don't start off too fast."

"I promise." How many times will I hear this? she wondered. This has got to be one of the biggest mistakes people make.

As they approached the starting point of the race, a few faint strands of first light peeked over the mountains to the east. They parked, got out, and began stretching. Anne found some people she knew, and jogged up and down the street with them. Debbie focused on stretching. She wasn't going to run any more than she had to. The announcer asked the runners to get into positions, and Debbie found herself jostled by the crowd. Then she became separated from Anne. Suddenly her stomach found its way into her mouth, and she quickly pushed her way to the sidelines, leaned over the rope, and rid herself of her Power Bar and coffee. A man came up to her and asked if she was okay. She nodded and took a swig from her water bottle to rid her mouth of the nasty aftertaste. She tried to get herself back to where she had been, but before she could the shot rang through the early morning air, and all the runners took off.

She found her body pushed by the force of the crowd, and she began to open up and started running the pace of all the runners around her. I think I'm running a little too fast, she thought, but I feel so good. She ran that pace the first few miles. I'm sure I'll be fine, she concluded as the adrenaline pumped through her body, and she continued to ignore the internal voice that told her to slow down.

She felt wonderful, and as the crowd began to thin out, she felt her body push faster and faster. This is easier than I thought, she concluded at the five-mile marker. I should feel this good for the rest of the race. I've trained for this. No sooner had the words crossed her mind, then she tripped over something in the road and found herself face-down on the pavement.

"Are you hurt?"

Debbie got up and brushed herself off and looked into the liquid blue eyes of a woman in her early fifties. "I'm fine, thanks. I don't know what happened."

The woman smiled. "It looks like you tripped over this stick. Let me move it." She pushed it to the side of the road. "Why don't we run together for a while. Is this your first marathon?"

Debbie fell into step alongside the woman, and they jogged forward. "Yes, can you tell?"

The lady blushed. "Why yes, I can. You have that first-marathoner's pace."

"Really? You can tell? I just feel so good. Maybe I should listen to what everyone has told me and just go slower."

The woman glanced over at Debbie. "I would. Take it from me–this is my third marathon, and you're going to be feeling it soon. I equate running a marathon to going through life. You have to think the process out and not try and rush the experience. If you push yourself too fast, especially on your first one, you'll burn out, just like in life. You also need to find your own pace, like your own style of living, and follow that, not the dictates of the maddening crowd. Enough philosophy. My name's June. Yours?"

"Debbie," she answered between breaths. "It's nice to meet you, June. Thanks for the rescue."

"You're welcome. Where are you from, Debbie?"

"San Francisco originally. I've been living in Tahoe for more than a year. And you?"

"I live in Carson City. How long have you been running?"

"A little over a year. When I moved to the lake last June after my husband left me, I started running to make myself stronger."

"And you're doing a marathon so soon! I'm impressed."

They ran side by side awhile longer. Suddenly Debbie found her energy starting to drain from her body. She looked at the mile marker. Mile ten. Shit, she wasn't even halfway way there yet. June continued to run with her for a bit, smiling and encouraging Debbie every so often. "Just remember, Debbie, don't focus on the pain; train the mind to focus on the goal. Push yourself through the pain like you push yourself through life."

All Debbie could do was turn her head and smile weakly. God, she was tired!

"Are you going to be okay if I go ahead, Debbie?" June asked gently.

"Oh, sure, I don't want to hold you up. Thanks for your encouragement and your help."

"You're welcome. Just remember, it's one foot at a time. Stop and walk if you need to, and there's an aid station coming up soon if you need something."

Debbie tried to smile, but it hurt even to do that!

June began to run faster, but Debbie didn't. She just stayed at her speed, slowly plodding along. Finally, she saw the aid station and stopped, filled her water bottle, and took a few swigs, careful not to drink too much so she wouldn't get a stomach cramp. Then she trudged on.

The hot sun beat down on her unmercifully, and she wiped her brow with her race T-shirt. Damn, I wish I would have slept better last night. She felt dizzy and slowed to a fast walk. You're not cut out for this! her body screamed at her weak mind. You should be home in bed! As she continued to power walk, she was passed by many runners, some who turned to offer her a smile or a kind word of encouragement, and others who were just focusing on their own race. Is this really necessary? her body shouted. Whose bright idea was this anyway?

It was yours, a small voice reminded her. You decided to run this race to prove that you were strong. You ran this to show Sam that he didn't destroy your life the day he betrayed you, and you ran this to show Jenny that women can be strong in adverse conditions. You also ran this to show your parents, who are watching from their Camelot above, that even though it felt like they abandoned you when they exited this earth, you're okay alone.

As she trudged along, one foot in front of the other, the theme song from Rocky playing in her head, she realized that she was indeed running alone. And the thing in life she had feared the most, being abandoned, had happened not once, but twice. But she had survived. As she continued on her run, she realized that the marathon was a metaphor for life. Everyone out here was running alone, just like everyone was alone on their own path of life. And she realized it wasn't as bad as she once had thought. In fact, she really wasn't alone, she was with her own best friend, herself, and as long as she realized this, she would never be alone.

Plodding along, she had another epiphany. The marathon, like life, was about energy management rather than speed and finishing first. She'd finish when it was her turn, when her body and will decided it was time. With that thought, she began to focus on her breath and tried to quiet her doubts, observing the litany of thoughts that crossed her mind, one right after another, like ants marching across a picnic table. Puzzled, she wondered where many of these thoughts came from, but she finally concluded that most of them were the thoughts and insecurities of the other people she had once decided knew all the answers and not her own feelings.

I think for too long I have listened to what others have told me and not honored my own truth, she decided as she focused on mile marker eighteen. Incredible, where had the last five miles gone? Eight more miles and she would be finished.

And with that thought she increased her speed a little more and sailed past the twenty-mile marker. I'm going to be fine, she told herself. But during the next mile, every muscle screamed again, her bones began to ache, and even her teeth throbbed. She hit the wall at twenty-one miles and felt she couldn't go any farther. She slowed to a crawl and felt the tears rush to her eyes. "I can't do this," she sobbed.

She heard a gentle voice from behind: "Yes, you can. Take a drink of water, breathe, you can do it, you're almost there."

She turned and was surprised to see an old man jog up next to her. She judged him to be in his early seventies, his silver hair catching the sun as he turned to her. "You've hit the wall. You need to push yourself through the pain. The finish line is close at hand. Don't quit now."

Debbie smiled faintly and started to jog again. She let the gentle man pace her for a bit, and then she slowed to a walk again. "You can do it," he reminded her as he jogged forward.

She walked for a while, gathering her inner strength, then told herself, This is it. It's time to suck it up and finish this damn race. You started it, and you can finish it, even though you've hit the so-called wall. The wall is a test of the self, and the goal is to pick yourself up, dust yourself off, and move forward. She reflected back to the wisdom that had seeped through her soul earlier; she was on the road of life alone, and everyone else was a mere passer-by. Maybe they'd accompany her for a short distance, but it was up to her to keep going. She was running the race solo.

With a throbbing knee in an uncomfortable, hot, and sticky brace, her body wracked with pain and trembling with fatigue, she now knew she was going to make it. With one foot in front of the other, she shuffled toward the finish line, humming the theme to Rocky out loud this time.

There it was in the distance. The finish line. Her eyes were blurry with heat and exhaustion, and as she felt herself push her weary body faster, she heard her daughter yell from the sidelines, "Way to go, Mom! You did it!"

Debbie ran toward the finish line and crossed with tears streaming down her face. She felt someone put a wrap around her and looked up to see a man place a finisher's medal in her hand. She had done it! Twenty-six-point-two miles all by herself.

Jenny and Aunt Jane came up to congratulate her and escort her to the refreshment table, where juice and fruit were waiting. "I'd hug you, Mom, but you stink," Jenny teased.

Debbie was too tired to smile. "That's okay. Thanks for being here, both of you."

"We wouldn't have missed it for the world. Did you hear your time?" Aunt Jane asked.

Debbie looked up. "No, did you?"

Aunt Jane smiled. "Four hours and thirty-two minutes."

Not bad. Not a world record, but Debbie felt satisfied. It was close enough to her four-and-a-half-hour goal. She had finished what she set out to do, and she realized that this had been something only she could have done for herself. Never had victory felt and tasted so good. She was a winner!

Anne quickly rushed up to her. "You did it, Debbie! I'm so proud of you!" She threw her sweaty arms around her.

Debbie gazed back at her friend. "Thanks. And thanks for encouraging me every step of the way. I can't believe I did it." Debbie bent over. "I just don't feel very well at the moment."

Anne put an arm around her. "Let's walk around for a moment so your body can cool down. You have just put it through quite an ordeal." She led Debbie around the parking lot of the finishing area.

"I feel like a horse being led around by its owner after a race," Debbie whispered.

Anne smiled. "It's the same theory. I've got to cool you down." The two of them walked around for a few minutes, then Anne led her over to the picnic area, where a group of them had gathered for a celebration lunch. "Don't sit down quite yet," she warned. "Your muscles still need to cool down some more."

"Mom," Debbie heard Jenny ask, "would you like some juice?"

"That sounds good." She took the carton of orange juice Jenny handed her and finished it in almost one swallow. "Is there any more?"

"We have enough food and juice for the entire marathon," Jenny laughed and went to get several more cartons.

Debbie hobbled over to the blanket Aunt Jane was sitting on and slowly lowered her aching body. "Can I get you anything, dear?" her aunt asked as she moved a few things so Debbie could sit down.

"No thanks. I'm not hungry right now. I just want to lie down and take off my shoes."

It felt like heaven to finally be sitting down, and she slowly started to unlace her shoes and slide her stinky feet out of her smelly shoes and socks. "My God, this feels wonderful," she exclaimed when her feet were freed from their constraints. "Phew." She looked at Aunt Jane, who chuckled and turned her head to avoid the smell.

She dug her toes into the thick, warm grass and massaged her aching feet with the green blades. "I don't know if I ever want to wear shoes again," she told Aunt Jane.

"Are you sure I can't get you anything to eat?" her aunt asked. "I can't believe you're not hungry."

"No thanks. I think I'll just lie back on the blanket, close my eyes for a moment, and relish the taste of success," she said as she lay back and turned her precious medal over and over in her hand. Suddenly her eyes felt heavy, and she felt her body drift off somewhere. She could hear the people around her talk about the race, their times, and how they would do next year, but all she could do was lie there and vegetate. She felt someone tap her shoulder, and she struggled to come back into her body. Opening her eyes, she saw Anne standing there with a plate of food.

"You need to eat, Debbie. I don't want your blood sugar to plummet."

Debbie shifted her body to an upright position. "I'm not really hungry. Maybe later."

"Trust me," Anne replied firmly. "I don't want you sick."

Debbie eyed the plate of food: a sandwich, grapes, potato chips, and some chocolate chip cookies. Suddenly, her stomach began to growl. Maybe food would taste good. She took the plate from Anne and slowly began to eat. Her body screamed, Food! Food! and she quickly began to devour the entire plate. Finished, she looked up sheepishly and saw her friends watching her. "Okay, I guess I was hungry." They all laughed. "Do you think I could have another sandwich?"

Debbie awoke late the following morning, and as she struggled to come to consciousness, she felt her body ache with resentment. "Ouch!" she exclaimed while she tried to straighten her legs, which felt like they had been run over by a garbage truck. She glanced at her bedside clock and saw she had slept until ten. As she lay in bed, the reason why her body was screaming at her came into focus. I can't believe I really did it, she thought, attempting to get out of bed. Yesterday seemed so far away. She limped to the bathroom, brushed her teeth, and gazed at her reflection in the mirror. "Good morning, marathoner. You are a winner," she told the unsightly vision gazing back at her.

Her quad muscles screamed as she attempted to walk down the stairs. She found it easier to sit on her butt and slide down step by step. "What are you doing, dear?" Aunt Jane asked when she came in from the kitchen.

"I can't seem to get down any other way."

Aunt Jane chuckled. "I wish I had a picture of this. Can I fix you some breakfast?"

"Love some," Debbie said when she hit the bottom of the stairs with a thud. "Scrambled eggs, toast, and sausage, if that's not too much trouble."

"Of course not." Aunt Jane went back into the kitchen, and Debbie hobbled along behind her and plopped down at the kitchen table. Aunt Jane handed her a cup of steaming coffee, and Debbie felt herself slowly come awake.

Debbie had taken the day off from work, having been warned by Anne and others that she would be tired and sore—which she was. It took her a while to hobble back upstairs after breakfast, shower, dress, and slide on her rear end back down. She planted herself on the couch and spent the rest of the day visiting with her aunt, who seemed delighted to be caring for her. Jenny was over at Kristen's comparing schedules, teachers, locker combinations, and boys. High school was starting soon, and they seemed to be best friends once again.

"I think I'm going to try and take a walk and see if I can loosen my muscles," Debbie told Aunt Jane, who was in the kitchen trying to put dinner together. "I'll be back soon."

"Take your time, dear." She looked at Debbie. "You know, I don't feel like cooking. Do you think we could go out to eat and maybe play some slots?"

Debbie grinned widely. "Of course, Aunt Jane. My treat this time." She walked slowly out the cabin and down the driveway, cringing with pain as her muscles talked back.

As she ambled along the road, breathing in the sweet fragrance of the pine trees and pondering the mysteries of life, she decided that the mountains were indeed a part of her soul, and the decision that she and Jenny had made last week to stay another winter would probably extend indefinitely. She didn't think she could leave the mountains. It was up here in the clear, pure air that she had found the lost part of her self she had subconsciously been looking for since childhood. Even though she didn't live an elaborate lifestyle any longer and her needs and wants were few, she was much happier. She had stripped herself of all unnecessary clutter, redefined her goals and priorities, and dug herself out of financial debt. Completing the marathon had been a test of her will, and she now knew she could do anything she focused her mind on.

She continued her slow walk and felt her muscles begin to relax and the ache disappear. She took several deep breaths and smiled.

The Summit
part 3

JENNY'S NEW SCHOOL YEAR

coincided with Debbie's offer on a three-bedroom, two-bath A-frame house. As she filled out the paperwork, she reflected back to where she had been a year ago and smiled. You've come a long way, baby, she chuckled to herself as she signed her name to the offer and held it out to the other real-estate agent. The agent scanned the offer and nodded. "This looks good, Debbie. I'll present it right away and get back to you."

Debbie went to her office, sat in her desk chair, put her feet up on the desk, leaned back, and exhaled. She gazed at a picture taken of Jenny last year on the pier in Tahoe City shortly after they had arrived. The young girl she lived with now had a great deal more self-confidence than the girl smiling tentatively in the picture. Like her mother.

Debbie smiled and mentally patted herself on the back. In one year she had achieved more inner growth and accomplished more goals than in the entire time she had been married. She now rejoiced in being her own woman, paying her own way, earning her own income, and not relying on another soul for support. She had learned the hard way what happens when you abdicate your own inner growth and use money as a substitute for love and security. She was determined never to make that mistake again.

Would she ever marry again? Honestly, she didn't know. She had discovered she liked being on her own and focusing on her own growth and development instead of trying to be the perfect wife and have the perfect home. Marriage should be a partnership, and she now realized her marriage had lacked many of the critical elements a partnership needed in order to survive. She accepted full responsibility for her contribution to the failure of her marriage. But she didn't view the marriage as a complete failure now; it got her to this point. She also realized she had only four more years until Jenny turned eighteen, and with such a small window of opportunity in which to help shape her daughter for the future, she didn't want to share that time with another man. She knew where her priorities were—Jenny and work.

It was now time to put running in its place. While she had been thrilled with the sweet victory of completing the marathon and displayed her medal proudly on her desk at work, she didn't think she had the time in her schedule to devote to training again. She was going to keep running, but a more realistic mileage.

She and Jenny were planning a vacation to Mexico with Aunt Jane for the Christmas holidays. The only dark cloud on Debbie's horizon was the trip to San Francisco in October to take Jenny to Sam and Donna's wedding. Jenny had protested going, but Debbie was firm. "This is your father, Jenny, and he wants you there," she had told her.

"But what are you going to do when I'm at the wedding?" Jenny had wailed.

Debbie had smiled and assured her that she would be fine. "I'll see Aunt Jane and run some errands. Don't worry about me. These people are a part of you. You need to be there." But Jenny was having a hard time with the concept of Sam actually marrying Donna.

Debbie was surprised at how indifferent she felt toward the upcoming wedding and her fortieth birthday at the end of September. Last year her birthday had come and gone without much celebration. While she had always dreaded the big four-oh, she now found the closer that she came to that day, the less it bothered her. Last year she had been worried about being divorced and forty. This year she saw forty as the beginning of the second part of her life. She had already arranged to treat herself to a spa day at the Resort at Squaw Creek to celebrate the event.

I don't think I'd want to go back, she told herself as she glanced at her appointment book and saw she'd better get moving if she was going to make her eleven-o'clock meeting. She smiled at her reflection in the mirror and exited her office. Not bad, she decided. You're going to be just fine.

"Mom, Dad and Donna's place is there, over on the right." Jenny had been directing Debbie to her father's, and they had taken a few wrong turns. She was due at ten for pictures. Debbie pulled up along side the elegant townhouse, as Sam came rushing out to greet his daughter.

"Hi, Daddy," her daughter said none too enthusiastically, getting carefully out of the car as not to harm the purple silk bridesmaid dress Donna had picked out for her to wear. "Yuk," she had told Debbie earlier that morning at Aunt Jane's. "I look so ugly. I hope there are no cute boys there to see me in this get-up."

"Hi, Jenny," Sam exclaimed as he threw his long lanky arms around her. Debbie's heart fluttered softly. He looked so handsome standing there in a white tuxedo with tails. Damn, I thought I was over him. But part of her knew she'd never really be over him. After all, he was Jenny's father, and they had created her.

"Can I talk to your mother for a moment?" he asked Jenny. "Why don't you go up and help Donna. She's having problems with her dress."

Jenny glanced over at Debbie. "It's okay." Debbie assured her. "I'll see you later tonight. Have fun."

Sam slid into the front seat. "I thought it was bad luck for the groom to see the bride before the wedding," she pointed out.

He turned and looked at her with those piercing blue eyes. Damn, he's still so good looking, she thought. She noticed the gray hair at his temples, but it only served to make him more handsome and distinguish.

"It's pretty hard to accomplish that tradition with the baby. Besides, that's an old wives' tale. We didn't see each other, and look how our marriage turned out." He quickly tried to cover up his mistake. "Sorry, I don't know where that came from. I guess I'm just nervous. Anyway, I just wanted to say thank you for bringing Jenny down. It means a great deal to me and Donna to have her here, and I just want to tell you that I'll try and be a better father. I'm just a little overwhelmed with the baby and Donna, and I do apologize."

The fluttering in her stomach stopped. He hadn't changed. He was still the same old Sam. What had she been thinking when she married him? "I think you need to tell that to Jenny, not me," she answered.

He seemed startled by her detachment from him. Did he think she was going to beg him not to marry Donna and to come back to her? As far as Debbie was concerned, they deserved each other. He fumbled for words. "I'm sorry, I just wanted to tell you that. I will talk to Jenny."

"I've got to get going, Sam. I do wish you well. Have a great life, but don't forget, you have two children now, and one is fourteen and still needs a father in her life."

"I won't, and I am sorry I was late last month with the support check. This wedding has taken a toll on me and my checkbook."

Debbie started the engine and made motions to leave. "I'm sure it has. But one thing you need to remember, Sam: you did all this. You're the one who fell in love, filed for divorce, and got Donna pregnant. Ultimately, you're responsible for this outcome. No one else. See you."

Sam got out of the car, and Debbie sped off. She glanced once in the rearview mirror and saw him standing in the middle of the street, watching her drive away.

It was a clear, warm, perfect October day, and the idea of shopping repulsed Debbie, so she steered her car in the direction of the Golden Gate Bridge. With the windows open and the wind rushing her senses, she turned up the volume on the stereo and sang enthusiastically to the Doobie Brothers as she sailed across the bridge. She parked the car on the other side, laced up her running shoes, and headed off over the hills. Breathing the fresh sea air, she rejoiced in the epiphany she had finally reached and felt herself closer to wholeness as she ran down the hills toward the blue Pacific Ocean.

Catherine MacDonald was raised in California and currently lives in Nevada with her husband and children. She teaches writing and literature and started her writing career as an elementary school teacher. **Reaching the Summit** is her first novel.